LAMENT FOR ADONIS

LAMENT FOR ADONIS

EDWARD THOMPSON

To
THEO JESSUP

LONDON ERNEST BENN LIMITED

First published in 1932

PRELUDE

ON APRIL 30, 1918, A MAN BRINGING IN A WOUNDED comrade, in the British failure East of Jordan, was hit in the spine. His case was hopeless, and his battalion, hard pressed, were retreating down a terrain where no stretchers could be carried. There was nothing for it but to leave him to die.

His death closed a chapter in many men's lives, I being one. The manner of his dying deepened its poignancy. He had fallen down a precipitate glacis swept by fire and could be spoken to but not reached. In answer to comrades he gave the assurance that he was 'quite cushy'; and his spirit turned to face the terrors of desertion and oncoming night in a wilderness occupied by an enemy whose character he knew.

I heard the news in Jerusalem, three or four days after. The memory stayed with me for ten years, until in 1928 the mood which could express something of what I felt came to ripeness. In pre-War years thought would have moved into the immemorial medium of verse. But that world has gone far from us. I tried to see if fiction, the form that the age imposes on all we write imaginatively, would serve for elegiac; I wrote *In Araby Orion*.

Writing *In Araby Orion* I had no further horizon. But the fictive medium involved, naturally, the creation and introduction of other characters than my friend; and I found that when I finished some of these seemed to have taken on, for me at any rate, a reality that asked for extended life and experiences of their own. So this book had to be written to satisfy their demand.

If the reader will remember merely that before *Lament for Adonis* opens Warren Remfry and Martin Chapman have been in the fighting in Transjordan; that Arab women selling oranges when their battalion, the Brentfords, broke up camp before marching into Transjordan had carried off Remfry's water-bottle and haversack (the latter containing shaving tackle, sponge, and brushes); and that Lance-Corporal Henry Bateman was left to die; he will find this story straightforward and in no sense a 'sequel.' He will please accept it as fiction; and not assume, as many readers do, that what an author calls fiction is in fact diluted autobiography.

LAMENT FOR ADONIS

I

Some days elapsed before Remfry could make the shopping trip to Jerusalem that the Arab women's visit had necessitated. He was fastidious as to his person; the delay and discomfort irked him. A sponge at a pinch might be borrowed, so might soap and even shaving tackle. Not toothbrush.

He made the time of waiting vocal with complaint. 'I have sad reason to fear,' said Father O'Hara, 'that in our friend Warren's heart the seeds of *years* of anti-semitism to follow are being planted. The words he has been using of these poor ontutored children of the desert have been most onchristian. Ye've sore need for repentance, Remfry me boy!'

'I've sore need for a shot-gun that'll fetch down some of the blighters! By the time I've spotted them they're too far for my revolver. And my batman's rifle never seems handy.'

The London Division was under orders to leave the Wadi Kelt, for the barren uplifted country north-west of Jerusalem. Remfry wangled it to go two days ahead, on May 5th, to choose the Brentfords' camping-site. With him went Martin Chapman. Martin's clerkly past had come to exalted ears and he had been seconded from the brigade to serve as Field Disbursing Officer. Henceforward he was to live on the Mount of Olives and to run about in a car, acting as Corps banker.

This was withdrawal to the safety zone. After four months on the Somme, a spell in Salonika, and the successive rock-stormings by which the British had gained Jerusalem and had even flowed (to ebb again) as far as mid-Gilead, he need not feel squeamish about accepting it. Chances of return to regimental duty were slight. The intolerable, interminable boredom of battalion life, absurd misuse of time in an existence solely physical yet devoid of all physical delight and interest, was gone.

Yet sundering of comradeship brought shame. Moreover, Martin had found his niche in war's routine; he was now the hermit-crab outside its shell.

'Quarters' sent ahead his kit. Then the two friends jumped a lorry plying between Jericho and Jerusalem.

'I feel an awful outsider, Bunny, to be leaving the fellows.'

(Warren, by association of ideas, had resulted in the nickname Bunny.)

'Rot! You've earned your reprieve, if ever anyone did.'

'You chaps have to carry on.'

'No reason why *you* should continue to be cannon-fodder! We want a few uncontaminated spirits to survive, to carry civilisation through the moral breakdown our thinkers predict. It follows every war, you know.'

'I'm leaving you and the rest——' persisted Martin.

'To the thinning-out parades? What of it? My dear Martin Puzzlewit, for the last time, don't be an ass! No one thinks *you* haven't done your bit.'

'What about you? And a whole shute of other fellows?'

'Oh, well! Anyway'—Remfry whistled, then lapsed into unusual seriousness—'I'll bet I had a softer time *before* the War than you had. It's as Father Abraham said to Dives.' He brightened up. 'Can't you see how the old buffer enjoyed saying it! Just like my old Head, stroking his saintly beard before he flogged the life out of you! Son, remember! thou hadst *thy* good time on earth. Now thou hast to pay for it! I was in Scotland, and due to go up to the Varsity, when the War came. And that summer I'd played twice for Somerset, and notched a couple of quite cheering scores, thank you! and Plum Warner had told me I should be playing for the Gentlemen in a couple of years. Fat lot he knew about what I should be doing in a couple of years! But what was little Martin doing,' he concluded triumphantly, 'when that silly chap began letting off revolvers somewhere in the Balkans?'

'Quill-driving. In Shoreditch.'

'You see! So now he shall quill-drive on Olivet, with a nice little Ford to race about in. Son! *remember!* While I supervise the digging of useless holes in solid rock and the useless ordering and sloping of arms and useless route marches when everyone merely wants to be allowed to lie down and die without any fuss. And ask men why the hell this, and why in thunder that, and generally make C Company's life a burden to it!'

Jerusalem in May was not much more attractive than Hades may be supposed to be at the same season. It was a seething pot over which a dust-smoke swirled. Its main human ingredient appeared to be the sheikhly folk (even then beginning to be glorified by Hollywood) for whom Warren held that an unnecessary war was being waged. As the lorry lumbered up to the Holy City his disapproval went out to them.

'*Look* at them! the crushed nationalities for whose liberation I've been sneaking behind rocks, and tramping till my feet were raw!'

'I see them,' said Martin. 'But I don't particularly want to.'

'Do they look like stuff you could ever make anything decent out of? A pinching, slouching, lousy lot! I bet you couldn't collect a respectable soccer eleven, let alone a rugger fifteen, from the whole of Jerusalem!'

'Oh, chuck it, Bunny! They haven't *all* got your beastly toothbrush. You're losing all sense of proportion. You'll be writing to Allenby about it.'

This seemed to give Remfry an idea.

'By Jove! but there *will* be trouble, if Allenby doesn't do something to stop all this bloody pinching that goes on! You mark my words! These Aussies'—he pointed to a group swaggering magnificently past—'will be cleaning up an Ayrab village one of these days.'

'Well,' said Martin, 'you'd better have a notice shoved in Aussie Orders, that when that time comes all units are to keep an eye open for Lieutenant Warren Remfry's toothbrush.'

'Don't try to be witty, Martin Chapman! And don't show a nasty temper to your superior officer!'

But Martin pointed triumphantly to the third pip now his in recognition of his quasi-headquarter status. Warren, despite the April casualties having raised him to command of a company, remained a lieutenant, though the order for his acting captaincy rank might come through any day.

They descended at the Damascus Gate, where a motley tide flowed round them, many-complexioned, many-statured. It included the emu-feather-hatted, superbly limbed, insolently self-sure Australian; the cautious Highlander; the stocky, humble English county soldier, Cinderella of all wars but wanting Cinderella's ultimate emergence from the scullery; the dwarfish Gurkha, controlled, watchful, enigmatic; the Sikh, ungainly, finely raffish, stiffly rakish. These, and a score of other human variations, through all the Empire's graduated changes, made their way amid a crowd which may be compendiously dismissed as 'Oriental.' That capable and kindly person Thomas Atkins was in charge, in the shape of a corporal of the Welsh Division. He grinned tolerantly at a bulky 'Ayrab' riding past, his burdened wife trudging beside the donkey.

"These people, sir,' he observed, as he saluted Martin, 'treat their women ass if they wass birds of prey.'

They paused to chat and show friendliness. Warren asked, 'Where are your chaps now, Corporal?'

'Oh, the boyce iss before Nablus, sir. Here!'—to another noble Arab, who was belabouring the head of the ass he bestrode—'whateffer are you toing?' He wrenched the cudgel from the amazed peasant, threatened him with it, then snapped it across a muscular knee. He returned some six inches of it.

'That's all the power that you beggars iss fit to be trusted with.'

'Stout fellow, Tommy Atkins!' said Warren, after they had gone on. 'Or, in this case, Taffy Atkins. How good to hear again the accents of Tonypandy! Chohn Tavis, iss thatt *you*, man? Whereffer haff you peen? Haff you seen Hlewethlyn Shenkins, the Paptist minister of Merthyr? Yess, inteet, to goodness! Fery powerful in prayer, whateffer, but an awful liar, whateffer!'

With which ancient libel on his sinful lips, Warren Remfry, in high spirits, entered the Holy City. Somewhere within it, he knew, he would find a place where he could buy sponge and toothbrush and even shaving tackle. At shocking prices, it is true. 'But haff I not with me the Tiffisional Tisbursing Officer, Captain Martin Chapman, of Abertillery? And he will supply, surely, all I neet, overlooking that little matter of an alleged oferdraft. Yess, inteet! A goot man and a kint, but untruthful!'

But the righteous Gods with indignation marking his jaunty carriage—noting, sad-eyed, that his loss of toilette had been a judgment vainly sent—had prepared disaster for him. A car swept up to the Gate. From it descended two officers; with almost feminine swiftness of disapproval Remfry noted their triple offence of flawless uniform, scarlet tabs, and courtly demeanour assuredly not won from trench experience. With them descended apparitions lovelier yet, Miss Cynthia Cameron, of Lackawanna County, Penna, and Miss Valerie Connett, of Roandoke Wilderness, Va. When the celestial Cynthia confronted her shepherd she took him at this added disadvantage, that he awakened on bleak upland, where never an Oread peeped from misty crag and heather's monotony. So now, to poor Warren, fresh from Jericho's sandy wretchedness and the death-humming rocks of Moab, shone this cool perfection. He flushed, conscious of his battle-stains and drab inadequacy. Martin heard him say,

'My God! Women! Not nurses!'

The unchivalrous distinction calls for explanation. Nurses Remfry had seen and knew. He had been in hospital for fever and colitis, and there had been that matter of a flesh wound in his arm at Second Gaza. (Jacko, to use his own expression, had 'notched' him on two other occasions, but not seriously; for only one of these hurts had he left his unit, and then for a very brief period.)

But a snowy uniform and sisterly impartiality had cloaked their femininity. Miss Cameron's case was other. With her, femininity triumphed over even the uniform of the American Relief Force of which she was a member. This uniform was a grotesque amalgam of ordinary tropical sun-wear and the British Army's quickly soiling and soon unlovely kit. But to the artist intractable material is a challenge. The pith helmet, for example, as the Englishwoman in India long ago learnt, can be worn ensnaringly; Miss Cameron had stumbled on this great truth at once. And the brown folds of her dress were made to suggest, not intolerable heat and discomfort, but neatness and elusive modesty. It quickened the beholder's sense of humility and obeisance due, that such divinity should be content to hide itself!

Remfry, aware only of tabless tunic and dusty
knees, did not know that he and his comrade
possessed what was worth even a goddess's eye and
for a moment flung a shadow on her escort. Only
athletic youth moves with such offenceless swagger,
and limbs that do their owner's will so easily and
unconsciously. The ladies, though none caught the
flicker aside of an eyelash, appraised all this. They
noted, too, the bronze that comes from sun and
exposure, and the expression which valour wins
from death confronted before its time and from the
fear of death cast aside, yet remembered. Youth in
this generation carried such eyes as it has hardly
carried since. Those who imagine that war brings
degradation only know nothing of the thing they
presume to discuss.

Entering the Tyropaean Valley, Warren said, more
to himself than to Martin, 'Wonder who they are?
That little one was an absolute picture. They'd be
bound,' he added bitterly, 'to fool round with red
tabs, anyway.'

'Of course they would. Wouldn't any girl? You
and I are navvies.'

An idea struck him. 'If you don't use your giddy
new elevation to get to know them, you're a bigger
fool than I care to think any friend of mine. Do you
want me to continue to look you up, now that you've
joined the brass hats!'

'What do you mean, Bunny?'

'Ass! dolt! idiot! Nonconformist ass, which in-
cludes all the rest! I mean, if you don't find some
way of making me acquainted with them, I've no
further use for you!'

'Why? Do you think they've pinched your tooth-brush?'

Warren stared at him blankly—so completely had the vision of Miss Cameron cleansed his brain of its old obsession. Then he remembered. They were passing a foliated pillar of Hadrian's time; in its recesses lurked a fruit-seller who seemed to be offering baskets of flies for sale. It was the work of a moment to trip Martin, who subsided on to a heap of prickly pears, over-ripe and yellow. There was no appearance of anything but sheer accident in the episode, a big man's clumsiness in sloping slippery paths.

Martin arose, damnation on his lips and in his heart. His rueful face met, however, not Warren's—Warren had sauntered on—but Miss Valerie Connett's. The taller of the two deities, in the blaze of her companion's splendour she had been obscured. She was making a valiant effort to refrain from mirth. It failed, but in her failure was an appeal to Martin for forgiveness. There was nothing to do but to laugh back.

II

THE WAR HELD NO SAFER, QUIETER NOOK THAN Jerusalem. No aeroplane dared violate the sky overarching the sacred city of three religions. Yet the battle's fringes swept so close that you heard the guns thudding at your frontiers.

The contrast with his former experience turned Martin's mind back to Henry (so confident of surviving the War), whom they had left in that

B

pocket of the hills. War meant this kind of dying. You were on a wiring party or night patrol, and the random shot out of darkness took you, no one saw you fall. You were hit in an attack and had to be left between the lines. No one knew how long it took men to die, so; or with what slow accumulation of misery.

He had been so close to the possibility himself that the fact was horrible. Thought was apt to work upon it and try it in new lights. But as the days passed it sank into the mind's background. He was only twenty-two, and a whole fresh existence was opening for him, one of absurd leisure and ease. Youth demanded that his entire life should not be given to vanished friendship or the wrongs of the dead, however dear the dead had been. He began to realise how jolly war can be.

First came rest and release, precursors of active happiness. His billet and office were on Olivet, in the house of a Scots baronet normally resident in Palestine but absent during the current unpleasantness. A series of rooms fronted with verandas had been built round a square shaded with pepper trees. He was one of a miscellaneous officers' mess, whose members realised Burns' description of himself, 'Contented wi' little, and canty wi' mair.' They had survived—which seemed to them a great deal. And here they were on Olympus—not in the Synod of the Great Deities, but in what Shakespeare rightly thought must be a circle of jollity, the session of the petty gods. They no longer cared to guess how distant peace might be. Probably the War would drift on and on, until a generation arose that had forgotten how it began, and in sheer indifference mislaid it in Flanders and Poland and Palestine, where it would die down and away gradually, as the combatant armies also grew old and feeble and weary, and disappeared. Meanwhile, this was Jerusalem, with an unhurried, lazy battle muttering at its doors. And they had jobs of sorts to get done; and the world's loveliest city invited them to saunter through its less insanitary regions, when the day grew cool. Ambition did not enter their lives; but then, neither did fear nor hope.

This island of human flotsam temporarily swept together and poised above the tides of war was a school for tolerance. Knowing well that the Higher Wisdom had seen to it that queer and useless jobs abounded, no man bothered as to what his neighbour was alleged to do. Not only was ordinary life in abeyance, the extraordinary life of war's lunacy was in abeyance also. Accepted into their company, Martin was content to be a convalescent.

After purchase of what Warren lacked they had had a drink in one of Jerusalem's two tolerable hotels; had pottered round the narrow streets; and lunched at the other hotel.

This, like its rival, was adorned with a stuffed hyena above the entrance. Warren, surveying the Oriental world from his soul's watch-tower of malevolence, growled, 'Evidently the regular badge of the Ayrab hotel-keepers' guild!'

'But this place is kept by sheenies, not by Ayrabs.'

'What's the difference, damn it? Sheenies *are* Ayrabs, conies *iss* rabbatch. Anyway, they shove a beast of ravin up to give you fair warning that they intend to dutch you to the bloody limit. Very decent of them!'

Then Martin had made his way to Olivet and reported to his new Commandant, Major Austin-Gary. In a few colourless words his arrival was noted and he was handed over to Captain Ralph Mackenzie, Assistant Commandant. This functionary lay in the depths of a chair, his eyes winking in friendly somnolence. He liked Chapman's looks.

'Mac'll look after you, Chapman,' said Austin-Gary. 'So long, then! You'll see me when I'm hard up, which you'll find will be pretty often.'

He yawned, started to say something more, thought better of it and decided to yawn again. He waved a hand of dismissal and restored his attention to the *Tatler*. Mackenzie slowly collected outlying members of his person, and when fully assembled rose, revealing a tall athletic body. 'I'll show you your place now, Chapman. It's only a step from here.'

At dinner Chapman sat between Austin-Gary and a vacant chair. Opposite him were two men excellently contrasted: Wenyon, ex-Fellow of Wadham and now in Corps 'Q' branch, lean-faced, long, with features wrinkling up into a charming pose of discontent, and Garratt, ex-architect, an irreverent little image of the jolly friar of Victorian semi-humorous portraiture. Garratt was Signals. Mackenzie sat the other side of the vacant place.

Major Austin-Gary interpreted Chapman's glance of enquiry at the empty seat. 'Major Blundell sits there. You are in Garratt's old place and have taken on the newcomer's job.'

'What's that, sir?'

'Buffer between me and Major Blundell.'

'The rule of the house, Chapman,' said Captain Wenyon. 'And no injustice to you. We've all had to do our turn. "All's love yet all's law." Be a man and don't grouse.'

'Why should I grouse?" asked the bewildered Martin.

'Ah! you'll learn soon enough!' said Garratt.

'Major Blundell,' Wenyon explained with grave courtliness, 'is a scientist and philosopher. He will address himself exclusively to you as the newest mind present; and Mac on his other side will have a period of peace while you receive infinite enlightenment and have your crass and idiotic delusions dissipated.'

'You'll be lucky,' said Garratt, exploding mirthfully, 'if all you receive is enlightenment. Take a word of advice from me, and try to get old Blundell to do his discoursing *between* courses. He discourses in more senses than one.'

In this concurrence of human atoms whirling lazily round in this diminutive vortex of the Great War there was nothing to call out emotion or earnestness or serious discussion. You met for casual fooling and chatter and meals that were no matter for excitement. Then you drifted back to your office or to read some magazine.

A fire of desultory chaff sputtered.

'Jacko,' Garratt pointed out, retorting on Mackenzie's reference to him as 'our cheery cheeky midget,' 'is too religious to shell this place. We get Mac to stand on the Mount of Olives and survey the whole enemy trench-system. Mac's seven feet four, and another eighteen inches when fully extended and on tiptoe.'

Martin, involuntarily half-turning towards Mackenzie, was aware of a figure sagging into the vacancy between them. What seemed its shoulders had on the likeness of a major's crown, rusted almost out of recognition. The body subsided, as its voice arose. Martin was confronted by fanatic eyes burning deeply in pits.

'You are wrong, Garratt,' said Major Blundell, kindly adding, 'And I'll tell you why. It is not possible to see the enemy trench-system from Olivet, partly because visibility is defective on account of the dust, still more because the Turkish positions are hidden by the nature of the terrain, with its intervening mountains.' He warmed to his theme, with the scholar's impersonal indignation. 'It is a false and foolish way of talking, to speak of *surveying* the enemy trench-position. Strictly speaking, all that even aeroplanes can do is to photograph scars on the earth's surface which we *guess* to be trenches, though it is, humanly speaking,—Major Blundell made a great distinction between 'strictly speaking' and 'humanly speaking'—'certain that many of them are merely natural ridges or even just natural discolourations. I have made a special study of these natural discolourations, and there is no doubt that they are of very particular interest and that science in the near future will have to pay close attention to them. For example, in the Jordan Valley——'

'Major Blundell,' said the Commandant, interrupting, 'I think you haven't met Captain Chapman, the new D.D.O.'

Major Blundell, his exposition momentarily deflected, expressed his pleasure at Captain Chapman's arrival; but hurriedly, as one anxious to return to business.

'I've come from the London Division,' said Martin; and was ill-advised enough to add: 'We've been in the Wadi Kelt. You know, sir—the place where the ravens fed Elijah.'

The fanatical eyes gleamed fiercely. 'You are wrong. And I'll tell you why. It cannot have been ravens that fed the prophet, for no ravens are known to exist in the Wadi Kelt.'

'Why shouldn't there have been some in Elijah's time?' asked Wenyon belligerently.

Major Blundell quelled him with the scowl of a tiger interrupted in its meal on a fawn, and proceeded to tell him why.

'Tradition says nothing about ravens in the Wadi Kelt. The word translated *ravens*——'

'Isn't the Old Testament tradition?' asked Wenyon, recovering.

'Will you kindly listen to me, Captain Wenyon, and not persist in pushing your theories before us? The word translated *ravens* undoubtedly should be translated jackdaws. There is a species of jackdaw that is peculiar to the Jordan Valley. "And the Jordan jackdaws brought him pancakes and gazelle flesh in the morning, and pancakes and gazelle flesh in the evening; and after eating he rinsed his mouth in the brook." I am translating the passage as it should be translated, to bring the meaning before the Western reader. Possibly, "scoured his mouth" or even "scrubbed his mouth" gives the meaning still better. And while we are all discussing the Jordan Valley let me explain the nature of the bituminous shale which forms a large portion of the surface of Eastern Palestine. By an inexperienced or unscientific photographer it might very readily be mistaken—especially where it lies in regular lines of thickening—for the work of man, even for trenches. This bituminous shale——'

For the complete text of Major Blundell's lecture, which occupied the rest of dinner and some time afterwards, I must refer my disappointed readers to the Royal Society's transactions; I cannot infringe a valuable copyright. All except Wenyon and Chapman disappeared early, the latter chained by politeness, the former by a grim cussedness that sought occasions to jerk the speaker out of his course.

When at long last the audience escaped, Chapman asked Wenyon, 'What's the Major's job?'

'Scientific observer.'

'What on earth's that?'

'Ah! anyone can see that you've just come from the ignorant and uncivilised infantry! You'll have to get used to the military fauna of these more alpine regions. How the devil do you think the cost of the War could be run up to eight millions a day, if we proceeded on the narrow lines of your kind of thought? He's *scientific observer*, I repeat. Sent by the Tasmanian Government. Used to be attached to the A.S.C. But the A.S.C. refused to get attached to *him*. So he was sent here and attached to Corps Intelligence. And I must say he fits in very splendidly.'

III

AND NOW THE CITY GATHERED MARTIN UNDER ITS spell. The amazing pity and beauty of the past seemed at hand, as it does in Umbria or Palestine, as it does not in Oxford or Winchester. You cannot believe in Waltheof led up Castle Hill to die, or in Cranmer being degraded on the tiny plat of grass and stones by Christ Church. You cannot but believe in Santa Chiara confronting the paradisal wonder of the green plain, and the Saracen bullies by celestial grace awed into an episode only, not (as elsewhere) a menace but mere sound and fury, foil to one divine girl! The aged olives of the Temple area, mistletoe-crammed, linked the ages. Martin, haunting the sun-comforted tangle of flowers, could see a Figure, moving on the outskirts where the common crowd gathered, telling of the Father who sent rain on just and unjust alike and cared for the sparrows as they fluttered to the ground to peck their food. Herod's aery bridge spanned the valley between City and Temple: Roman legionaries watchfully patrolled streets that held potentialities of unknown mischief. Here was the Tower of Antonia, here the cobbles before Pilate's Palace. Over there the Maccabbees had held out for freedom; a long stone's throw further had been the first Zion, which Job had scaled 'by the gutter'.

His duties were unexacting. There were hours when he was on hand to pay out to individual officers or to representatives of units in his area. He ran about in a Ford, as Remfry had predicted. For the rest, he was free to loaf, to read, to wander. Time became one eternal contemporaneousness. The Grecian tomb and Athene's owl on the olive that partially screened it, the fountain where Adonijah had been anointed king and the place where Godfrey had burst over the walls, were to him all part of the glorious City's present. Coming late in time he confronted the ages as one and indivisible.

Wenyon and Mackenzie both owned George Adam Smith's *Historical Geography of the Holy Land*, a book studied raptly by many who campaigned in Palestine. Wenyon had also the same author's two-volumed *Jerusalem*, known almost line by line. It was Wenyon who introduced Chapman to the City, on the afternoon of his second day at Corps H.Q. 'I never get to the end of it. There's always some new tomb to look into, always some fresh site to explore. I worship the old place and shall be half sorry when the War ends.'

The City divides mankind into fools who in blindness pass her by, and lovers who can see nothing mean or insignificant in her infinite variety. Wenyon was a lover.

'Why, even these new brick red houses on the hills, that you hear folk cursing, there's nothing wrong with them! They merely show that the wonderful town is alive. It's still growing, Martin! I like to think of Jerusalem the *living*—the one place in all the world that has a soul inside it!'

Mackenzie was invited to join their party; and he good-naturedly gathered in a group of soldier sight-seers sent from a Division in the line. These had been sheep with a fool for shepherd; Mac rescued them from a scowling, incompetent guide with a juggle of incomprehensible gutturals which he gave out as English.

They passed down the Tyropaean Valley to the Temple, where Wenyon traced out the varying fortunes of that tiny plot which has seen Jebusite and Maccabbee, no less than Hebrew and Crusader, defending possession. Mounting thence they had reached the Jaffa Gate, and Wenyon discussed the fortress called David's but built by Herod.

Round the corner came Major Blundell, who joined them immediately. To Wenyon's obvious vexation he waited listening, grimly keeping down impatience till a decisive point in the exposition had been reached. Wenyon, examining the problem of where the old city wall ran and its bearing on the further question of whether the Holy Sepulchre could be a genuine site, was allowed to commit himself to the hilt and to say be believed it was. Then Major Blundell smashed in devastatingly.

'You're wrong, Wenyon. And I'll tell you why.'

This he proceeded to do.

Thereafter he accompanied the party, at each pause waiting till Wenyon had interpreted and then giving him the lie direct. It was clear that it never occurred to him that his presence was other than delightful or his auditors other than grateful for the enlightenment uncompromisingly poured upon them. Marking a homicidal glitter in even Mackenzie's patient, lazy eyes, Chapman understood why Authority had given Blundell a majority. Army Regulations discouraged the slaughter of field-officers by those who ranked below them. As thousands who were not field-officers in the Great War can testify, this was a fortunate thing for very many field-officers, who have presumably spent the last fourteen years hiding in as civilian a disguise as they can find.

'I will explain it all to you very simply. Very simply, Wenyon. I have one principle: that Tradition

is always right. Our so-called scholars' (a phrase he
loved; he was always particularly down on Wenyon,
the ex-Oxford-don) 'think it is always wrong. But
if it were wrong how could it have arisen?'

Major Blundell paused triumphantly, as any man
who has reached a decisive point in his argument is
entitled to do.

'But Tradition *says* the Wall ran here, sir,' said the
exasperated Wenyon. 'Why, it's here still! It runs
through that line of shops. You can trace it for
yourself!'

'That is another wall altogether. Your tradition,
Wenyon, is a false one, a later one. And I'll tell you
why. I have three strong lines of proof. Josephus
tells us that the besieging Roman forces encamped
before the Wall.'

'Naturally,' said Wenyon. 'The Jews would hardly
have welcomed them *behind* it.' Mutiny blazed in his
eyes and speech.

'Attend to me, please. I have given you my first
strong line of evidence. My second is this. Tradition
says they encamped over there, about four hundred
yards from where *your* wall is. *Your* wall, I say; and
say *your* wall advisedly. For it is not *the* wall. It
cannot be. If *your* wall had been the wall of the City
when the Romans besieged it, they could not
possibly have encamped where we know from
Tradition that they did.'

'Why on earth not?' said Wenyon, in the intensity
of his emotion not adding 'sir.'

'Why?' said the scholar gleefully. '*Why?*' He had
evicted his quarry from cover and was about to run
it down in the open. 'I'll tell you why. Attend to
me, please. This is my third line of proof.' And

Major Blundell, who had never seen a shot fired, continued: 'Because it would have been too dangerous. The Jewish troops would have been able to shoot arrows at them.'

Chapman made a contribution. 'The Romans would be entrenched, sir.'

The great scholar was good enough to consider this suggestion before rejecting it. But reject it he did. 'Tradition says nothing about that. And, even if they were, the trenches—with the appliances of those days, when you must remember that they had none of our devices for ensuring the safety of our troops—could not have been made entirely arrowproof. No Roman general of repute (and Titus was undoubtedly in the first rank, in my judgment above Cæsar and only a little below Pompeius Magnus himself) would have allowed his men to be entrenched where they would suffer casualties by the enemy's desultory hostility.'

'I wish *we* might be commanded by some Roman general of repute,' observed Mackenzie. And gave a manifestation of incipient insanity, bursting into a laugh that was a paroxysm. He did not trouble to apologise.

The laugh startled into attention a sight-seeing group of whose presence Martin was already nervously aware. It was the two deities, with their attendant Red Tabs. Martin knew he was instantaneously recognised, one in this infernal agglomeration—hilarious giant, beaked impostor, and 'other ranks' visibly sagging in the loosened tape of discipline, possessed as they were of a giggling secret, in knowledge of the major's imbecility.

Greater vexation yet followed when the two companies flowed together in the Jaffa Gate defile. The well-bred and adorable neatness of the one stood off from the shambling and reckless miscellaneousness of the other. Martin's foreboding became justified. An awful thing happened.

'This is what they call Zion,' said the Senior Red Tab, Carruthers, a young-looking major. 'Shouldn't you think it must have been the original centre of the City, Ferguson?'

The ladies waited, their faces tilted in charming interest. This interest, before Ferguson could reply, was heightened by the irruption of Major Blundell. Scholarship knows (and ought to know) no conventions. He had heard a heretical opinion; his work was to contradict heretical opinions.

Martin, horrified, loath to trust the evidence of his ears, heard him say, 'You're wrong. And I'll tell you why.'

Several conflicts sprang into instant activity. One, of which Martin was at once aware, was personal between him and Major Carruthers, the boy with the spoiled, insolent face, whose surmise as to the origin of Zion had been so tyrannously quelled. With dislike peering in his eyes, he recognised Martin as one of two bounders in the infantry who had once before (even if only momentarily) drawn off attention due to those who exemplified the higher civilisation. Another conflict (of which Major Blundell was entirely unaware) was the one too common, between British public-school regular army officer and slack Colonial. The ladies' escort noted the emu feather and the slouch (perhaps the only

Aussie marks that Major Blundell possessed); and they seemed characteristic of a clan whose bearing was all saliences, loud, aggressive, bullying, contemptuous. Nose and eyes were the more obvious offences, but the whole man was an offence. And on the privacy of delightful ciceronage he had thrust his following of over a dozen, that dozen composed of beings whose job was to salute and keep to a distance.

Wenyon tumbled to the situation and drew off his party to note the spot where the Turkish gallows used to stand. This rid him of his tormentor; but he followed it with a deed that will befriend him at the Last Day. He called loudly to Major Blundell, 'I say, Major, have you seen this?'

The Major merely vouchsafed one indifferent glance. He was engrossed with his new prey, stirred under all his bumbling busyness by the attractive audience he had captured. He waxed eloquent over the folly and ignorance of their escort, and with joyful derision pointed out that Tradition placed the City's centre elsewhere. From now on he was a member of their party, and had done with his old one.

Weynon's shout, however, drew over Miss Valerie Connett, who was finding proximity to Major Blundell's excessively happy voice overpowering. She could hear him with greater convenience from across the road. Besides, she wanted to see what it was that Wenyon was drawing attention to.

Martin would have been well content with the exchange. But it proved no exchange, since Valerie's defection resulted in both groups being made inextricably one.

To the girls, unaware of the gulf set betwixt Political and Combatant, it meant nothing that Wenyon, Mackenzie and Chapman, though now promoted away from the fighting line, still bore the letters of their regiments, badges of their ignoble origin. And they were further unaware of the yet vaster gulf that yawns between the officer and 'other ranks'. They were more than willing to be merged, especially since Wenyon and Mackenzie knew the City, whereas their escort merely knew that there was a city and that it was a well-known one.

Major Blundell, the solvent who had made the parties indissolubly knit, continued to correct fallacies —Wenyon's now, since Carruthers had sunk into fuming silence.

Martin found Carruthers' face close to his. 'Take your damned menagerie away,' he was told in a hissed undertone.

'I've no authority over the Major,' he replied. 'He joined us as he joined you—uninvited.'

'You've no business to come barging in on other people.'

'If it comes to that, who's doing the barging?' asked Martin in a fury of cold contempt. 'We've taken our crowd off at least twice. Speak to the Major yourself. I'm not a field officer.'

He turned his back indignantly.

The ladies exchanged glances, awakening to the fact of hostilities. They were aware of insipidities in their escort. The newly acquired officers looked interesting. Cynthia, sometimes more noticing than Valerie, had seen that they had made genuine efforts to free them from a complication assumed to be unwelcome.

She was not going to have Chapman snubbed. She slipped to his side and began to draw him out, first about general matters, then about himself. Learning that he had been in the East of Jordan fighting whose mutters were just dying down when the American Relief Force reached Jerusalem, a few days previously, she called out her discovery to Valerie. Everything about war was exciting to them at this stage of experience. Presently Major Blundell was glaring disapprovingly at interruptions that broke up the full proud sail of his exposition. He sometimes wondered if the ladies were listening.

Chapman and Mac and Wenyon, once conscience was satisfied that they had done their best as gentlemen, were by no means unhappy. The Red Tabs drifted along with them, in their unsuccessful rearguard action of disentanglement.

Cover showed at length in the Fast Hotel. Captain Ferguson suggested tea to the ladies, and the suggestion was accepted. Wenyon's force drew off.

But without Major Blundell. They carried away a confused vision of him pertinaciously maintaining to an audience now both profoundly uninterested and exasperated his thesis that *semper, ubique, et ab omnibus* Tradition is worthy of acceptance.

IV

I

THE GOVERNOR OF JERUSALEM HAD SENT MAJOR Carruthers and Captain Ferguson to meet the American Relief Force on its arrival, and to oversee

their settling in. They proved the swallows to an
April of British kindness; Valerie and Cynthia almost
at once seemed to know scores of officers, British
and Anzac, and were invited to a succession of
delightful jaunts.

But here the Relief Force needs a word of introduction.

The U.S.A. came into the War with characteristic
rush and enthusiasm. 'Lafayette, we are here!' This
generous fire scattered widely. Even Palestine
(though America never went to war with Turkey)
must have a force, though it could work merely
among civilians; and this force must be strictly
military.

It had two colonels, a missionary and a man of
letters. Under these were other ranks, of many
degrees and kind. There was 'Store-Major Schwartz',
'Staff-Captain Firelli', 'Transport-Commandant
Gleeson'.

And there were many ladies, who proved a complication at the outset of work in Jerusalem. They all
ranked as privates or merely non-commissioned
officers, whereas every man was a commissioned
officer. Since the leaders were strict about saluting,
and, moreover, held that a private should salute a
lance-corporal and a corporal a sergeant, the British
Army was given some surprising spectacles. 'Store-
Major Schwartz' would be lurching down Zion's
ancient ways, his khaki bulging in unauthorised
lumps, when he would come face to face with an
oread who had drawn all masculine eyes in her
gracious progress. Promptly the oread would click
her heels and salute; the unmilitary bulk so notably

honoured would wave a fat paw and slouch on. Or
the girl just out of Vassar or Wellesley would meet
the matron who had guided the Women's Club of
Toledo (Ohio) in their researches into 'Europe's
Monarchical Systems and the World War' and
'Dante and Emerson as Masters of Life and
Thought'. And just graduated Vassar or Wellesley
would gravely salute the Toledo Sibyl, bearing
herself humbly and obsequiously, as adolescence
should in the presence of wisdom and ripe experience.

It was magnificent; and it was war. For war is all
kinds of nonsense, as well as fighting.

The Relief Force by reason of Mediterranean
submarines divagated via South Africa and Ceylon,
on its course from New York to Port Said. It had
done picturesquely and enjoyed itself immensely.
There had been a march through Colombo, headed
by the two colonels and Store-Major Schwartz and
completed by Privates Cynthia Cameron and
Valerie Connett, the whole meinie chanting 'The
Star-Spangled Banner' (which is a very difficult
hymn to sing, owing to a wide variance of opinion
as to the correct pitch of the opening 'Oh, say!').
There had been experience of delightful hospitality
in Natal, with glimpses of real hippos in a real river.
There had been earnest classes on the long voyage,
on Arabic and French, on military deportment,
rules of behaviour towards officers and men of the
Allies, social technique as employed in an alien
country, the keeping of diaries. Finally, the Force had
taken up work in Jerusalem.

Having reached Jerusalem, the Relief Force began
to behave in an entirely American fashion. The

earnestness and enthusiasm persisted, but immediately sank into a full stream of energy and useful-
ness. Its members were amateurs, collected from
many sides of life—schoolmarms, missionaries kept
out of Syria and Palestine by the War and eager to
return (these predominated), engineers, business
men, students. Yet they were astonishingly efficient.
They were also exceedingly unselfish, as is America's
wont when its heart is moved with pity. They did
not stand out for honour or for individuality; their
leaders saw the British Commander and the Corps
authorities on Olivet, and asked frankly where their
own zeal and their country's money could be best
used. Since America was at peace with Turkey, it
was felt that the Relief Force had better leave
British needs alone. So it took over the miscellaneous
misery of the land's inhabitants, and almost from
the day of arrival the Force was running orphanages,
hospitals, food distribution centres.

Its members, during their tortuous trail across the
world's seas, had received lectures enough on the
necessity of tact towards those touchy folk the
British. The lectures must have been very good and
deeply pondered, for the Force gave an exhibition
of flawless courtesy and thought for others. Their
garb may have been queer, but its wearers were
quickly respected; and, once the Englishman has
decided that he respects you, it does not matter
what you wear, for after the first time he will not
see it. There might be a glint in the eye of the British
captain in charge of local transport, when Miss
Cameron, coming to beg the use of a motor lorry
(she called it a truck) to give her orphans a run down
to the fountain at Ain Karim, was seen at close

range to be 'dressed like nothing on earth' ('but, by God! she wore it as if it suited her! and it did suit her, too!') But he noted very speedily that this divinely pretty girl 'did her job', for which reason alone (there were others reinforcing it; but this would have sufficed) she had no difficulty in getting a 'truck' any time she wanted one. Presently the Relief Force had plenty of trucks of its own. But the friendly relations she had set up in the first truckless days persisted.

Once interest awakens, souls look at each other from argus-eyes. There is more than the glance of person to person; there is the watchfulness of differing generations and nationalities. Between Cynthia and Valerie, daughters of one country, was the distinction between Daughter of the Revolution and Daughter of the Confederacy. Both had (or thought they had) historical memory in their homes. But for one this was legend; for the other, living tradition that had scarcely begun to be tradition, scarcely ceased to be experience. Pressed by Cynthia's keenness, the Camerons had persuaded themselves and the local chapter of the 'Daughters of the American Revolution' that they possessed a link with one Ramsay Cameron, whose name appears in the lists of men who served fitfully from New York State; he had soldiered for a few months in 1780. But Valerie's people had had their homestead burned by Northern soldiers, before they had moved to Norfolk. Two uncles had fought under Lee, and one had been killed at Chancellorsville. Her father, too young to fight, had grown up bitter in the shadow of the Civil War. When she looked at the statue of the Confeder-

ate infantryman that the Daughters of the Confederacy have raised in Charlottesville, her heart
swelled with pride and grief for the inscription, 'Love
keeps their memory immortal'. Love did keep their
memory immortal. This was how, in her visualisa-
tion of it, her own beloved South, her own dear
State of Virginia, stood at bay, defeated yet
confronting still this new age that misunderstood
its values.

The vanquished are twice unfortunate, for pride
forbids them to cast away any part of their heritage;
they are apt to stand resolutely on all the ancient
ways and all the ancient evil. However that may be,
in Valerie's gaze towards life there were shadows
that the Northern girl had never known that there
lay on any spirit. Yet her own generation was fast
shedding the scorn and anger which her father's
generation felt towards the arrogant victorious
North. She could view Cynthia's naïvely happy
unconsciousness of everything except her own
excellence and the excellence of the world in which
she had been brought up, and could be glad as she
saw it.

Their alliance had begun in the offices of the Relief
Force, in New York, when they had met as applicants
for places in its Palestine expedition. Valerie had
found Cynthia a fountain of delightfulness, before
ever they spoke together. She was a humming-bird,
one tremor and glimmer of colour and activity, an
iridescence hovering at flower after flower. Valerie
noted that she had been spoiled, but would have
added, as Dr. Johnson did of Kit Smart, that her
infirmities were not noxious to society. That she
had always had what she wanted had not inflicted

any hardship on anyone who was visible, for most people had been reasonably eager to give her what she wanted.

II

The Relief Force established themselves in Jerusalem's northern suburb, in a mass of temporarily deserted buildings where its members, male and female, commissioned, non-commissioned, uncommissioned, had their first rooms (before half of them scattered to independent jobs of their own) and fed in monastic community. It was out of this communal existence that trouble arose.

I have said that the ladies were all 'other ranks,' the men all commissioned. Yet no one suggested that the ladies ought to take their meals apart; the men were too gallant to stress the yawning social gulf. War compels sacrifice, but not sacrifice such as this. All would have gone on well if in Jerusalem itself three civilian Americans serving with the Y.M.C.A. had not approached the two colonel chieftains and asked to be taken into their national unit. They were young men of good presence, all three had been at universities of repute, all three were useful. They were taken on as motor engineers and drivers, to do the same work as commissioned members of the Relief Force.

Unfortunately, only the U.S.A. Government could commission them, so perforce they joined as the first male privates. And in their thoughtless American fashion, at dinner the very first day they proposed to sit with the rest of the Relief Force. Two of them had found a couple of members of their own

Fraternity, and had made with them a cheery bunch.

It was the soldierly eye of Store-Major Schwartz that fell on this unseemly breach of discipline. If the uncommissioned once begin to eat beside the commissioned, there is no army in the world that will not disintegrate. Witness the fate that overtook Bolshevik Russia. Ladies—Store-Major Schwartz's glance did for a minute note that Miss Cynthia Cameron, chatting with a most undisciplined vivacity and freedom with the newcomers, was not even a lance-corporal—were different. He had a feeling that to drive them into outer darkness, while it might be war, would be considered by his fellow-officers an act of unnecessary austerity and purity. He checked for only a moment, though. Then he coughed to ensure silence, before sternly observing: 'This is a mess for commissioned officers of the U-nited States Army. Privates will take their meals in the basement under the clothes-room?

Store-Major Schwartz, though public speaking was his delight and hobby, was not as a rule an effective orator. On this occasion, however, he achieved a startling success. Not Sheridan flaying Warren Hastings, not John Bright in his 'angel of death beating his wings' peroration, can have produced a more shocked silence. It was profaned only by a matronly 'Well!' from Sergeant Maria Hunsecker of Poughkeepsie. Then the three culprits, privates of the Relief Force, sullenly humped themselves to their feet and prepared for extradition.

Cynthia and Valerie had risen with them. 'I don't know what the rest of you girls are going to do

about it,' Miss Cameron announced, 'but Val and
I are going with these boys. Jim and Alan and
Willard are privates, says Store-Major Schwartz. I
guess that's *right*, there's no getting round *that*! But
so are I and Val'—in moments of emotion Miss
Cameron, despite her Wellesley training, relapsed
into the order of the personal pronouns which Latin
prefers. 'And so are most of you girls. And even
Mrs. Hunsecker is only a sergeant.'

The party of the expelled, thus reinforced and compensated, went with a joyousness hard to endure by
those left behind. The rest of the women followed
almost on their heels, all except three.

Marooned in their nearly Eveless Eden, the men sat
unspeaking, while the work of dinner paused. Then
Lieutenant Wilbur Frobisher spoke.

'I make it game to the girls, Major,' he said. 'I
guess they've overtrumped you. They had all the
cards, and you didn't notice it.'

Store-Major Schwartz glowered. 'We are repre-
senting the military forces of the U-nited States,
and it is essential that we should show ourselves as a
disciplined body.'

Lieutenant Frobisher thoughtfully helped himself
to an olive. Its saline sharpness seemed to bring
decision. 'To Hell with discipline!' he remarked at
last. 'I'm going to have supper with the girls.'

'That is a grossly improper way of addressing your
superior officer, Lootenant Frobisher. If a lootenant
spoke so to a major in the British Army, he would be
placed under arrest, sir!'

'That so?' enquired Frobisher indifferently, trying
another olive, and rising at the same time.

'I'm with Frobisher,' announced Captain Wardell. 'No offence to you, Store-Major Schwartz. You are our commanding officer here to-night, sir, and we admit it. But we don't want British Army ways here, sir, and I guess that's the sense of us all.'

'The girls are right,' pointed out Transport-Commandant Gleeson. 'There's logic to what Miss Cameron said. They *are* privates, and if the privates is to eat separate, why, Miss Cameron and Miss Connett are privates, like she said. And so are half the other girls.'

Logic carried the day, the commissioned rejoined the uncommissioned, the schism was closed. Store-Major Schwartz made a gesture of necessity. 'I reckon we don't *want* all those stilted British ways here, after all,' he conceded. 'Why, Miss Cameron's right when she says you girls are privates too. I hadn't noticed it that way till she put it straight, the way she did just now.'

Pending formal sanction from Washington, which came in due course, the three masculine privates were made temporary second-lieutenants, losing a pre-eminence of abasement that had promised to be very enjoyable. Order was restored. The Relief Force was once more a disciplined body, observing all rules and practices of the Ancients.

This affair cropped up and was settled when the Force had been less than three days in Jerusalem. Those three days had been eventful. Rarely can any girls, even in the Great War, have come to their work in such unmeasured excitement as Valerie and Cynthia experienced; and all the excitement was pleasurable.

The enthusiasm with which their country had at last entered the War was almost hysterical; and they themselves had formed the wild, deep, sudden friendship of adolescence. A mist of glory was over everything. And no words can convey the experience of being in Jerusalem, after their protracted and tortuous journey which seemed to take them into all corners of the known world! Of starting work in Jerusalem, with the real War so close to them!

In Jerusalem were the men who had taken it. Beyond those eastern hills were the Arabs, a nation now, and led by a figure of legend—for the first time they heard of Colonel Lawrence. Allenby himself, a giant of a man with a giant reputation destined to tower yet higher, was often in Jerusalem, and from the beginning was a friend of their unit and its leaders. In the streets were all the 'thrills' possible and in company. The Bedouin and his camel moved side by side with the Gurkha and the Sikh—so diverse in appearance, so famous for war; from their officers they learnt of the prowess of these men who had come from India, a name of magic, to fight for the Raj.

They had not seen officers of the British Army before; here they were, veterans from four years of wide-flung battle, men who talked familiarly of the Somme and Gallipoli, of Gaza and Baghdad. The Army was Indian and Scots and Welsh and Irish, as well as English, every race represented by its own dour and war-tested battalions, with their varying traditions and details of dress and custom. It was also Australian and New Zealand; Jerusalem paths were thronged with these men whose every move-ment spoke recklessness and devil-may-care independence, accepting all experience without wonder and without hesitation. Did not men say that Captain Francks, the German counterpart of our own Colonel Lawrence, the gallant spy whose mother was English, would one day be caught when he swung into our lines from the desert borderland, because he overdid the swagger of his favourite disguise, an Aussie Camel Transport officer? The foreigner of genius picks out some saliency of deportment and imitates it. But his very skill undoes him; it is very difficult for him not to exaggerate in just the extra trivial detail that gives him away. The Aussie would no doubt ride past a covey of brigadiers without saluting; that was all right. But he would not as a rule call them 'a bunch of bloody old——' for blocking his way. Francks had done this when he came in by Beersheba.

Cynthia was greatly interested in 'problems'—'the problem of capital and labour', 'the problem of India and her demand for freedom', 'the problem of European imperialism'. These had been set before her in outlines of an austere, awe-inspiring simplicity, by the master-minds who had taught her, whether in school-days or in the Women's Club of her home town. She sometimes wondered why they continued to furnish fuel for protracted and even embittered discussion, why new problems did not come on. Like most educated Americans, she was especially puzzled as to what the European fuss was all about.

Valerie's mind had hitherto passed over 'problems' as belonging to a world far outside Virginia. Yet in every American woman sleeps a gift for generalisation, which the right wind can fan into a flame.

Coming to Jerusalem—even before she came—
Valerie had begun to reflect on the accidents which
had drawn her so far from her orbit. She could on
occasion be more maddeningly doctrinaire than
Cynthia; a vigorous dislike could make her con-
clusions run into a hard mould. Their new experience brought complication as well as delight, it
awakened antagonism as well as admiration and
excitement. They were meeting so many officers,
Anzac as well as British. They sympathised with the
free and independent manners of the former; had
the same readiness to come to swift decisions
expressed vigorously even if not deeply rooted; found
equally much that repelled them in the British
Army and its customs.

All this, however, came later. In this month of
May, 1918, that sees the opening of our story, each
day began in a haze of pleasure, with the scarcely
realisable thought that it was in Jerusalem that they
rose from sleep.

They managed (easily) to combine hard work
with abundant play. On June 1st Val and Cynthia
were invited to watch a cricket match played on
Olivet. It was all local colour, part of the enchant-
ingly strange habits of the English, deserving of
study by modern American girls wishful to understand the outside world. During the match there
would be tea—tea on the Mount of Olives! At
night, dinner with their escort—in a house which
had belonged to an English baronet—and a concert
afterwards. Major Carruthers called this last a
'gaffe', in inverted commas, but explained what it
really was. It would not be up to much. 'Still, you
and Miss Cameron may find it not altogether too

boring. And there's no chance of Fergy and myself being bored!' It would be very, very interesting to see how the British Army amused itself.

V

THE MATCH WAS BETWEEN CORPS HEADQUARTERS AND the London Division. Major Austin-Gary, skippering the former team, sent out a facetious Plan of Operations, which directed that 'vigorous and concerted action be taken against the enemy strong points', among which it enumerated Captain Remfry, 'who has played for Somerset and made a century for Winchester against the M.C.C. He should be dealt with as expeditiously as the attacking forces can arrange'.

Olivet, in response to infinite pains, had yielded up a good matting pitch, though the outfield remained a rockery. Both teams were to be the guests of Sir Philip Chetwode, the Corps Commander, at dinner after the game. The printing department had found a special fount for the word 'champagne'.

Warren, who had not yet changed, hooted with delight at his friend's metamorphosis, when Martin, in all the amenity of flannels, met him at the Damascus Gate and swankily took him off in his own car.

'Who would think that this Beau Brummel— staring offensively at his old commander!—was ever one of the brutal and licentious soldiery!'

Martin sighed. 'You've no idea how good it is to be out of khaki! Jump in, Bunny my boy. It'll be a treat when I see you in flannels, too!'

The car began to get up speed to take the winding road that skirts the side of Kedron and climbs up Mount Scopus to Olivet. 'You beggars must have had a hell of a time since it began to get really hot!'

Warren agreed. 'It's perfectly putrid. And we've villages of Ayrabs all round us. It's as Lloyd George said in the Cabinet when Bonar Law asked him what was doing in Mesopotamia. "Oh, the flice is too awful, whateffer!"' He proceeded to fall back on his conviction, traceable to a doubtful drip of Wicklow blood in his veins, that he could echo the elegiac notes and cadences of the Poor Woman. 'It's meself that has had the harrd times,' he crooned, 'all through the nights and days of Samhain, when the great winds do be blowing and the rains falling as if the Lord God (and He in His golden chair, beholding meself as it might be meself beholding a Connemara sparrow)—'

Though he had passed through a famous school, it would be a mistake to regard Captain Warren Remfry as entirely uneducated. He chose to conceal the fact, but he read poetry, and had been caught enthusiastically into the Synge cult that preceded the War. (Does anyone read Synge now? We all read him in 1910.)

'Chuck this imbecility,' said Martin firmly. 'You are not ragging Father O'Hara now. Try to remember,' he went on with severity, 'that you're talking to a grown man and may be talking to others presently. I don't want the fellows up at Corps to think I'm pals with a half-wit.'

The main lines of personal abuse, as of the other fine arts, were laid down long ago. Martin's sole weapon for this warfare was the gift of facial control, lines that he set sternly and refused to relax. Warren, for once outfought, could reply only with the threat of a brawl. 'Well, of all the outstanding cheek! From *you*—Martin Chapman, Martin Luther, Martin Puzzlewit—to me! O-oh! If you weren't driving round a hairpin bend, it would be my joy and duty to give you that painful malady known as a thick ear, to match your thick head. By the way,' he suddenly remembered, 'are you going to introduce me this afternoon to the two girls who saw you staggering about in that fruit-shop?'

'I'm sorry, Bunny, but I haven't managed to get to know them. At least——'

'Ass! idiot! notorious dolt and imbecile! You sit there and tell me that for a whole fortnight you have been loafing on Olympus without getting to know the local oreads! Do you mean to say that you haven't invited them to see me play?'

Martin related the incident of the Jaffa Gate. Remfry disapproved that he had made so little use of it. 'All the same' (brightening up) 'it was an introduction of a sort. Let's hope for the best. They *may* have been asked up by those fellows, and you may get your chance of proving that your acquaintance isn't solely among the criminal classes.'

Cricket on Olivet is the most nearly perfect sport in the world. The outfield being a chaos, the fieldsman can combine almost as many varieties of manly healthy exercise as there are. A rock to be leapt thrusts up suddenly between him and a catch; more painfully he has to mountaineer to collect a drive gone to ground in a wilderness of crag and thorn;

a masked pyramid precipitates him in full career, and he skis or dives into a bush of long needles.

Martin, placed on the boundary as tribute to Remfry's known prowess—in a chaos which Austin-Gary, doing a preliminary survey of the field, has nicknamed 'the Grampians'—feels the thrill no one but an Englishman ever experiences, seeing the fielders dispose themselves into attitudes of deceptive casualness, the body seemingly slack and indifferent, the hands anywhere. The batsmen come, moving with easy, elaborately impersonal carriage, each mark of individuality subordinated to the quiet tones of this festival of sight and quickness and skill. That boy is Warren Remfry, from whom Somerset expect great things if ever this absurd War finishes. And his friend, waiting in a ghastly trap of peaks submerged in a sea of thistles, knows what pride is as he sees Remfry's gaze, sweeping the circle of the ground, pause noticeably on him, and understands the resolve in the brain behind. 'Better keep clear of Martin till you get set! Old Puzzlewit can generally be relied on to deliver the goods. The odds are that a chance sent his way will be a chance gratefully accepted.'

And for several overs Warren does beware of Martin while he cautiously learns the tricks of this unique ground. But it is not in Warren to be cautious for long, and soon—in contrast to his partner, who plays as if he were an Aberdonian and had to buy every run with a pound sterling (pre-National-Government value)—he is opening his shoulders. Suddenly one of his shots comes racing towards the Grampians. Martin has sprung on to what (he thinks) is fairly true surface and is ready to gather the ball, when it hits a cistus-covered reef, rises straight like a ten-

D

foot serpent, and is over his head to the boundary. Overbalancing in a last insane effort to prevent the tragedy, Martin tilted backward disappears into an underworld of stabs and prickles. In the throes of extrication he is rattled by joyous laughter. He turns to retrieve the ball from the spectators, and sees it has been picked up by Carruthers, whom he has twice met as Miss Valerie's escort. Carruthers is in the same high service to-day.

No one is laughing at Martin, really, except that you cannot help smiling a bit more at a tall man than at a short one, when he comes to physical grief. He looks so much more astonished and disconcerted at the ball deserting all proper ball-like behaviour. By a frantic elongation to his utmost Martin had all but caught it; and to the uninitiated the good fielder when he does just miss a sheer impossibility —having drawn it almost within the category of possibility—*looks* like a bad fielder. Your real bad fielder will not get within arm's length, and will *seem* to have done all that man could do.

Martin is still dazed by annoyance with that treacherous terrain and with knowledge of what eyes were on his failure, when Remfry, on good terms with himself, decides to knock Austin-Gary off his length. Here on Olivet the odds are with the batsman. He has a pitch scoured of its aboriginal roughness and matted down, while the fielding side are dotted amid alps and andes of sharp edge and varying altitude. Remfry steps back to a good length ball and sweeps it magnificently to the leg boundary. The next ball is several inches short, and he bangs it through the covers. After two fours in succession he feels a six is due, and by the least perceptible withdrawal of his bat behind the block he makes the next ball nearly a half-volley. He has got well under it and sent it soaring. Not quite enough under it, though—or, rather, too much! It is speeding towards Martin. But Martin, with only half his mind returned from that group by the boundary, in the fraction of a second when the ball rose from bat into the background of the dazzling blue, has lost its flight. He is in the wrong place, and has misjudged it! Not quite a six, it reaches the ropes over his head; and though he live to be a hundred and outlive everyone who has seen him play to-day the agony of his knowledge that but for his momentary hesitation when he caught the glare full and lost the ball's course he would have been on the boundary when it fell will never leave him. This time the uninitiated do not know that he has been a bad fielder. But Martin knows, and there is misery ahead of him. That missed catch has gone irrevocably into eternity. Remfry has notched twenty-six runs; and Martin Chapman, who for the last eight years has not failed to get to and to hold a possible long-field catch, has let him off. He notes the consequence of his folly, notes it with a stabbing at his heart, as he sees the bowler's slight droop of despair when he takes up the attack again.

The fielders crossed over. Martin was drawn back from the isolation of the deep field, into proximity with his fellow-men whom he had so grievously offended. He was in the gulley, and Austin-Gary, off whose bowling he had missed Remfry, was his neighbour at slip. To poor Martin it would have been relief beyond the power of speech to express, if the wronged man had walked across and put him to death. He was an outcast, with all righteous eyes seeking to avoid him. His deed has been wide-reaching; the bowler at the other end also realises that it is hopeless to expect Remfry to make another mistake for long enough to come—and even if he did, some rabbit would put it on the floor, as the last fellow had practically done.

Remfry has backed up well and stolen a single. Then, joyously greeting a full-pitch to leg, he has swung it far over the southern boundary, where Olivet slopes precipitately into Kedron. The ball lands on a tomb of late Roman times, and rebounds on and on, into the Valley of Jehoshaphat. It is a gorgeous hit; the ranks of Tuscany do not attempt to refrain from cheering. Even two American ladies, nurtured on a literature which stresses humour and finds cricket one of the saliencies in that thing of jest, the English make-up, and inured to the thrill of seeing the champions of baseball accomplish their mighty strokes, know they have seen an epic deed. It was 'swell'! and Warren Remfry, swaggeringly modest, leans back on his bat, waiting for a fresh ball. (The ball that has gone is not recovered; two privates are despatched after it but make only a perfunctory search, being anxious not to miss the rest of Captain Remfry's knock.)

The nearest fielders gathered about the batsman in friendly rueful congratulation, all except Martin. Remfry, who has seen his friend in so many distresses and has memory of Martin, grimly self-controlled, sweeping back the Turkish attacks through night that is falling on the Moab hills, sees and understands his sorrow and forbears to intrude upon it.

The new ball arrives; Warren hits a single, then the last two balls of the over pass without incident. The game continues to be a one-man display; Captain Remfry is exercising the dashing gifts that have delighted the Somerset selectors. It does not in the least matter what the sound potterer at the other end does, or what his successors elect to do or try to do. Captain Remfry is in charge of the game, and his eye is in.

At last Major Austin-Gary, who has tried four new bowlers, goes on again himself, this time bowling round the wicket, with Martin in the Grampians but further on the leg and deeper. Warren disdains to accustom himself to a bowler he has already once dismissed. He throws all his youth and strength and courage into Austin-Gary's first delivery. The ball gets up somewhat, and for the second time the batsman is too much under it. It soars up gloriously, but it is not going to pass the boundary, and for what seems the passing of ages Martin waits beneath is, all eyes upon him, so that he does not notice the absurdly chivalrous action of his friend. For Warren, once he sees that the catch is coming to hand this time, breaks off his run and is sauntering to the ropes, his warfare accomplished. 'What are you doing?' shouts his amazed partner. 'The ball isn't caught yet! Run, man!' Warren shakes his head, answering loudly, 'No. But it will be! I know that fellow. He's as safe as houses. Good-bye!'

Martin's whole existence is in that sphere tumbling and twisting downwards towards him. The bowler's existence is there also; he, too, is waiting almost hysterically while one red spot is swaying superbly

up, up, up into the Syrian blue and then diving and
swerving earthward after its parabola. Is it possible
that this Chapman fellow, who mugged the earlier
chance, will hold a second one? Austin-Gary does
the unforgivable thing, never done by him before,
never done by any Englishman who is an Englishman
and knows what cricket is, in every sense of that
glorious word. We can excuse him only if we believe
(what is the fact) that he does not know that he does
it. Just as the ball is on the point of reaching Martin's
hands, a despairing appeal escapes him. '*Now*,
Chapman!' Martin's startled senses are tripped off
their track. He looks up like a shot rabbit before it
goes over, the ball bounces from his fingers. By the
mercy of whatever gods haunt these Judaean hills,
by the kindness of whatever spirits waylay the wan-
derer and in the last minute before he plunges into
unsuspected mine or over the bramble-masked cliff-
ledge set him straight, by miracle he recovers it!
It is a grand catch, nonchalantly held! See how
carelessly and easily it was tossed up in sheer
bravado, to be caught again! Swank, of course, and
to be frowned on; yet not frowned on too austerely,
when the swanker has shown you such accomplish-
ment. These lucky people on Olivet have been
seeing some cricket! Warren Remfry has made 74,
and made them in a fashion that would have done
credit to Frank Woolley. And he has been given
an epic death, in that splendid bit of work on the
boundary. No wonder the spectators cheer.

But Martin knows no other feelings but anger and
renewed humiliation. Two people exist for him, himself and the fool who has been bowling. He walks
up to Major Austin-Gary, and in a white passion

says, 'If I had dropped that damned catch it would have been your fault.' Austin-Gary, shocked out of his ease, looks up and in a moment realises that the holding of the catch was a fluke after it had really been lost. He flushes with answering rage, which is not less because of his knowledge that it was he who began the quarrel by doing 'a thing that isn't done.' Martin now has done three things that aren't done—he has affronted the skipper of his side and been guilty of gross offensiveness to a field-officer, and that field-officer a friend.

When the innings closed for 129, Martin, dragging his way to the ring, found Warren at home with everyone there. He had come to them a benefactor, after having given them a crowded forty minutes of exciting cricket; and he is seen in person to be exactly what his deeds proclaimed him, an eager, rapid boy, swift and glowing in speech and movement. He ought not to be in this shamble-furnace of Armageddon, where youth grows drab and stained and is flung down broken and done with. But you forget all this, seeing him modestly swing up just in the very heat of your cheers for the catch that dismissed him. He has all but lost his ovation by his generosity, slipping in while you were wondering if that fellow would hold the ball.

'Oh, well played, sir!'

'Jolly well played! I don't know when I've seen a nicer knock in all my life.'

A general, a really 'nice old buffer,' seizes him by the shoulder and faces him with fatherly disapproval. 'Damned pretty work, sir! But, you know, my boy, that catch might easily have been put down. Why on earth did you take it for granted that the fellow was going to hold it?'

Warren, touching his cap in acknowledgement, replies to Brigadier-General Hauksbee. 'Thank you very much, sir! Oh, no, sir, I know that man in the deep field. He used to be in my company, and I knew I was a goner when I saw the ball was going to him.'

He is taken up enthusiastically and introduced to many charming people. General Hauksbee, who regards all nice girls as his honorary nieces, takes him up to a group of ladies who are delighted to make a fuss of him, he is so boyish and young. 'Captain Remfry!' No doubt your feeling that he ought to be still at school is right, but, you see, this is the Great War. Yes, this is really *Captain* Warren Remfry, and men twice his age look up to him as a veteran and are glad to be commanded by him in a tight place. If you find it hard to believe that he is actually twenty-one, watch his eyes carefully; they have learnt only too well what strain and fear and sorrow are. He is not worrying about those disquieting companions now, he is too happy to be where he has nature's right to be, in the midst of gaiety and beauty and friendliness. He is still worrying about his chum, though; and when the London Division's innings closes he runs out to bring Martin also into the circle of nymphs and deities to which the hero after death attains by right of prowess.

'Miss Cameron! Miss Connett! you must get to know Martin Chapman, the fellow who did me in with that topping catch!'

The ladies, being American, saw no harm in owning that they were 'pleased to meet' Captain Chapman.

Captain Chapman, being English, although excessively pleased to meet them, suppressed the fact.
Moreover, he was still wretched over his loss of
control when he had let himself down in that brawl
with Austin-Gary. The sense of sin, whose passing
is rightly deplored by earnest people, flourishes in
youth and not in age. Martin's soul was overclouded,
and until it was at peace he was not able to be happy
even beside a goddess, though that goddess was in
gracious mood.

'Your catch was *swell*!' Cynthia told him. 'I always
thought that cricket was a kind of slow motion
dance played without music. But it was great to-day.
I'll say it was great, won't you, Val?'

Valerie assented enthusiastically. 'My heart went
into my boots when I saw you standing there in that
thistle-patch, waiting and waiting.'

Martin wanted to get his soul clean in every respect.
'I've been longing to meet you—I mean, meet you
properly,' he said; and reddened. Then marred this
blunt but excellent beginning by adding, 'You don't
know how I've been wanting to apologise for barging
in on your party.'

Valerie's brows knitted. 'You mean, when we saw
you before?'

'Yes. That *dreadful* time.'

Cynthia saw a chance for mischief. 'Oh, but,
Captain Chapman, you didn't barge in on us. We
were very, *very* sorry, when we saw you fall that
day, weren't we, Val?'

'Very sorry, indeed,' corroborated Valerie; but
hardly looked, even now, as if the memory were a
sharp distress.

Martin remembered—there had been an earlier

encounter, when they had seen him rising from a basket of buzzing flies. He explained confusedly that he meant the day of Major Blundell's incursion. And blushed yet deeper.

Valerie took pity. 'We knew perfectly well that it wasn't your fault, Captain Chapman.'

Martin, batting in the place generally reserved for an unknown quantity, Number One, had to go to get on his pads.

Warren followed him. 'What's up, old chap?'

'What do you mean?'

'You know what I mean.'

'Damn that catch I bossed!' said Martin, rejecting one of two left-leg pads and hunting for a right-leg.

'I shouldn't let it worry me. Any other fellow on your side would have misjudged it. Besides, that outfield is *wicked*. It isn't fit for human consumption.'

'I know that.'

'Then don't let the business worry you, old man. You made up for it magnificently, and everyone knows you did.'

'It isn't that, Bunny.'

'Then what is it? Hurry up. I ought to be out in the field.'

Martin hesitated.

'Buck up, old Puzzlewit!'

So Martin told him.

'Right! I'm coming!' Remfry called back to his skipper summoning him. 'Do you know what I should do in your place, Martin? Austin-Gary looks a decent enough chap. If he is, he must know that he acted like an out-and-out sweep in yelling at you when he did. I'd apologise. If he accepts—and he will—you'll have a load off your mind and will probably hit me all over the place. If he doesn't— well, you've done what you ought to do, and you'll have to let him be as a heathen man and a publican to you henceforth.'

'He's absolutely savage with me. I saw it in his face.'

'*Of course* he's absolutely savage. But tell him you lost your temper and are sorry. If you go in as you're feeling now, I'll toss you up a dolly and you'll spoon it back like a baby. If you won't speak to Austin-Gary,' Warren concluded, 'I'm going to do it myself. Now!'

Martin's decision was taken. 'You're a brick, Bunny,' he said; and strode up to the still reddened face of his skipper, and said, 'I'm awfully sorry, sir. For my rotten loss of self-control. There was absolutely no excuse for it, and I apologise.'

Austin-Gary had been bitterly offended, not least because he knew that he had been first in the wrong. But the ancient chivalry of cricket is a strong argument to every man who has come within its noble laws and legend. Besides, the major, as Warren surmised, was a decent fellow—in all probability, would have been a decent fellow even if he had never learnt to play the game. Some men are.

'That's absolutely all right,' he said. Seeing Martin's remorse, a flood of sympathy came over him and swept the last vestiges of hesitation away. 'It's I who ought to apologise to you, Chapman. I know exactly what happened. And please believe that I honestly don't know how I ever came to shout out at you like that. I must have gone crazy. Now you go out and proceed to clump your pal Remfry all over the field, until he feels as wretched as you and I have been feeling.' He walked out a few paces with him, and dismissed him with reassurance. 'It's really all right, Chapman. Now you tell *me* you've forgiven me.'

'Why, of course, sir! You've been an absolute brick, sir.'

Sheer happiness overcame Martin. His mind, released, went singing into battle. He did not care what happened. Austin-Gary was a decent chap, a jolly decent chap. He was glad he had held that catch from Warren. My word! but he was glad! It was a fine knock of Bunny's. Miss Connett had said that the catch was wonderful. Well (complacently), it *was* a good catch.

He took middle and leg. Warren Remfry, that promising medium-pace bowler, was digging a hole in the Mount of Olives terrain ('turf' you cannot call it), to mark the end of his beat before he started to run to the wicket. There was a look in his eye which said, 'No quarter for you, Martin Puzzlewit!'

Martin was a steady bat, with streaks of recklessness that usually cost him his wicket. To-day he wanted to make a gesture of response to the universe that had been so generous to him, scattering Olivet with this pinky-tinged blue borage and superb thistles, strewing its slopes with these excellent fellows and setting such golden ladies at its side. He therefore assumed that Warren's first ball was going to be a half-volley, and by good luck it was. Martin's tremendous swipe met with a worthy reward, and the ball went out like that splendid lift of Warren's, far over the dipping hill, and presently (as Warren afterwards put it) was 'rousing the

eagles in the screes of the Valley of Jehoshaphat.'
How can cricket be brightened, our papers ask each
summer. Here is the answer. Let the M.C.C. make
a very simple rule, that it be compulsory for the
batsman—every batsman as he comes in—to take
a swipe at his first ball. Six or nothing! Either way
the spectators will get their money's worth. Martin's
six was greeted as it deserved. Here was a batsman to
watch, and the company settled down to watch him.

Warren as a bowler was also worth watching.
Walking from the wicket to where he began his run
he wore a philosophical look, as of a young disciple
of the Buddha who has not yet come to enlightenment
but is steadily pondering his way thither. Arrived at
the end of his walk, as he turned to run back, the
gravity jerked into sudden energy, the body rose on
invisible springs, the limbs began to sway easily into
increasing activity. Halfway to the wicket the ball
was transferred from the left hand to the right, and
then—you saw that right hand high up, and the ball
was on its way. If nothing happened, Warren re-
collected the ball, and a young philosopher was
soberly seeking the forest where he could meditate
untroubled by these others now vexing his peace.

If you once noted the process, it was apt to fascinate
you. We English, accustomed to such sights, ignore
them for the blatant moments when bat and ball
or ball and stumps coincide. There was Warren
Remfry, whose muscles obeyed instantaneously what
the brain commanded, now in the mere bowling of
balls of which only a small fraction would take wickets
betraying the watchful self-control that had salvaged
even youthfulness out of the folly and savagery of

war. And the spectators were seeing him idly, their vision quickening only after the ball had left him! Of a truth we deserve to have our countryside ravaged and all beauty swept bare by democracy's scythe! Yet, as I say, if you once by any chance did note what Remfry was doing, you were likely to make the eye wake up sooner. Sophocles would have watched him for hours, never caring whether the ball went to the boundary or hit the stumps.

Warren's second ball was not a half-volley. It was the ball which came with his arm—pitching a matter of perhaps three inches outside the off stump it turned in those three inches and a trifle more—the ball with which he bowled Mr. Percy Perrin when Essex played Somerset in 1914. Martin made the mistake of huddling back to play at it; it beat him, and—it must have been just a little *more* than three inches outside the wicket, for it missed the off stump by 'a coat of varnish.' Warren threw up his hands in despair. The third ball Martin drove hard at the bowler. In his exuberance he fancied there was going to be a run in it, and followed up his drive a good yard. With a lightning movement of his arm, Warren picked the ball up and broke his wicket. Martin was back in his crease just in time.

The two friends confronted each other laughing. In that interchange were how many memories! These two who had proved each other in the regimental absence of reserve and privacy which can be so insupportable, who knew each other when death and terror struck at their helpless bodies and also when the days and nights drew out a chain of

interminable boredom and fretting for wasted time
—now knit in rivalry for the olive-crown of England's
summer game, in that strife were rejoicing to beat
each other down. And because the things that are
eternal and go their way under the mask of our
dying lives break through when they find both the
man and the moment worthy, in that gesture of two
boys drawn up in mutual defiance and mockery
Youth and Valour and Friendship deigned to stand
manifest. There was sense in playing cricket on
Olivet during the Great War! Here was 'the civilisation for which we were fighting'—when two men
could exchange a challenge in which no hint of
self or of jealousy could hide, for if either went
down the victim would rejoice in the victor's luck or
prowess, whichever it might be. Yet, if we may judge
from the memoirs of the great minds that directed
the War, most of us think that civilisation is an affair
of noise and lights amid which elaborately dined and
wined animals move chattering and smiling.

Martin's contribution included no more sixes. But
it amounted to a useful 24, out of his side's total of
123. He was out just as the tea interval was due to
be taken, caught in the slips off a ball he ought to
have left alone.

VI

I

BOTH TEAMS WERE GUESTS OF THE CORPS COMMANDER,
Sir Philip Chetwode, at dinner. At the elaborate
gaffe afterwards Valerie and Cynthia reappeared;
and Cynthia, seeing Martin, generously co-opted

him and Warren into their party. The arrangement did not please her legitimate *cavaliere servente*, a fact noted by Cynthia but dismissed as of small importance. Knowing that she gave a vast deal of pleasure to the masculine world, she held herself entitled to recompense from that world. Why should this 'dumb' Captain Ferguson regard himself as entitled to a monopoly of her company?

She knew he was fuming, and she watched for an opportunity to set affairs on a proper basis. It came when Warren, swifter than Ferguson (and also, if truth be told, assisted by the lady, who turned to him when she was ready), was taking her wrap to the improvised cloak-room. Ferguson, too blind with annoyance to be wise, whispered savagely: 'Why need those fellows come butting in all the time where they aren't wanted?'

'I beg your pardon?'

'Why do you and Val—'

'I and who, Captain Ferguson?'

'Why do you and Miss Connett want to pick up these bounders?'

'Captain Ferguson, shall we get this *clear*? *I* asked Captain Remfry to sit with us. *I* choose to think Captain Remfry and Captain Chapman a sight more interesting than you and Major Carruthers, and Miss Connett agrees with me. For one thing, they are not always thinking of their splendid selves. For another, they are gentlemen. Oh, thank you so much, Captain Remfry!'

Then they settled down to enjoy the gaffe.

The ordinary man, though so numerous, counts for nothing in literature. This is a pity, for, had he taken after the War a part commensurate with his numbers, we should never have been bothered with fifteen years of fuss about complexes, inhibitions and the like. The British soldier does not suffer from inhibitions, but only from the quite flat and definite suppression enforced by army discipline. A gaffe is his saturnalia; thought is free, and is given wings to wander where it will.

At first all was reasonably well; the smuttier sallies were momentary. The japes were tried and tested favourites. Two funny men came on, and one accepted a cigar from the other. He drew a couple of whiffs, then asked, 'What brand do you call this cigar?'

'Oh, that's a very fine brand. A very fine brand indeed! Why, it's one of the most *remarkable* brands on the market!'

'Ah! I know it! It's an Adam and Eve cigar, isn't it?'

'Adam and Eve cigar? What d'you mean? Adam and Eve cigar?'

'Yes. Adam and Eve. When you've 'ad 'em you 'eave.'

Martin, with some qualms, but in deep happiness of spirit, turned to his neighbour and saw that her eyes were smiling. 'I was thinking,' whispered Valerie, 'that this is the Mount of Olives.'

Time and the War had certainly played an excellent jest in juxtaposition. This, as the girl pointed out, was Olivet. And a band of gleeful batmen, dressed as pierrots, were swaying arm-in-arm and singing through a lugubrious forecast of years of conflict still to come. The poet who had composed the chant

E

reached 1929 before he decided that the War really
might end; the song took on a brisk joyance:

> ' In the Year Nineteen-twenty-nine,
> Instead of our drinking Quin-ine,
>   We'll be filled up with cheer—
> (*Crescendo*) We'll be filled up with BEER!
>   In the Year Nineteen-twenty-nine! '

The prediction went home with power and zest-
fulness. Sweetly the listeners lifted their voices, and
repeated the words of hope. Followed that fine lyric,

> ' What do you want to make those eyes at me for.
> When they don't mean what they say? '

At the last stanza a colleague of the singer ran a
paper screen on to the stage. It was suddenly burst
by a hideously masked face, lolling a scarlet tongue.
The Trojans roared applause, the singer's voice rose
to a yell of mock terror:

> ' What do you want to make THOSE EYES at me for? '

Xerxes, gazing on his host at Salamis, wept for the
realisation that in fifty years all that youth and
courage would have passed away. We who saw the
gathering of the peoples, England's valour and
lovable recklessness coming in her time of peril from
every quarter of the globe, seek to tell a new generation what we saw, and cannot.

It was perhaps because something had touched the
deepest springs of pity in her that the next item

jarred unbearably on Valerie. It jarred on Cynthia too, if in sharper, more conventional fashion. Both girls had this in common, that they had been given a rigidly puritanical outlook on life. It was understood that in Europe—drinking, licentious, undemocratic Europe—things were not well done. For example, British troops, it was known, could not attack without a rum ration which was commonly stated to be so stiff that it sent them over oblivious of danger. France, similarly, was known to inculcate naughty ways of thought and action. All this apart, there was oafishness in what followed.

An artiste whom Martin knew in private life as a sober and blameless clerk in his own department came on the stage in a preposterous parody of a small boy's dress, in bright sash and short skirts, and dragging a wooden horse. He gambolled to delighted encouragement, trolling a song whose burden (delivered with a leer of lascivious anticipation) was:

> ' I'm getting a Big Boy now!
> I'm getting a Big Boy now!
> They say, before long
> I'm *bound* to go wrong!
> Oh, I'm getting a Big Boy now!'

Martin, fuming and uncomfortable, was startled to see that Valerie had risen, and with one quick look to the other girl, was going out. Cynthia went too, and all four of their companions followed perforce, in an amazed silence which they were painfully aware had drawn all eyes on them. The silence, as they reached the door, was broken up by a couple of derisive cat-calls.

Having made a mistake, Valerie took refuge in rage. 'I shall be grateful if in future I am not invited to witness the British Army's idea of amusement.'

Her escort and Cynthia's assured them that the whole business was caddish and scandalous. Martin and Warren were silent, a fact that added pique to fury.

'So you think the business is all right, Captain Remfry!' said Cynthia challengingly.

'No,' said Warren. 'I'm more sorry than I can say that you were here.'

This did not satisfy. 'Answer me, Captain Remfry!' said Cynthia. 'It was because Miss Connett and I were present that you and Captain Chapman think it was rotten. You aren't really upset otherwise.'

'It's only fair to remember that no one thought about the possibility of ladies being present.'

'Answer me, Captain Remfry,' Cynthia said imperiously.

'Then, if you want my honest opinion—'

Cynthia interrupted him angrily.

'Please don't keep us waiting any longer. We want to know what you think.'

He raised his face and looked her full in the eyes. 'I don't think there was anything much really wrong, if you hadn't been present. The fellow was playing the goat, of course. But no one who wasn't an ass—no man, I mean, would have taken it as anything but a rag.'

'I agree with Remfry,' said Martin loyally.

'Thank you, both of you,' said Cynthia. 'Now we know that you think Val and I are—asses!'

'No!' said Warren.

'You called us that, Captain Remfry.'

'I beg your pardon. I did not. I was speaking of men only.'

'Then you think there are different standards for men and women,' said Valerie.

She was looking at Martin; and Martin unflinchingly said, 'Yes. In some things. Not in those that matter.'

'Martin and I,' said Warren, 'are not going to pretend to misunderstand what we understand perfectly well. We take a business like this gaffe in its context.'

'Which is, Captain Remfry?" asked Valerie coldly.

'The background of those fellows' lives, which is pretty dull and stupid. What they've gone through, and what some of them still have to go through."

And saying this he hated himself, for having said one word that seemed to ask for pity or for allowance for his comrades, from these outsiders who knew nothing about their world. Not that he was thinking of the girls, of course. They could not help their ignorance and it was right and natural. But the fellows beside them! That painted rubbish!

Major Carruthers thought the time had come for decisive word.

'That's all rot,' he said loftily. 'What *have* they gone through, if it comes to that?'

'The truth is,' Captain Ferguson summed up, 'if fellows have foul and low minds they'll keep them, whatever they go through. I shouldn't waste time arguing, Miss Connett. My car's outside. I'll get hold of my chauffeur and we'll take you both home.'

'By God!' said Major Carruthers admiringly, 'but you two have taught some of us a lesson to-night. Those who needed it, I mean.'

This was just what Valerie was beginning to doubt.
'I suppose you think,' she said to Martin, 'that we
both made an unnecessary fuss by going out?'

Her voice and manner were meant to be scornful.
They seemed half wistful, and uncertain.

'He has said that he thinks we are asses,' said
Cynthia, looking furiously at Warren.

Warren again met her gaze without flinching. 'We
both understand perfectly,' he said, 'and we don't
blame you.'

'You did the *only* thing to do,' said Ferguson
vigorously.

Cynthia, unaccustomed to the shadow of any masculine criticism, in her rage had lost all dignity. 'If you
want Val and I ever to speak to you again, Captain
Remfry, you've got to apologise for that word *asses*!'

'I never used it—except,' said Warren as he looked
at Carruthers, 'of *men* who pretend to be deeply
shocked at a thing they understand perfectly well.'

Valerie's anger had passed, and been succeeded by
a sinking feeling that she had made a mistake.
She saw, too, that nothing could be more humiliating
than this protracted argument. It was again Martin
whom she addressed, as she asked dispiritedly, 'Then
you think I made a fool of myself by going out?'

Martin shook his head. But he felt he had to say,
'I think it would have been better if we'd paid no
notice and waited, once we were in.'

'That's enough, Captain Chapman,' cried Cynthia.
'We know now what you think, and will wish you
and Captain Remfry good night.'

As they went off, Warren and Martin could hear
that they were being comforted with the assurance

that those fellows were no gentlemen. 'A bounder'll always show himself in his true colours if you give him time,' was Major Carruther's summing up of the situation.

'That's torn things,' observed Warren sorrowfully. 'But I wasn't going to tell a lie, or pretend that I saw anything wrong where there was nothing wrong —except that ladies should have been there at all. Besides,' he added, 'the worst of lying is, you don't take anyone in—anyone with any brains, that is. At least, I never do.'

There was nothing but to go to Martin's billet, where they lingered until the gaffe finished. It was close on eleven when the cars filled up to take the London team back to their division. There had been enough champagne in circulation at the general's dinner to make the crowd a cheery one.

'I say, Remfry,' said one of his fellow-players, 'your crew made rather a scene, didn't they? Where did you pick up those jolly-looking girls, though? You never said a word about knowing people like that in Jerusalem.'

'What was the trouble?' asked another. 'You all strutted out in the middle of the show, the girls looking as if they'd like to see the place blown up. What had you been saying?'

'Shut up,' said Warren morosely.

'I say! I say! I say! Is it as bad as all that?'

'Oh, dry up, Pettigrew! You know as well as I do that a gaffe isn't a place for decent women. Now shut up, if you don't mind.'

'Oh, it was that, was it? Why, there wasn't anything very steep, that I remember.'

'Oh, wasn't there?' said Ashdown. 'What about that song the fellow sang about "Divided Labours"?'

'Ah, yes, that *was* a bit thick.'

In the midst of the argument Warren got in, and the cars moved joyfully off, a shouting, racing noise in the starry silence of the Palestine night. The London eleven returned home singing.

II

Martin, dispiritedly contemplating the necessity of bed after what should have been a good day, had an unexpected visitor. There was a knock and a query, 'You in, Chapman?'

Major Austin-Gary entered.

Martin rose hurriedly. 'What'll you smoke, sir?' he asked, bringing cigars and cigarettes, seeing that Austin-Gary had obviously come to stay.

The major dropped into a long chair. 'Thanks. I'll carry on with a pipe.'

Still disquieted about the breeze during the cricket match, Martin took it for granted that his skipper had come to reaffirm his plenary absolution. He did him injustice, although conversation opened as he expected.

'Topping game we had to-day. That was a hefty swipe of yours. I didn't know you were such a slogger, Chapman.'

'I'm not really. As a rule, I'm a rather dull old stonewall.'

'Then you didn't play true to form. We ought to get on fairly well against the other divisions, after making such an adequate show against the Londons.

Your pal Remfry's played for Somerset, they tell
me.'

Martin knew that the speaker was aware of this.
But it was decent of him to have come in to make
friendly conversation.   Something of its drabness
began to leave the ghost of the day that remained.

'He made seventy-five against Essex.'

'Not much of a team, Essex,' said Austin-Gary
reflectively.   '*On paper* they often look almost good
enough to whack England. But you can put your
money safely on their collapsing when the push
comes.'

'He made fifty-six against Middlesex.'

'Ah! Middlesex. Now *that* took a bit of cricket!
I hope he'll find time to play when the War's
over.'

'Oh, I think so.'

'His people got money? Do you know what they
are?'

'His father's a retired colonel.'

'What was his regiment?'

'Indian Army. One of the Piffers, I forget which.
But Remfry's the only son, and his mother's side
are pretty well off, from what he's told me."

'I expect he'll keep on in the Army,' Austin-Gary
decided. 'Pity, when a chap's meant to be an England
cricketer. Now may I be very rude?'

Chapman looked his bewilderment.

'I want to be very prying and impertinent. Do
you mind?'

'Rather not. It's jolly decent of you to come in
like this, sir.'

'What's your idea for *après la guerre fini*?'

'I suppose I shall go back to my old job. I was in

a London Bank. I expect I shall end as manager of some suburban branch.'

'Don't. Wenyon and I have a better idea for you.'

'Wenyon?'

'Yes. Wenyon, the wise old don. We had a chat about you just before I came in.'

Martin coloured. He need not have done. The conversation had sprung up by accident and the cricket unpleasantness had not come into it. He remained silent.

'It's just as well to begin thinking a bit now. This damned War won't actually go on for ever, you know, though we've all got used to the idea that it will. What about staying on out here?'

'No. I'm not keen on staying in the Army—even if I could get a regular commission when the War finishes.'

'There are worse places than Palestine.'

'I should say there are! But you couldn't expect to stay in one country if you were in the Army.'

'I wasn't thinking of the Army, as it happens. You've got a good deal of spare time, haven't you?'

'Heaps. This is the softest job I ever had.'

'Why not learn a bit of Arabic?'

'Arabic?'

'Yes. Other fellows are doing it. Only one here and there. Most haven't the sense. The average subaltern is too happy-go-lucky. He doesn't bother to look beyond the next cigarette.'

'And that's true.'

'Listen to me, Chapman. And remember, it's Wenyon's notion that's behind what I'm saying. We've already bitten off a goodly chunk of this goodly land. Supposing Allenby does another big push this autumn?'

'I don't see how he can, sir!'

'Perhaps not. But supposing he does?'

'Then we shall only get shot to pieces in those hills east of Jordan, as we did before.'

'It won't be east of Jordan. The Bull's got a lot of sense, take it from me; I've been on his staff. Having caught his head—'

'It was *our* head,' said Martin softly.

'I'm speaking metaphorically.'

'Sorry, sir. I didn't mean to interrupt.'

'Having, as I say, whacked his head hard against rocks *twice*, this animal is intelligent and says, "Those things are *hard*. Bloody hard! I'm not *meant* to butt past them." The push will come up the coast. Wenyon, who's a diligent Bible student, says that ever since fighting began in this land every offensive has been up the coast. If you once get going there you go like billyo. And you capture the *whole* of Palestine automatically.'

'Sounds like a play to me, sir.'

'All right. It *may*—go like a play. You're still the sceptical infantryman. Get Wenyon to let you see the Intelligence Reports. All is not so well with Jacko as it used to be. And ask Caleb'—for such was Wenyon's misfortune of a name—'to fix up one of his more or less trustworthy local thieves as an usher for you. *Put in your spare moments at Arabic.* You'll find yourself glad you did, some day. Now I'm going to turn in. Good night, Chapman.'

'Good night, Major. It's most frightfully decent of you.'

'Not at all. It was Caleb's idea. By the way, you

know you played a jolly big part in the very respectable show we put up against those experienced
ruffians, your pal Remfry and the other profession-
als. Well, so long till to-morrow! And thanks for
being so patient while I butted in on your private
business.'

VII

SUNDAY; AND OVER JERUSALEM, FROM BELFRIES
Armenian, Coptic, Greek Orthodox, Russian, Mar-
onite and Roman Catholic, the day was heralded
before it dawned and accompanied with acclaim
until it ended. Less intemperate in its piety, the
bell of the Anglican Cathedral called to Early
Communion at 7, to Matins at 11, to Evensong at 6.

Valerie and Cynthia, their spirits ruffled from the
mischance and annoyance of the previous night,
were glad that they had resolved to attend the
earliest service and had kept to their resolve. When
they left the silent corridors of the A.R.F. for the
morning-cold streets that skirted the City and led to
St. George's Cathedral, the sun was already warming
the white walls and the airs around them; but in
the shadow of trees and houses the dewy chillness
lingered.

The walk home was hotter; the streets dustier,
under a tricky, pricking, whisking wind. But they
had bathed in peace deeper than sleep, more potent
to knit up the ravelled sleeve of care and to calm
and strengthen them to face the encounters, exas-
perations and excitements of another week. They
came contented, though late, to a cold breakfast

served amid the remains of breakfasts of the less energetically religious who had finished and gone. Only two of the unit were left.

One of these, Captain Hergesheimer, seemed out of sorts. 'Thought you were a Methodist!' he grunted, when Cynthia explained their lateness.

'I am. Miss Connett's Presbyterian,' she answered.

'What's that got to do with it?'

He laughed aggressively. 'Well, well, well! What would the padre have said, if he'd guessed that "Nonconformists" were taking "mass" right under his nose?'

The girls stiffened. This was not the man to invite to explain the outrageous thing he suggested. Explanation, however, came uninvited; Captain Hergesheimer was of the philanthropic clan who make their meaning pikestaff-plain. As he often observed, he didn't believe in milling about and being so darned particular about people's feelings; what he thought he said *right out*. Cynthia's cheeks flamed as he turned to his neighbour now for confirmation of his opinion; in Valerie's flushed an icier wrath and indignation.

'Wouldn't do at all, would it?'

But Captain Jenkins, a Baptist missionary normally stationed in Galilee and longing for the day of release from the secular work of the A.R.F., rose and edged doorwards, faltering unconvincing palliatives. 'Why, Captain! I don't know anything about the padre this morning. The Bishop's pretty good, anyway. And when you see the other European sects and the way they carry on in Jerusalem, you can understand that they are bound to feel a bit superior'. 'They' was not 'the other European sects.'

In his heart he knew that the padre, whoever he was, would not have recognised him, a Baptist from Wisconsin, as a genuine 'reverend'. He dreaded his rowdy table mate and regretted the confidences given during a more than usually sea-sick and dismal interval of the journey they had shared as cabin companions from New York. The life of an American Baptist missionary in a region where numbers and political prestige were all on the side of Anglican neighbours—for sixty years it had been the tradition and practice to go to the British Consul for help, in preference to your own—had not been an easy one. Hurrying off to his food distribution at Bethlehem he blushed and winced with thought of Captain Hergesheimer forcefully and colourfully elaborating his indiscreet complaints.

Captain Hergesheimer was not staying, however. He lurched upright and dusted breakfast crumbs from what had been his lap. 'I guess,' he conceded gallantly, 'you two girls can go where you like. The Bish would find an excuse for *you*—ignorance or bad education. *I* would, anyway, if I saw you at my service. And it's War,' he concluded impressively, 'when rules don't matter so terrible much.'

He strode away unconscious of the cloud of disgust upswirling in his wake.

Valerie's unexpressed humiliation was the deeper, that she had been tricked by peace and beauty and stately order—the white vestments of the padre radiant before a sunlit altar, the erect military figures at the front, the dignity and composure and sureness of the English acknowledging a celestial *imperium in imperio*—into confidence in a priest and a God who felt themselves too good for her. For her

—a girl of Virginia! Valerie Connett of the Connetts of Roandoke Valley and Wilderness Mountain!

They laughed annoyance off, and left the dining-room. But the glory of the day had gone, they were sore at heart. Never had either felt more belligerently American.

Monday brought temporary forgetfulness, with an exciting job.

In the Turk's eyes the gallows is a considerable part of good government; and he makes diligent enquiry into the demeanour of recovered subjects after any absence from them. This was why Jerusalem in addition to its ordinary embarrassments—a populace work-shy more than any other in the world, more even than that of Benares, living by acquired sanctity, on charity from outside eked out by sale of 'objects of piety'—now carried an unabsorbed crowd of starving Arab refugees from Es-Salt beyond Jordan. They had been evacuated by the troops in their retirement at the end of April.

Deserted buildings in the Armenian quarter were set aside for these unfortunates; and the American Relief Force took over the job of making these buildings sanitary enough to be lived in and the 'Salties' sanitary enough to live in them. The latter promised to be the more complicated task, bad though the other was. The Salties' clothes (and this is a very remarkable fact) were even dirtier than their persons.

Miss Masterman had taken Val and Cynthia with her, to oversee a staff of carpenters, scrubbers, whitewashers, fumigators. A revolting fauna had been made unhappy and driven into crevices. This had taken up the preceding week. Val and Cynthia had gone to the cricket match in a glow of self-esteem for duty well and truly done (also, with nerves tenser than they knew). The place, as Val had remarked, 'looked fairly ready for the seventy times seven devils that are coming in on Monday. There's not much more that can be done in the sweeping and garnishing line.'

The Salties had been kept in ignorance of their glorious haven, or they would have taken possession tumultuously, brushing aside the formality of its and their own scouring. Which would not have been according to plan. Monday morning was appointed for a massed expedition to the public Turkish Baths.

Now the Arabs, though a noble, are not an aquatic people. Zero hour had to be postponed, for protracted argument. Standing dark and watchful as desert hawks with their broods, the Salties were at last won over by the promise of new clothes for everyone.

'Darn them, they won't get a stitch unless they march at once!' shouted Store-Major Schwartz. 'Tell them,' he yelled at the interpreter, 'that the clothes are *at the Baths*. Yes, sir! *There* ! ! ! Or will be before they come out. Waiting for them!'

Male and female contingents were formed, the latter commanded by Val and Cynthia under Miss Masterman, who in pre-War years had taught in Tripoli and knew some Arabic. But another delay ensued.

'What's that silly old sheikh fussing about *now*?' demanded Store-Major Schwartz.

He was wanting assurance that sundered families would be reunited.

'Damn him! *Yes!* Ask him for the love of Mike who in thunder would want to steal a lot of Janes like these?'

The words of comfort were translated. The patriarch professed himself satisfied.

The women's section of the Baths turned out so much smaller than the men's that Miss Masterman thought it might be necessary to wash the little girls separately. While she explored the Baths' capacity they were temporarily segregated and given to Val and Cynthia as an independent command. It is charitable to suppose that sudden promotion went to Cynthia's head, though the American girl's dislike of watching time go by unoccupied had a share in her folly.

She pointed to a stone sarcophagus, in use as a drinking trough, and fed by a well of sorts, one of the mosquito-ridden rock-pools in which Jerusalem abounds. 'What do you say, Val, to bribing that attendant who's lounging there doing nothing, to give them a face-and-head dip here? It'll make a start on what promises to be a tough all-day job.'

Val agreed. Then humanely hesitated. 'It's going to be hard on the camels and donks that drink here afterwards.'

'They're really rather darling, though!' she added, surveying the ragged and enchanting throng of dark-eyed girls and babies marshalled before them.

When their captors revealed their fell purpose, the children set up a sturdy wailing resistance. Their

F

mothers, in defiance of all discipline, broke their
ranks and ran to succour them. The hubbub brought
Miss Masterman hurrying out from the Baths. Val
and Cynthia acknowledged defeat. But worse than
defeat had happened. Confidence had been lost,
peace had been shattered.

The attention of Captain Martin Chapman—who
every Monday visited units in the Holy City's
vicinity—was arrested by a voice of lamentation
wild enough to suggest that some communal massacre
was in progress. He told his chauffeur to drive
towards it. 'For God's sake, hurry, Bennett!'

Valerie's face, red from unsuccessful battle, looked
up from the melée, completing his astonishment. It
was not friendly, and turned away without vouch-
safing the least hint of acquaintance. She had no
intention of admitting that the planet owned him as
a fellow-inhabitant—this was very plainly conveyed
to him.

There was nothing to do but to drive off, which he
did.

But his mind remained on the scene he had left.
He ought to have thought of its richly comic side,
but did not. Possibly Warren's deplorably undemocratic outlook had infected him; he felt it was not
good enough that two girls should be wrestling with
a band of female hooligans who would be better
sheep-dipped by fishwomen instead of washed one
by one by ladies. Or, if it had to be done thus,
someone should be standing by with an ash-plant,
to see that they went through it without behav-
ing like demons. He reminded himself that the
recalcitrants were small girls (though, as *he* saw

them, sufficiently ruffianly; and with excited mothers supporting them), so that this thought was wrong and unchivalrous. It stayed with him, nevertheless.

We know that divine Artemis and her nymphs, on hills deliciously thyme-and-cistus-clad like Judæa's, pursued the wild swine with arrows, which imagination finds a reasonably poetic occupation for celestial litheness and beauty. But not even a post-War poet has ever thought of them as scrubbing the same wild swine in the wayside fountains.

His unhappiness would have been deepened if he had known the humiliated resentment—indignation, as if that odious Captain Chapman had appeared on purpose—with which his presence had been noted. Had he offered to help he would have been icily and efficiently snubbed. Yet when he went away heavy-hearted and reluctant Valerie gave him bad marks for this also—so unfair and illogical is the mind of woman.

Miss Masterman explained that it would be the tightest squeeze on record, but they could—just—get in their twenty-two small girls and thirty older women. She announced that all clothes were to be removed at first entrance. 'And then,' she added in a shuddering undertone to Val and Cynthia, '*burned*.' The Bath attendants had instructions to bring the discarded garments outside surreptitiously.

This clothing business, into which the A.R.F. had put generous funds, had given the unit's workrooms a great start. Mrs. Frobisher, who had overseen the making, had enjoyed having all these definite orders

—for Salties of ascertained bulk and age—instead of merely instructions to produce 'clothes'. On Sunday evening Val and Cynthia had seen the results, all neatly labelled and docketed—men's sizes 1 to 6, women's sizes 1 to 6, boys' ditto, girls' ditto. By Monday noon a complete village of Arab families, clean and in their right garments, would be renewing relationship, and thankfully entering their spick-and-span new quarters, with spirits one incessant hymn to American goodness, efficiency, and managing skill.

'What did Lootenant Frobisher say, Miss Connett?' Miss Masterman asked Valerie, who had made the last arrangements.

'He said he'd deliver the clothes promptly here at eleven.'

'That's fine!'

They had not yet, however, drained to its dregs the bitter cup that Fate had prepared.

Once begun, the work went well, and the show became the jolliest of romps. Val and Cynthia would catch a laughing young peri and send her flying back into the steaming room. They were radiantly happy.

It was astonishing what white skins had been hidden under the black desert rags.

But the clothes had not arrived.

Soon Miss Masterman came up for frenzied consultation. Valerie offered to find Mrs. Frobisher and ask what had happened.

'For pity's sake get Wilbur Frobisher to hustle! Or these angels will become brigands again and tear us in pieces!'

From the tropical heat of the Baths Valerie passed into the baking, dusty street. She traversed short-cut lanes and bazaars and endured the novel humiliation of a crowd staring at an American girl in hurry that was close to panic.

'Why, the clothes have *gone!*' Mrs. Frobisher exclaimed. 'Wilbur took them an hour ago. They'll all be at the Baths.'

'There isn't a single piece there,' gasped Val; and felt like crying. It was she who had officially fixed things up; this bad staff work lay at her door. She ran back, this time undisguisedly, dignity flung to the winds—hoping that somewhere, in some unsuspected coign or nook of a tiny overlooked room at the Baths the clothes were waiting all the time. But she knew that this was not so.

Store-Major Schwartz, his face crimson with Jerusalem's June and with anger, was outside the men's section of the Baths. He bellowed at her, 'Where are those darned clothes? Where's Frobisher? What's he think he's doing?'

Cynthia, who had left the pink results of her own toil, joined them. Seeing behind Store-Major Schwartz wrathful and alarmed faces peering over the shoulders of the attendants (who were gesticulating and clamouring that the Baths were needed now for their normal clients and could not be occupied all day by their present incumbents) she giggled helplessly. She had seen the lords of the desert moving off with such stately disdain, a little over two hours ago. She did not know how the business was going to end; but for the moment their predicament had compensations.

'It isn't so darned funny, Miss Cameron!' She had forgotten that beside her stood a spirit in torment.

'I can't understand a word that these bath specialists are saying, but I guess they want the place free, and double quick. I gather from that darned fool of an interpreter that this is Jerusalem's day for getting laundered and that the Moslems want the next two hours, and the Greek Christians after that, and then a whole shute of dagoes and sheenies. Tell me what in thunder we are to do!'

Cynthia, even in this solemn moment irrepressible, said, 'We ought to organise indoor sports of some kind.'

She never realised how close Store-Major Schwartz came to murder; and murder, moreover, of a kind that American opinion recognises as genuinely reprehensible, that of a beautiful young woman. She did, however, grasp perfectly clearly that he was not in a mood when light-hearted jesting appealed to him.

'I'd like to wring my sheikhs' necks,' he said. And passed a hand between his own and its collar. It came out dripping with perspiration. He had never been hotter in his life, both within and without.

Then the children in the women's baths did a terrible thing. Half of them escaped from their guards, whose surveillance had lost its first enthusiasm, and made a rush for their former clothes, a pile lying dedicated to the fire. Their guards followed them, so did the unescaped younger prisoners; and the spectacle ensued of twenty Arab little girls standing in the June sunlight, clean and naked and mutinous, besieging four people who kept a heap of blood-curdling garments. Valerie had seen their purpose and forestalled them just in time. How long they could hold off their attacks was doubtful. From over the attendants' shoulders their parents hoarsely encouraged them. The interpreter stood aside, neutral.

Martin, mournfully reflecting on the price that is exacted for loyalty—'We tore things somehow, Bunny and I. But it was too thick, to have to let down fellows you know about, just to put yourselves right with others who don't understand'—had been doing his job remissly. The only units who saw him were those on the road to the railway station. Then he raced back worried, to the Baths.

There was some excuse for wondering if there were visions about. Certainly there *seemed* to be no mystic quality in this clear June sunlight. But . . . but? Was this dream or reality—the imps of his former imagination now washed but more outrageous than ever, were standing mother-naked and indignant, sensitive at the spectacle they were presenting to the considerable crowd enjoying the show!

What would you feel, reader?—what should I feel? —if when we were in the helplessness of unhappy sleep an angel should arrive in the very crisis of our nightmare?

'Why, there's Captain Chapman!' exclaimed Cynthia, forgetting his offensive sinfulness.

The flash in Valerie's eyes recalled the memory to her. But Store-Major Schwartz had heard, and he shouted for assistance.

Captain Chapman jumped down from his car, and saluted. Even in their wrath the girls were conscious that the act of homage saved them. The dreaded uniform, with a real warrior inside it, calmed the watching senior mutineers and made even the children pause.

He took charge quietly, listening to Store-Major Schwartz's volubility, to Miss Masterman's urgency, to the interpreter's anxiety to make his importance and innocence clear—three simultaneous and eloquent addresses. 'This officer set a splendid example to all ranks, by his resource and self-control.'

The girls grew riotous again. '*Iskut!*' ('Shut up!') he shouted fiercely, using one of the few words of Arabic that he had acquired (the British soldier applying himself to a foreign tongue is a practical person in what little he learns.) He noted mentally that Major Austin-Gary's advice to master this local lingo was good; it enabled you to assist Miss Connett and Miss Cameron in distress.

If he had been thinking of his audience's femininity, he should have said '*Iskuti*'; if of their plurality, the form '*Iskutu*'. But we need not be pedantic. His hearers understood him; and understood also, which was more important, that he was going to eat them alive if they did not shut up.

'I'm afraid we've still got this city in a most awful mess,' he said apologetically.

It was tactful, this assumption that of course the whole ridiculous circus had come by act of malign mischance and was not part of the Relief Force's normal operations (which, the girls were ragingly aware, often provided what these British took to be welcome comic relief just as Palestine was growing tedious and dusty).

Instinctively his eyes had sought Valerie's. She knew she ought not to acknowledge that he existed, but the provocation was too great. 'These,' she said resentfully, 'are your leavings. Rubbish the British Army brought in from east of Jordan.'

He nodded. Then his glance fell on the noxious pile that the children were seeking to resume. He gingerly poked it with his foot, and asked, 'Are these the old clothes?'

A wail went up from the temporarily silenced children.

Val had to laugh. But enough genuine annoyance remained to bring up the frown that he so richly merited.

'*What* did you say had happened to their new clothes?' he asked.

She was astonished at his dumbness. Then she remembered that three people had all been explaining things at once, and at cross purposes; sometimes even an Englishman is not as stupid as he looks and behaves.

'We've skads of clothes for them somewhere in Jerusalem,' Cynthia said. 'And the arrangement was that they should be here at eleven. And here it is nearly one.'

'Perhaps they've been left at one of the other Turkish Baths, sir,' Bennett, Martin's chauffeur, suggested.

Everyone stared at the speaker.

'*Are* there any other Baths?' asked Valerie.

Bennett explained that there were.

'That's it!' shouted Store-Major Schwartz. 'That darned fool Frobisher has gone to the wrong Baths! Say, Captain, will you lend us your automobile to find them?'

'Rather,' said Martin. 'Bennett, you stop here till I get back. You may as well have my revolver as well as your rifle. No need, of course; but just as well, with this crowd of ruffians all about, and those bandits in the Bath over there.' He handed it over ostentatiously. 'And I say'—to the interpreter—'make it clear to these kids—these children—that they are not to stir one step towards this pile of garbage, or I'll have General Allenby after them. And they're not to annoy the ladies, mind, or they'll hear about it when I get back.'

With ferocious and eloquent gestures the interpreter interpreted. Martin drew his hand across his own throat and produced a fearsome scowl. Then he took him over to the Baths and explained on the honour of the British Army that the whole thing was not a vast practical joke in the worst of taste from the victims' point of view, but that clothes *would—be —shortly—forthcoming*.

He all but crashed, three minutes later, into Lieutenant Wilbur Frobisher, who had learnt from his wife of the dreadful thing that had happened, and was careering dangerously round Jerusalem with a lorry, along streets never meant for any traffic swifter or broader than an ass carrying two sacks. Martin, whose brain was working well this morning, even in the moment of barely averted collision saw what the lunatic driver was bringing and jumped out and impounded them.

'I say, are these the clothes those American ladies are wanting?'

'Yes!' shouted Frobisher.

'Are these the lot?'

'No. There's another heap I had to leave to make a second trip for.'

'I'll fetch them. Tell me where they are.'

Martin, leaving Frobisher to help with the distribution, made two trips to fetch the rest of the clothes. When the job was done, he asked, 'Now won't you all lunch with me? I wish you would!'

'Why, you come along and take your dinner with us!' said Store-Major Schwartz. 'It's all ready, waiting for us at headquarters.'

Miss Masterman and Frobisher earnestly seconded the invitation. He badly wanted to accept it.

But pride said, No. Miss Connett and Miss Cameron had not said a word. He was damned if he was going, unless they wanted him as well.

In face of the others' hospitality he stuck to his refusal, finding excuses. He went.

'He was too shy to come with us right off,' Miss Masterman decided. 'It was fine, the way he came right in and helped us.'

'He's what I call a real fellow,' said Frobisher.

At his going even the girls were stiffly courteous. Their manner would have done them more credit if they had not (unjustly) felt sure that he would presently be laughing at them. It was an unkind jest of chance, to cast them for such ridiculous parts at their first meeting with a young man after they had dismissed him into the outer darkness of denial of their favour for ever.

They ought to have felt shabby; but truth compels the statement that they did not. Even in these days of uniformity, a difference remains between masculine and feminine psychology, thank God!

VIII

I

THREE DAYS HAD PASSED WHEN MARTIN IN HIS MAIL, which was mostly 'Signals' and official, noted a letter addressed in an unknown, neatly feminine hand. Valerie invited him to a picnic supper on Olivet next evening but two, June 9th. His surprise would have been deepened had he known the heart-burning that had gone before the making of this overture, which had been possible at all only because Frobisher had suggested Martin's inclusion. We have seen Frobisher twice, once in a deed perilously close to mutiny, blunt and almost coolly insolent, and once blundering through Jerusalem roads in search of a goal he did not clearly know.

Cynthia had flatly refused to have the invitation extended to Warren, even if Warren had been within reach. Valerie, knowing that her heart was sore and angry and that she wanted him back, if merely in proxy in his chum's person, had asked Martin. Through Martin an olive-twig might be extended, and yet honour preserved.

They were not yet decided that they meant to extend even an olive-twig. Neither of the last two encounters had gone exactly as it should have done. Martin, in particular, was deplorably far from having

experienced adequate humiliation. Still, there were
reasons why he (but certainly not Captain Remfry)
might be given another chance. If he should presume
that all was forgiven opportunity could be provided
for him to realise the enormity of his miscalculation.
But he could come back for once, at any rate to the
outer circle of their acquaintance. There would be
other girls and men in the party; perhaps some of
them would talk to him.

Some of them did. In fact, it was painful to see how
quickly Martin seemed to become quite popular.
Captain Wilbur Frobisher (he had been raised to
this rank, temporarily, like the three new lieuten-
ants, pending sanction from Washington) and Mrs.
Frobisher were largely responsible for this. Frobisher
in real life was in charge of a Presbyterian Church
in Maine, a pacifist, an idealist, a passionate believer
in the United States, youth, and humanity, the
degree of his belief being correctly indicated by that
order. He could be sticky when his ideals were
opposed by unimaginative and stupid action—we
have noticed an instance of this. But this was not his
natural mood, which was one of that eager kind-
liness which seems to flourish so much more luxuri-
antly in America than in the cautious Old World.

He had cause to like Martin already. His warm
welcome and his obvious expectation to find in a
fellow-man a fellow-idealist won Martin immediately.
There was enough of deep enthusiasm in both men
to ensure their friendship.

This age has forgotten. Rather, it never knew. But
now, go back to the age out of which the pre-War
generation came.

Set your hand on your heart; think, remember, and be honest. Between 1870 and 1900 was there a thing happened or was there a thought thought, which rose above the dead, shameful-shameless mediocrity of the time? It was a shabby, poor generation, not the men and women themselves, but the bewilderment, the mean ideals, the complacency, the resolute contempt or crushing out of minorities, the dull untruthful doctrine which fed their minds and hearts. Its idealist was Gladstone; and its cynic, Disraeli, by all standards that involve what the human spirit suffers and endures, was the nobler man. We have seen what the age achieved in India, and the storm it has set our generation to weather if it can. We know what it did in South Africa. We have seen how it worked in and through the United States. And in Europe—what happened beside wars? Wars that really were made by politicians—ignoble, sordid wars deliberately launched by men now in Hell.

The Great Queen died in a blaze of sham magnificence, amid the mutterings of the last imperialist campaign. And as the glory that was Victoria passed into the ages a sense of shame and repentance stirred in her people. We had learnt that we were ill-led, ill-educated and ignorant, that outside our borders were countries with compensations for falling short of our aggregate opulence. The young men and women whose leaders were swept away in the World War were touched with a fire from God. They honestly believed they could bring into being a decent polity and citizenship; that they could abolish war and poverty and exploitation, and heal the nations. They saw a New Jerusalem and were passionately eager to live for it—which they proved by the way they died for it.

We who knew that generation tell youth to-day that it can never get from its prophets the thrill that came to us from ours. There was an evangelistic wrath, reaching out for martyrdom, in the despair of our John Davidson, that our successors will not find in their own preachers that all is vanity. They will never know the exultation with which we listened to Ibsen and Tolstoi, or the sacrificial awe and exultation with which men answered the call to arms. Those who had dreamed and planned and worked vanished. Will Redmond and Sorley and Alan Seagar died; the politicians and society ladies and you and I, middle-aged reader, lived.

But these men were our companions.

Martin had gone through experiences that ought to have killed all memory of the pre-War fire. But drawn into this warm friendliness in a moment he leapt back. Not eight years before, he had been caught into excitement over the New Theology, which was going to give mankind a religion that would never clash with science and fact, that would be free from all superstition while making the major superstition, the one that at the heart of the Universe there is Mind and Love and Purity, safe for the intellect! Yet he had seen his friend deserted by God and man, left to die in a pit of the hills. He had himself prayed, and not for selfish or material ends, and his prayers had been so much chaff dispersed. He knew, more exactly than the schoolmen could tell him, how closely clamped down on man's good-

ness are that goodness's limitations. Yet—the old
fire revived, the old belief returned, as he was
welcomed into this earnest hope and charity
nourished in the boundless West. The Americans of
1918 had not yet lost their great tradition, of hospitable arms opened out to the whole world.

Cynthia's heart was still angry, and she vouchsafed
only the chillest 'How do you do, Captain Chapman?' and turned away to talk to another man.
Neither did Valerie do more than barely recognise
old acquaintance. He was left to begin all over again,
on the footing of the chance visitor of an evening.
He had no further word from either, as the party
made their way into the Kedron Valley and up the
steep lane to the 'Hic Dominus Flevit' inscription.
  But the others accepted him at once. He had had
four weeks of Wenyon's companionship and coaching; their eagerness to know all about the Holy
City lit the flame of his own eagerness to tell.
Though it is possible for the man who is enthusiastic
to be dull, his enthusiasm is a handicap unless he is
a perfect fool. It is not possible for even the perfect
fool to be dull if he is enthusiastic about Jerusalem.
Martin was not a perfect fool, far from it. And in his
earnestness was a personal modesty and loyalty
that won affection, as it had long since won Warren
Remfry's. You could not help feeling this beauty of
spirit, laying itself open to the beauty of both worlds,
both the seen physical world and the unseen moral
world.

  The party came to rest at length on Olivet's summit,
where a vineyard ran up into the native wilderness

of thymes and mints. Fragrance of the Syrian air, which if you once experience you never forget, filled the evening. The last golden, peaceful light was on everything, on the marvellous City and the hills and over the Dead Sea Valley. Only Jordan's thickets, that green lushness thrusting a twisted finger through the desert—this and the depths of the Vale of Jehoshaphat lay in shadow.

Against Martin's memory of two anguished and despairing retreats through that seeming quiet and lovely terrain, his present security was unearthly, as if he had died and could recall life's sufferings merely as dim figures on the mind's wall.

In France his countrymen were in the long agony of the fierce last onslaught of the German Army; his friend of youth was plundered bones in those desolate mountains. He was on Olivet, with kindness and graciousness his neighbours. Seated on the sweet thyme-carpet, he became blissfully aware that Valerie was next to him and that the trouble between them was over.

The moon rose above the Moab hills, an enormous orange-red orb. No one wished to talk while that superb glory slowly lifted itself free of earth's shadow that deepened its glowing brightness. Fireflies flickered in the vine-leaves.

Valerie touched his arm. 'See!' she whispered.

A fox, smaller than the English kind, had sauntered up and paused to look fearlessly at the generous banquet that the girls had spread on their incense-strewn table. It watched them as they looked back silent, then slipped away as unobtrusively as it had come.

G

'I wonder what the Dead Sea died of?' said Frobisher.

'It died of depression,' said Valerie, making a joke first-class in every way.

In the general laughter that followed Martin met Cynthia's eyes. They tried to look angry and scornful, but had to smile.

'Captain Chapman?' queried a girl, as she offered him olives.

Then Cynthia made peace in her own magnificent way.

'We're all Christian names here,' she said. 'Is it all right to take a liberty with a real British captain?' she asked. 'It's not like *our* captains—no offence meant to you, Captain Frobisher——'

'None at all,' said Frobisher cheerily. 'I'm just what the British call a padre. I haven't seen war, thank goodness!'

Martin accepted an olive, and said, 'Thank you, Miss Williams.'

Cynthia clapped her hands furiously. Valerie, acting on the cue, arrested his arm. 'Put that olive back, Martin. Now take it again, Martin, and say "Thank you, Jean." You heard Cynthia's order, Martin.'

Martin said, 'Thank you, Jean.'

'You said that quite prettily, Martin,' said Cynthia.

Presently, strangely talkative, he was annotated by Cynthia.

'Warren Remfry's the boy we saw playing cricket last Saturday. You know, Jean, the one who plays as if he were a baseball cracker-jack.'

'He does not,' said Martin indignantly. 'He's a beautiful cricketer.'

'That's what Cynthia said,' said Valerie. 'You are not to contradict Cynthia so flatly, Martin.'

'Yes. But I say——'

'Well, he gave me a new idea of cricket, anyway,' said Cynthia.

'He seemed a nice boy,' said Jean impartially.

'He rather thinks that himself, doesn't he?' said Cynthia, indicating to Martin that she was still officially at war with his friend, who had not yet been so fortunate as to come in and make his submission.

'He doesn't,' said Martin.

'Oh!'

'No. Even if he did—and he doesn't—he's got a right to think well of himself. If you knew Bunny as well as I do——'

'Knew *who*?'

'Warren. They call him Bunny.'

'Why?'

'Why? Because rabbits live in warrens.' It hardly seemed an adequate explanation.

'I see. I thought it might be because he looked such a baby. They call him a captain,' Cynthia explained, 'but anyone who saw him would say he ought to be going to school.'

So Warren's state of unforgiven sinfulness was made clear to all. But he had a champion present. Few themes arouse the eloquence of generous youth as friendship does. The company heard something of Warren's prowess and fineness.

'It's nice to hear that there *is* another side to him,' said Cynthia in tones that were a sigh indicating the deepest scepticism.

After supper the party amused itself in ways that would never occur to an English picnic-party. Cynthia recited Masefield's 'August 1914,' throwing herself into its grave slow rhythms. Another girl recited 'I have a rendezvous with death' and the whole of Rupert Brooke's *1914.* Then Mrs. Frobisher suggested some singing; and under the full moon now high over Olivet the Americans sang—plantation songs, sentimental songs, comic songs—and finally, with feeling and solemnity, 'My country, 'tis of thee.' 'Martin can sing "God save the King" if he likes,' said Cynthia, 'since he doesn't know anything about a "sweet land of liberty," but comes from where tyrants reign and they still have a House of Lords and a Court.'

'But if I sing something different won't it put you all out?' he asked.

'They're both the same tune,' said Valerie.

'You've stolen our tune for your National Anthem,' Cynthia explained.

Cynthia told the story of their meetings. 'We've put a hoodoo on each other. It all depends on who sees the other first. If it's Martin sees *us*, then we're in a wild skirmish with ruffians whose clothes have walked out on them. If we see *him* first, why, Martin is trying to do the fakir stunt on a heap of prickly pears; or has a dreadful man chasing him round Jerusalem.'

'Well, after the queer way you came to the Holy Land—via Japan and Kamschatka, wasn't it?—'

'Don't exaggerate, Martin,' said Valerie. 'The *facts* are quite funny enough.'

'You might *expect* signs and wonders to continue after you got here,' he concluded.

'No bigger signs and wonders than we've seen,' said Cynthia. 'We almost did a circular tour of the British Empire. You'll never get me again to believe that your Empire's a gathering of really independent nations. We've seen it in time of war.'

'Durban's what I shall remember as long as I live,' said Frobisher. 'What we saw taught me something—something that I don't believe America will ever know happened. You couldn't know unless you *saw*.'

The Relief Force had reached Durban in the first appalling success of the German Offensive of 1918. Careless of this, from their remoteness in America and the silence of the long sea trip that had enwrapped them, they had planned a grand dance ashore. Natal opinion had been shocked, but in quick courtesy had understood and forgiven; kindness overwhelming (but without a dance) had been poured out on these who represented the newest Ally. They had seen—and Valerie could almost imagine that she was living through the tenseness of which she had heard since her earliest days, when her beloved Virginia had steeled herself for the invasion and overthrow that all her valour had not placated the gods to avert—the courage and love welling in these younger nations of the English. From these people, so far from the thunder of the guns advancing to the narrow seas, had gone up passionate loyalty and unconquerable resolve; their own sons were dying ungrudged. Durban's heart was in mourning, but its manner was gaiety—a gaiety which some of these visitors had seen for what it was, gentle condescension as to children whose days need not be darkened by the sorrow fallen in eternal cloud upon our own.

II

When at last they decided that they must get back, the night seemed too lovely to leave. So Martin felt, standing alone with Valerie, about to descend the steep narrow way.

'I'd love to stay out all night,' he said, 'and just wander all over this mountain in the moonlight.'

She answered with sudden frank impulsiveness. 'If you were an American boy whom I liked, I'd do it with you. I'd love it, too.'

'Why wouldn't you do it with me?' he asked eagerly.

'No British boy would understand.'

This he would not admit. He was piqued by an Eden of intimacy being indicated as shut to him and his kind.

'A British boy would think I was doing something out of the way and wonderful. He wouldn't understand just straight friendship, as we have it in America between boys and girls.'

Youth will not confess that where boy and girl play together Eros makes himself of the party. Martin protested, 'Of course I shouldn't misunderstand it, Valerie.'

She accepted his arm down a slippery place, naturally and with comradeship.

'We didn't treat you badly to-night,' she said thoughtfully. The path was better, and his arm was relinquished. 'We took you in on the ground floor—although you were British.'

'You've been perfectly ripping to me! All of you. Especially you and Cynthia.'

'Well—there's something you want to trust in a man who sticks up for his friend as you do. And who stuck up for his opinion, too, as you and Captain Remfry did to us. I tell you, Cynthia's been spoiled, and she isn't accustomed to having any man tell her he thinks she's wrong. Especially when she knows that man likes her. Captain Remfry does like her, doesn't he?'

'Bunny's crazy about her. And who wouldn't be? She's an absolutely topping girl. She was dear to me to-night.'

'Oh, well—'

'So were you, Valerie. Just as ripping as any girl could be!'

'That's better. I thought perhaps you were forgetting that everyone had been friendly to you.'

'No, I wasn't. But it was you two who really took me in. I'll never forget it. Never!'

The conversation was becoming dangerously tinged with emotion. Valerie, the exponent of frank, simple comradeship between the sexes, thought it better not to accept Martin's arm again, though they had come to a place where she had to scramble down by help of a broken wall.

'I say! Valerie!'

'Yes?'

'If you'd go over Olivet with an American fellow, why won't you go with me?'

'The others would misunderstand,' she said evasively.

'Wouldn't they misunderstand if you did it with one of your own fellows?'

'No.' She paused, and looked at him. 'Not if I picked my man—as I should do, of course. I wouldn't do it except with a boy that I trusted *absolutely*.'

'And you don't trust me!'

'Yes. I do. When I saw you suddenly go away from us all and go off thinking by yourself as you looked at those hills, I felt that I simply had to make things up, Martin. I didn't want to go on quarrelling with a man I wanted to have as a friend.'

'Come with me, Valerie! Please! Because I want to have you as a friend. You don't know how much I want it.'

'I can't, Martin.'

'We'll probably never have another chance. Of seeing all over this wonderful mountain in this heavenly moonlight, Valerie! Just look at the grey olives,' he pleaded, 'and the rocks and the shadows— and those white towers—and this sky—and that glorious, glorious city! There isn't another sight like it in the world. It's a chance we shall never get again—just like this! Why won't you share it with me, Valerie?'

'I've told you why.'

'You said that I couldn't understand friendship.'

She stopped and looked him full in the face. The mountain, like some ghostly shepherd, lay shadowy in moonlight, pasturing his olives and his memories. He was ready to accept one story more, of a boy and girl wandering through his crags and groves, gathering dreams from his peace.

They had reached the bottom of the Valley, by the Virgin's Tomb. The road was a climb from now on, right up to the Holy City's battlements.

'Martin! Isn't it true?'

'No. It isn't.'

'If I—if any girl——"

'No, No. No! Say "If I," Valerie. It's not any girl, it's you I want to come with me.'

'That makes it worse. Wouldn't you feel—before the night finished—that you had to make love to me?'

He was about to deny it, when the night took hold of him and made him tell the truth he had not known. The Syrian night, and the girl for whose courage and gentleness it made a perfect setting. Not without reason has Virginia prided itself on its women. If Wordsworth is right in saying that 'beauty born of murmuring sound' passes into the face that leans down listening to it, then there is a physical loveliness that comes from being nurtured amid beauty that is one with old-world memories. Her eyes had as many ripples and shadows as a woodland brook.

And Martin said, 'Yes, Valerie, I should. And it would be your fault. I don't see how any man could help wanting to make love to you if he saw you as I have seen you. I daren't ask you to come over Olivet with me. I won't ask you!'

She gripped his arm and pressed it in a quick impetuous gesture. 'I'd trust my life with you, Martin! You're a *man*—and you've got to be my pal. But you see, I was right. You *wouldn't* understand. Now I've promised to hand you over to Cynthia. She wants to walk up to the Holy City with you.'

He protested. 'Oh, but, Valerie——'

'No, sir. You've said too much to me to-night, Captain Chapman.'

'Martin!' he reminded her.

'Of course. Martin.'

She added, half teasingly, 'But perhaps we brought you in too soon.' (Hastily, seeing his look of protest) 'No, Martin, It's all right. But now you are not to be rude to Cynthia. Why, most men would be walking in heaven if she signified a wish to have their escort. So good-bye here. And do your devoirs like the lucky cavalier that you are.'

Cynthia up the steepness took his arm without hesitation. He knew that Valerie would not have taken it, and understood it as the measure of the impersonal friendship he was being offered.

'Listen, Martin. It was mean of Val to steal and keep you when she knew I was wanting to talk to you. But now I want you for a bit. I've been thinking things over, and I feel I was kind of shabby the other night. That's why I made it up. I wanted to go on being mean, but—oh, well, anyway, I couldn't. So I had to hand across the pipe of peace.'

'You were absolutely topping, Cynthia. I told Val that you were a dear.'

'Well,—I've made it up, anyway. And I'll make it up with Captain Remfry. It isn't that I think Val and I did anything *wrong*.'

'No, of course not.'

'*You* don't think we did anything wrong?'

'Rather not.'

'That's nice of you, Martin. But thinking it over
I remembered that it wasn't you and Captain Remfry
that asked us there, and you couldn't know the kind
of show it was going to be.'

'They never expected girls like you and Val.'

She considered a moment. 'But I think that stuck-up
idiot Major Carruthers might have known.'

'Oh, I don't see how he could, Cynthia!'

'But he'd seen those shows before. And it was he
and his friend who asked us—not you and Captain
Remfry. Could you manage to fix it up that he
could meet us again?'

'I should say I could! This is splendid of you,
Cynthia!'

'I don't like feeling I've behaved meanly to anyone.'

'He'll come in like a streak when he hears. No one
will see him for dust. He thinks you're the most
topping girl he ever met. If you and Val will have
dinner with us to-morrow——"

'Not to-morrow. Make it three days from now.'

'Righto. I know Bunny'll assassinate his colonel if
he tries to stop him coming in. And, I say, Cynthia
—let us take you two over Siloam before we have
dinner at the Fast. Bunny's never been, and I'm
sure *you* haven't yet.'

'I'll come, Martin.'

It was past midnight when he left them at the
Damascus Gate. Feeling that time was for dogs and
apes, he strode cheerfully into the Valley, instead of
taking the road, and climbed up over crag and thorn

to Olivet. He was going to go over the landscape of
Paradise again, before it vanished into the mists of
everyday. The moonlight made everything fairyland, where a man could not be wearied.

IX

FOR THE TRIP TO SILOAM THEY MET AT THE JAFFA
Gate; and took the circuitous path that goes amid
jostling memories of old unhappy things. But what
did Aceldama—or Hinnom's forgotten fires—mean
to them? To Warren, who swung so confidently and
arrogantly beside Cynthia making him the gift of
her undivided beauty and swift vivacious kindness?
To Martin who had been starved of youth's right to
admire and worship?

They reached the Virgin's Spring, whose curving,
slippery hollow receives the waters when they are
troubled by the Angel who drives them from their
hid recess. The girls' shoes were not made for such a
surface, a fact that did not disturb their wearers.
They ignored protests and went impetuously in and
on to the swelling polished rock above the pool.
They overlooked the fountain's source, their bodies
bowed in the perfect grace of their curiosity.

It was not Cynthia's way to make either peace or
war by halves. She was all radiancy and friendliness.
From the rock returning she all but jumped into
Bunny's arms, while Valerie ignored Martin's hand
outstretched to steady her. Valerie throughout was
chill and doctrinaire and vexing. She accepted
Martin as the boy who was talking to her, pro-
tagonist of opinions opposed to her own.

If the ramble proved maddeningly unsatisfactory, Martin found dinner almost worse. Even Cynthia noticed Val's ridiculous preoccupation with questions surely trivial to-night—why fuss Martin (who after all was British and could not help it) as to how far English land-grabbing had brought on the World War, conjointly with German bullying and imperialism? She rebuked her as high-brow. To-night Cynthia, her college education set aside for the time being, was rejoicingly low-brow.

Valerie hotly defended herself.

'If Martin joined up as a volunteer as soon as war was declared—he wasn't like Bunny, who had meant to go into the Army in any case—he must have convinced himself that the British were in the right. You wouldn't join up if you weren't sure of that, Martin, would you?'

'If 1914 came back again I would.'

'But how could you?'

'You don't begin to understand, Val——'

'Oh!'

'No, honestly you don't. Bunny and I didn't join up with the idea that our country was so magnificently in the right that we were going to whack a whole lot of other people. We knew she *was* in the right, but that wasn't it. I hated the notion of war, I was keen on peace and justice and an equal chance for *everyone* in every country, Val, I was really. But first of all a lot of fellows had to take their chance of dying and of being smashed up, before anything else could be done. Anyone who wasn't an utter skunk knew where he had to be.'

'Val, are you crazy?' asked Cynthia petulantly.

'How can you expect these boys not to stick up for
what England does, when England's their country?
I know I'd stick up for the States, whatever they did
and whatever other nations might choose to say.
And I'd know we were in the right, too!'

'I'd like them to stick up for something bigger than
just England,' said Valerie.

'We do,' said Martin.

'Well, but how, Martin?'

Damn! here he was back in argument, when
Cynthia had extricated him, if he had only had the
sense to keep quiet. He had not yet built up a bridge
of connection with Valerie's mind.

Afterwards, on the hotel roof Cynthia, her arm
pushed through Bunny's, was softly and happily
singing: 'Massa's in de col' col' groun''; 'Less than
the dust beneath thy chariot wheels'; 'Drink to
me only with thine eyes.' Valerie, bad-tempered
with herself for her cussedness, held Martin to a
discussion of President Wilson's Fourteen Points,
particularly the one concerning the Rights of Small
Nations.

Martin took refuge in a helpless man's resource.
He turned sulky. 'You'd best ask Bunny about that,'
he said. 'He holds views very different from your
President's as to what should be done to small
nations—especially in these parts.'

'If you ask *me*, he's one fine man!' said Cynthia,
glowingly uninterested. She was referring to President
Wilson. But Bunny may have had some share in the
enthusiasm she felt for the Liberator.

To Martin's further vexation, Valerie took his
advice seriously. She turned to drag Captain Warren

Remfry into exposition of his racial philosophy. But he was strongly placed in his ally.

'I won't have Bunny arguing so late as this,' said Cynthia. 'Besides, he's nicer when he isn't arguing. He isn't a thinker like Martin—or like you, Val.'

This was one of those happy remarks that manage to be unacceptable to all whom they concern. Bunny protested against relegation to the non-thinking portion of mankind. Martin was loath to be branded as one who thought and was therefore uninteresting to those whom he wished to interest. Valerie, though she alone said nothing, wondered at the implications of the 'highbrow' rôle so persistently allotted to her; she by no means ranked herself with femininity commonly supposed to be frowsy.

Cynthia silenced both protestants. 'Bunny, you are all right as you are—just for to-night. And, Martin, you argue with Val, if you must argue.' Which was rather hard on Martin. 'I'm as keen as anyone on all these problems,' she soothingly explained. 'When I was at college no one worked harder for our Political Association than I did, and we used to get down the most *interesting* people, women who'd done—well, they'd done just the most *wonderful* things you could think of and made contact with all the most dynamic and worth-while personalities you could find, in the Orient as well as in America or Europe. But you just won't get me arguing when it's getting on towards midnight. My brain kind of goes to sleep then."Massa's in de col' col' ground," ' she hummed.

Martin was giving Warren a bed at his billet on Olivet, borrowed from Wenyon on leave in Alex.

'Why the devil did you and Val argue about those silly subjects?' Bunny asked him before they turned in.

'Do you think I wanted to?'

'Well, you did it. Why, why, *why*, O Puzzlewit?'

'Oh, damn, Bunny! she *insisted* on arguing.'

'I shouldn't have let her.'

'How could I stop her?'

'Oh, you always can—if you know how. I know this much, if I were with a dashed pretty girl whom I liked as much as you like Val I'd talk about something more interesting to *her*. Do you know what Cynthia said to me, on the roof? She said, "Val isn't really keen on what she's talking about now. She's only ragging Martin, to keep him properly humble. She isn't going to give him any excuse for thinking that there's any danger of her falling for him." But you were an ass to play up to her, Martin.'

'I didn't play up to her.'

Bunny did not think it necessary to pass over the full interchange of comment between him and Cynthia. He had asked her, 'Would *you* make *me* what you call properly humble if you thought I were what Val thinks Martin is?' She had answered, 'Perhaps.' 'How would you do it, Cynthia?' 'Ah! that's asking questions! But you'd find I *could* do, jolly quick if I wanted! But just now you are just right, Bunny. All you have to do is to go on being nice to me. "Massa's in de col' col' ground."' He thought he should remember those words and that tune to his dying day.

X

DURING THE REST OF JUNE, MARTIN WAS GIVEN ONLY glimpses of Valerie. She passed him in a lorry, one of a group rushing happily off to some picnic. She was on the outskirts of a crowd watching the cricket match against the Seventh Meerut Division, and saw him ignominiously leg-before-wicket; he managed to speak to her—just. And that was all.

Cynthia he saw more often, yet not for much longer. She had advanced Bunny to the first place among her admirers, and he was wangling a surprising amount of time away from his unit. Not many men would care to act as battalion quartermaster as well as company commander, which was what he was doing. The Brentfords' normal quartermaster, a lethargic and middle-aged ranker, felt that if this boy were so keen on Jerusalem that he was prepared to volunteer to do the regimental business at canteens and stores he might as well be humoured. June is a hot month in the Judaean crags, very trying to those no longer young.

'I'd like to congratulate you, Warren me boy,' said Father O'Hara, 'on the noble interest ye've developed in the Holy City. Maybe ye'll escape Hell yet, if only because the place is full up with other Englishmen.'

'Jerusalem's a topping hole,' said Bunny enthusiastically.

'Now there's not many as young and inexperienced as you that would have the sense to see that. Is it Martin Chapman that has taught you this? I'd always a respect for that boy, though he's a heretic

like yourself. But if it's a heretic that he is, he has
the grace to be a Nonconformist and have no truck
with the church established by law in England and
the Army.'

'Martin's a topper,' said Warren, whose approval
was wide and generous.

'Since he does you so much good, ye're wise to see
as much of him as ye can,' Father O'Hara concluded.

He was not seeing much of Martin, nevertheless.
For the most part Martin had to be content with
a chance greeting in some Jerusalem street, a
'Hullo, Puzzlewit!' or a 'Why, Martin! how *nice* to
see you like this! I haven't seen Martin for ages,
Bunny!'

His lame enquiries about Valerie would be met
with vague, half-considered answers.

'Val? Why, Martin, I guess Val's just *busy*. I
hardly ever see her myself. There's so much to do.
Now that we've both got our own orphanages, we're
just about run off our feet.'

The momentary vision of Cynthia, friendly, cosy,
charming, was jolly. He would look after them as
they swung away, engrossed in each other's world.
With her 'peerless hunter, harper, knight' she was
a fitting Iseult. And yet——

'Iseult? Ah, not the Iseult I desire!'

He would have liked, too, renewal of the old leisured
intimacy with Warren.

Instead, 'Good-bye, Cynthia! So long, Warren!'

'Good-bye, Martin! I'll tell Val I've seen you.'

'So long! Bye-bye, Beefycheeks!'

It was not very satisfying.

July was in its first week when he was suddenly swept back into the life that had forsaken him. Just before sunset, he was on the moor contiguous to his billet, doing nothing in particular—idly twisting and breaking stalks of aromatic scrub, oppressed by vague knowledge of emptiness and uselessness. He heard a 'Coo-ee!' It was repeated; he looked up, and saw Remfry a couple of hundred yards away, his hands a trumpet before his lips. They both advanced; and as they met, Warren said, 'No, don't come in, old chap. I want a talk. Let's have it here, out of doors.'

The talk was punctuated by Warren's restlessness. 'I don't like the way things are going in France.'

'They're going better than they were.'

'Think so? I don't believe a single bloody thing they tell us. They've fooled us too often, Martin. It's a bad show, a bloody bad show.'

'It's better than it was last April. Remember how bucked our brigadier was when our fellows were retreating like hell? He argued that it was all a trap. That we were luring the Hun on! Everyone but the old boy knew better than that.'

"God! he *was* a half-wit!' said Warren bitterly. 'A bloody half-wit, if there ever was one!'

'No, he wasn't, Bunny. He was only arguing from the only premises they ever give us in our school-days. *You* never heard of any British defeat, or of any British army falling back. Then why should they begin falling back now, especially when we have the finest generals in the world? Obviously, there was deep purpose in it.'

'Oh, why the devil am I talking about France?'

Warren broke out. 'However, there's this in it. You heard any gup lately, Martin?'

'What kind of gup?'

'About sending troops from here to France?'

Martin *had* heard rumours. The white troops were to be sent from this Front and their place taken by Indians. Rumour was especially firm about the Londons.

'Out with it, Martin, old man. You *have* heard that our fellows are going. You needn't keep it back from me. I've been through too many thinning-out parades to get the wind up about one more.'

Then Martin began to think aloud.

" I see the Indians' point of view. It *is* a damned shame, a foul and beastly shame!'

'What's a foul and beastly shame? What's the Indians' point of view?'

'Nothing. I was only thinking aloud—about something else.'

'Nothing be damned! You were thinking aloud, were you? If the Delphic priestess was as explicit as you are when you start talking in your sleep, I wonder they didn't chuck her down the chasm, tripod and all!'

Martin explained.

'We've got a Sikhs' officer in my mess. He was telling me that when he was in regimental work what his fellows couldn't understand was that after a chap had been through it and got hit he wasn't exempt for the duration, as having done his bit. They simply can't cotton on to our system of patching a poor devil up and then telling him to go through it again. He said it caused more trouble than anything else.'

'No,' said Warren slowly. 'It *isn't* decent, if you put it that way. I agree with the Indians. For them, of course. Not for myself.'

'How often have you been wounded?' asked Martin, after a pause.

'About as often as you, I guess. We both copped it at Second Gaza, as you know.'

'Yes. And I stopped one at Nebi Samwil. You've had a worse record than that.'

'The Gaza one was only in the beefy part of my arm. No one could complain of that.'

'Go on.'

'I was hit at Wadi Surar last December,' Bunny continued, 'and spent Christmas in hospital. Jolly good they were to me, too. Then there was a shrapnel bullet just skimmed my chest, in our first Es-Salt show. I don't count that. The doc. ran a brush of iodine across it.'

'Go on.'

'There's nothing to go on about.'

'There is. You were hit in France.'

'Oh, France! That's ancient history. I didn't know you wanted to rake up old scores.'

'Flesh wound, wasn't it?'

'Yes. I've too much muscle not to collect in it the enemy's more loosely flung missiles. My sad case is the opposite of Corporal Wintersgill's.' (Corporal Wintersgill, a vaguely built skeleton of a man, was the Londons' jester.) 'He said to me when he was asking me yesterday if there was any truth in this yarn of our going back to France, "If we're for it again, sir, it's bound to be a compound fracture for me. It's the only sort of hit that anyone could score on me."'

Martin thought aloud, a bad habit of his. 'I hope I'm sent back to the battalion. Only,' he added, 'there's Valerie.'

Realising what he had betrayed, he went a deep unhappy crimson. But the words were a release to his friend's spirit.

'Never talk in your sleep to anyone else, Puzzlewit!' Warren cried. 'But do it with me every time! Your more ordered and deliberate periods are wild and wandering enough, God knows. But you simply *leap* to the point when you drowse off and start gassing to yourself.'

'That's due to getting an intelligent listener for once,' said Martin recovering.

'It's due to getting half-wit chatting confidentially with half-wit.' And Warren, in rising cheerfulness, tossed a chunk of rock his way, which Martin just avoided by a quick springing up. 'Now no rough-housing! That wasn't unfriendly, it was only to complete the work of waking you up. Listen, Martin! You said, "Valerie." Every thought in me says "Cynthia!" I've *got* to get her.'

'I thought you had done it. You've been with her pretty well every day for the last month.'

Warren was too wrought up to be deflected. 'I don't care a damn about going back to France. It's losing my chance with Cynthia.'

'If you lose it, it's only because you haven't taken it, Bunny. Anyone can see how Cynthia feels.'

'Because she goes about with me sometimes? There are a score of fellows who get her to do that.'

'Have you *asked* her to marry you?'

'Have I asked her anything else? And she won't

say anything except, "Cut that out, Bunny. I'm not
ready for it. I only want a good time, and you'll do
as well as the next fellow." And when I told her that
I jolly well wanted to do better than the next fellow,
she said she wasn't going to stand for being bossed
by any man, least of all by a Britisher, and that she
was her own boss. I've been jolly rotten to her,' said
poor Bunny, who had been nothing of the kind, 'and
she had a right to tell me off. Only it made me so
wretched to have had a row with her, that I borrowed
a motorbike from Signals and came in to see her
this afternoon. She wasn't in. But I saw her outside
the Jaffa Gate with another fellow in a car, and she
called to me, "Captain Remfry!" And when I came
across she said, as sweetly as you please, "Oh,
Captain Remfry, I am so sorry, but I shall have to
break my engagement with you for lunch this Friday.
I've made another engagement." '

Warren lingered on, pouring out the whole confused
story of excited weeks. When he went, he gripped
Martin's arm suddenly and fiercely.
'Listen, Old Puzzlewit! You're an absolute fizzer.

    " Though I've belted you and flayed you,
      By the Living Gawd that made you
        You're a better man than I am, Gunga Din!"'

'When have you belted me and flayed me?' asked
the justly indignant Martin. 'I am now going to give
your body to the fowls of the air.'
But Bunny easily evaded him, and reappeared on
the other side of a rock, asking for peace. 'I've got
crossed fingers, Martin. *Pax! Kamerad!* You *can't*

strafe me now! All I mean is, I've ragged you all these years when you've been a saint to me.'

'Rot! Don't I rag you back?'

'Yes, Martin. You do. But rarely effectively.'

They went together to Martin's billet, and made coffee, after which Warren returned to his unit, temporarily cheered.

Too desperately in love to be wise, Warren had assumed a masterfulness he was far from feeling. Cynthia had stood up to the half-hearted momentary bluff, and decided that he should be taught his lesson. In sequel a chastened Warren, humbly aware of his unmerited good fortune, was to be restored to favour. It was the oldest and most commonplace situation in the world.

That evening Martin's telephone rang with a call from American Relief headquarters. 'Can I speak to Captain Martin?'

'There's no Captain Martin here.'

'I mean, Captain Chapman. I made a slip.'

'Captain Chapman speaking.'

'Oh, is that you, Martin?' It was Valerie. 'Can you get away for lunch the day after to-morrow? Cynthia and I are lunching with an officer—Major Shawcross—do you know him?'

'Shawcross of the Corps Survey Group?'

'Yes. His people are somewhere overlooking the Jordan Valley.'

'I know him.'

'You sound as if you didn't like him.'

'Well, I don't.'

'Will you come, Martin?' Her voice seemed to have

a break in it, as if his hesitation brought surprise and some mortification and anger.

His own reply, though the words hung back ungallantly, by its tone told her that her voice, coming out of such long silence, had not found him indifferent. 'How *can* I come, Valerie?' he asked slowly.

'You've always managed to arrange your time pretty well as you liked, before.'

'But I haven't been invited.'

'*I've* invited you. I've told Major Shawcross you will be driving us down.'

'Of course I'll come.'

Late that night, as it happened, word came of the awards for the six months of fighting that ended in the April show. Austin-Gary and Wenyon congratulated Martin on a 'mention.' He asked eagerly for other distinctions to the Brentfords. They had got a D.S.O. and two M.C.'s, one of the latter Bunny's.

Since Martin had to visit the London Division periodically on duty, he antedated his next trip by two days and went down to congratulate his friends. Also, he wanted to cheer Warren with news that a connection still remained open with Cynthia, through his own invitation to the picnic with her and Valerie. His memory of a man haggard and tired, very unlike the Warren Remfry that a whole division knew, haunted him.

The Brentfords' colonel, asserting rights of command which he maintained had never lapsed, ordered Martin to stay the night, to share in a celebration of their honours. He could do this, and yet get back for Val's picnic next morning. The Brentfords were in the third line, the reserve area.

Bunny was rapt into something like normal cheeriness. During the forenoon he had been espied by the divisional general near headquarters, and put under arrest as 'improperly dressed'; and under the eyes of Jove himself had been carried into the general's mess-tent, and his coat stripped from him and handed over to a batman to return within ten minutes, 'complete with Military Cross ribbon.' He was a favourite in the division; and its commanding officer was a cricket enthusiast.

The Brentfords' officers' mess dined at a table cut in the sand, with shelved benches hewn out of the ditch's side. With each decoration in turn, mentions included, the same ritual was used. Every man sang in turn, looking towards his neighbour on his left:

' *I*—drink—to *thee*, *friend*—as *my friend*—drank to *me*!
   And as *my friend*—*charged me*, *friend*—so *I*, *friend*—
              charge *thee*!
   That *thou*, *friend*—drink to *thy friend*—as *my friend*—
              drank to *me*!
   And that *thou*, *friend*—charge *thy friend*—as *my friend*—
              charged *me*!'

The words and tune have been debased since. But they came then with a quiet repetition on that word 'friend' which made them come as close to the unveiling of their hearts as the manner of the English will allow.

The battalion doctor provided a stretcher, and Martin dossed down under the stars, next to Bunny. They talked deep into the Syrian night, lying side by side.

XI

VALERIE'S PICNIC STRUCK MARTIN AS GRIMLY FUNNY.
The enemy had discovered that by taking advantage
of the huge drop into the Jordan Valley he could
plaster Jericho from both East and West of Jordan,
with long range heavies. It became an infernal pit,
with six-inch guns concentrated on it, and twice
daily the handful of men unhappy enough to be
stationed there endured a manifold wretchedness.
The heat and dust by themselves were cruel in the
extreme; in addition, the crumbled earth was torn
into vortex and eddy spinning round and round as
long as the morning and evening torments lasted.
There was no cover—in the nature of things there
could be none. And no escape.

But from the western hills it was an interesting
show, if war was a novelty to you. This fact had been
discovered by a unit whose officers proceeded to give
lunch parties to the ladies of the American Relief.
The matutinal shelling usually became really bad
about half-past eleven. From then until lunch you
sat out in easy chairs and watched the shells bouncing
on to one devoted spot and vast dust-clouds sweeping
up. What you could not see was the human insignifi-
cance trying to obliterate itself in that demon-
searched plot.

The girls sat enthralled while their host explained
the presumed location of Jericho Jane, Nimrin
Nellie, and their unnamed coadjutor in Ephraim.

'I'll say that this is fine! Won't you, Val?' said
Cynthia.

Martin was amused. 'Especially for the poor devils who are being butchered to make this Roman holiday for us,' he said with a grin.

Valerie turned horrified eyes on him. 'Do you mean to say there are *men* down there?'

'Oh, only one or two,' said their host. 'And they'll be pretty well safe under cover—trenches and things, you know. They get used to it.' And Major Shawcross, who had once, by miscalculation, come within the range of a couple of desultory long distance shots, lazily and obviously dropping a quarter of a mile to his right, added, 'One does, you know. You get used to it and don't care a damn.'

'Yes, I suppose you get to look on it as just an extra little excitement,' said Cynthia admiringly.

She rose, following her host's lead. Valerie's fascinated gaze upon the seething inferno at their feet shifted to over Martin's shoulder. The other two were strolling off to get another view-point. Valerie spoke suddenly.

'Martin, listen! I asked you along to help Cynthia. I want you to look after her.'

'Look after Cynthia?'

'Yes. She's been treating Bunny pretty badly. Has he told you?'

'No. He said that he had been rotten to her.'

'Well, he hasn't. It's Cynthia who's been mean to him. She knows why I've brought you along.'

'Oh!' said Martin, damped.

'Oh!' repeated Valerie. 'What a queer set men are! And when I rang you up you kept me arguing at the telephone before you said you would come!'

'Does Shawcross know why you asked me
along?'

'I don't know. And I don't care. All he knows is
that I told him that I was asking you and that I said
I preferred you to any of his officers. And you say
"Oh!" Don't you think it anything when a girl
trusts you—as I trust you, Martin?'

'I think it's everything, Valerie,' he said, proud
and happy.

And this was the end of her resolution to resume
her birthright and be the aloof Virginian lady. She
cared so much for Cynthia that she was going to
keep her from being a fool. She might have foreseen, in her heart *had* foreseen, that if she took
Martin as her ally then he had to be taken with
utter frankness. She found she was not disturbed by
the discovery. Besides, there were questions she
wanted to ask Martin—a wide curiosity which only
an Englishman could satisfy.

She admired very much the way Martin kept
himself out of the conversation that followed. But
then (she was already noting) he always did. It was
this that made him so safe, though British.

They had both risen and were following the other
two.

'Cynthia knows why you've come,' she repeated.

'That won't please her.'

'No. It doesn't. Officially, she's annoyed, and only
on semi-speaking terms with you.'

'I've noticed that.'

'Yes, she meant you to notice it. Actually, she's a
bit glad. After rather less than a week of letting

Shawcross rush her, she's more than a little tired of him. Tell me, Martin——'

'Yes?'

'Your public-school type—that you make so much of—do you *like* it? I mean, is it something that *ought* to be liked?'

'Of course.'

'Of course why?'

'Look at their pluck and their——'

'I prefer to look at the pluck of your tommies who expect so precious little, Martin. And I suppose, when peace comes they'll go back to a life that expects as little—and gets it. Martin, don't you realise that just now courage is the cheapest and commonest thing in Europe? It's being shown by all kinds of nations that you and I have always considered absolutely third-rate.'

'Not pluck like this, Val.'

'In what way is it different?'

'It'll always take responsibility on itself, especially when it's responsibility for going forward into something rotten. Look at Bunny, for example.'

'Righto. I'm always willing to look at him. You'll have no difficulty in getting any girl to look at Bunny.'

'I've seen Bunny in heaps of tight places, Val. And always—whenever he could—if it's been a choice between sending someone else out to the chance of being scuppered and going himself——'

'I know. There's been no choice in it. Bunny has just taken on the job himself. But is *every* public school boy a Warren Remfry?'

'In this way, yes. There's been only the one kind of teaching, and it has left no room for argument.'

The other two were still in sight. Valerie, watchful, said only, 'Go on, Martin.'

He hesitated. Then, 'I'm not altogether what you'd call the public school type myself——'

'No. I discovered that for myself. You are far too decent.'

He hastened to disclaim, or at least to modify this unwelcome tribute. 'My school ranked as a public school, but it's not what the outside world understands by the term "public school". It was a day school, one of our big grammar schools, getting on for four centuries old, for that matter. But the fellows were none of them rich——'

'I know. Your hunting, shooting set, that does nothing but play and rule. That set's going to have a bad time when this War finishes,' said Valerie with conviction.

'I'm not so sure,' said Martin, who was to prove the better prophet. 'Not for a very long while yet, Val.'

'No. Perhaps not. I daresay they'll manage to do what they've always been clever enough to do before —hand on any trouble that comes to the people who've always carried it.'

Martin let this sedition pass. He said in a burst of confidence, 'This is really the first time I've come close to the genuine public school type.'

'Do you *like* it, Martin?'

'Tremendously. There's Bunny, for instance.'

'Leave Bunny out. He's a dear boy, and would have been if he'd never gone to Eton—or was it Harrow?' said Valerie, who was under the impression that the English public schools, like the Varsities, were just two in number.

Martin corrected her error.

'Never mind where he went to. If it was Bunny who was getting hold of Cynthia I shouldn't worry. You've told me all about the pluck. Anything else?'

'Heaps. They don't brag, they don't——'

'No. But when they get together they give one another certificates rather generously, don't they? Now listen to me, Martin. We're Americans, and the type is newer to us than it can possibly have been to you. We've never met it before. And—to be frank— we don't altogether like it. I don't believe your Dominions altogether like it. At any rate, the Australian officers that I've met——'

'Oh, for God's sake don't take what they say seriously, Val! Don't you know there never were such chaps for talking as if they hated the whole world and the British in particular?'

'All right. Do you know what the world is beginning to suspect about your much-admired English gentleman?'

'No.'

'That he isn't a gentleman at all.'

'Oh, I say!'

'I'm not talking about *you*, Martin. And I'm not talking about Bunny.' She smiled at him, all radiance, all deep friendliness. 'You are two dear boys, and we both love you. No, not what you mean by love, Martin——'

'That's just the trouble.'

'In Cynthia's case it *is* that, though. And she half knows it. Which is why she's being such a little fool —oh, not only with this Major Shawcross man. Well, they've dropped out of sight. We'd better join them.'

She continued. 'You didn't guess that the outside world was beginning to take an analytical interest in you, instead of being content merely to admire and envy you!' She laughed at him. 'In the States you are becoming one of our "problems", along with the Filipinos and Hungarians and Indians and other semi-savage races. There'll be degrees given presently for theses on "The Problem of the British Public School Boy." I suppose you have been so wrapped up in fighting for your lives that you never imagined that people who weren't in the business had so much leisure.'

'I knew something. That other nations were saying we weren't keen on ideas. And all that sort of thing.'

'And, like the sensible people that you are, you dismissed it as just jealousy. All that sort of thing!'

'No. I know there's a lot in it. We *are* taught to distrust the clever fellow.'

'And aren't you taught to distrust ideas as well as the bounder—that's what you call a man who isn't public school, isn't it?' (Martin winced, but was not permitted to protest)—'the bounder who has them?'

'Maybe.'

'In America we're crazy about ideas,' said Valerie self-approvingly.

Martin, so long on the defensive, at last got in an effective shot.

'Yes. But you don't stay long enough with them to get familiar with them quite, do you?'

'Oh!' Tone and look warned him of his near approach to lese-majesty.

I

'Look at the absurd notions that you—yes, even you, Val'—he said abruptly—'have got about us. That time when you and Cynthia dined with us you both insisted—and insisted that you knew better than Bunny and I, who have been over the top a dozen times, if we've been once—that the British were all made drunk before they could attack.'

At this time the Prohibitionists were striving to persuade their great country to 'change her sins', with the ultimate success that Brooklyn and Chicago and the whole world mourn. The British rum ration (that exiguous potion which you and I, reader, sober men both of us, have been glad to take into chilled bodies lying out in wet and frost) was represented as a fiery draught which made a soldier blink obliviously at erupting death around him. Or else run red-eyed and murderously into it.

Valerie was not prepared to let go sound doctrine. 'Well, everyone knows about rum being served out to men before they go into battle. Mind you' (generously) 'I don't say that British troops wouldn't be just as brave without it. But I do say that your people up on top think they wouldn't.'

It is very difficult to tell a charming girl that she is talking nonsense. But Martin risked it.

'You honestly know nothing about it, Val. You don't *begin* to understand, really.'

'You're rather getting into the habit of telling people they "don't *begin* to understand". I think it's a bad habit.'

'Please don't be insulted. No one *can* understand unless they've been in modern war. If you don't mind I'd rather not talk about it—even to you.'

She was nettled. But seeing his reproachful face she saw that he was hurt. And remembered how she was sometimes hurt by the high ethical criticisms of her Yankee friends—so unanswerable on any plane that the critics' thought inhabited, so rigidly sound in that cast-iron world, yet so unfair! She realised afresh how deeply she respected Martin, and though a woman in a civilisation that has spoiled and adulated women, she recognised that she had no right to resent frankness answering her own frankness.

'You're the one man I won't quarrel with, Martin,' she said. 'I want to ask a question no lady should ask.'

'Well—you can ask it, Valerie.'

'I know that. What's your public school attitude towards women?'

Martin was troubled. 'That's just the one thing I don't care for. You see, I was brought up as a Nonconformist.'

'So was I. At least, we don't have them in America. But I know what you mean.'

'I was given all sorts of strict ideas about what was right and what was wrong. And the men you are asking about seem to me queerly unimaginative when you get out of their class. Unimaginative about everything—about the way subject races, for example, are bound to feel if they have any sort of intelligence at all. Resistance to their rights or what they take for granted as their rights strikes them as merely wickedness or a sign of low civilisation.'

'And women?'

'They would always regard a woman of their own class as sacred. You or Cynthia, for example, would be absolutely safe with them.'

'I wonder.'

'Oh, *yes*, Valerie!' he said protesting, 'Yes! Really.'

'All right. What about others?'

Martin hesitated. 'I'm afraid they'd look on others as fair game.'

'That's what I thought.'

'Oh, I'm only speaking of the rank and file, the fellows who are the average. Not of the best fellows. But isn't it the same in your country?'

'No. You see, we haven't the others who are "not of our class." We have only Americans—and negroes and foreigners who haven't become Americans.'

'It seems to me to come to the same thing.'

'I'm not going to argue with you, Martin. I want you to help Cynthia. She's up against one of your rank and file—I should say, one of the rankest of them. Rankest and vilest,' said Valerie, pleased with her wit. 'And she knows *nothing*! Though she thinks she knows everything!'

'What's she doing?'

'She's having what she calls "a swell time." She can turn a man's head, if she wants to, in quicker time than any girl I know. What's your opinion of Major Shawcross, Martin?'

'He's a solid cad. And he knows—and I don't care to think of the ways he learnt it—the exact value of every one of his qualities, which are all for show. But Val, he isn't an average public school boy,' he protested. 'He's known and despised for what he is, even if we say nothing. He's skrimshanked all real active service. I don't think much of Cynthia's taste, turning down Bunny for a fellow like Shawcross.'

'Oh, she doesn't think she *has* turned him down. She intends to have him back, properly humbled and put in his place. If Cynthia thought any other girl was going to grab Bunny,' said Valerie reflectively, 'she's fight like a Kentucky mountaineer to haul him back. Why doesn't he pretend to take up with some other girl? She could just about stand it for one week.'

'Bunny couldn't stand it for one day. A man in love can't do that sort of thing, Val. He simply can't pretend that he doesn't care.'

'Why not? Any woman can.'

'Well, no man can.'

'No,' she said thoughtfully. 'And of course he couldn't fool the girl he was pretending to make up to. I suppose it's God's way of protecting women.'

At lunch, had Martin been less anxious, less unsophisticated, he might have found amusement in the drama in which he had been unwillingly given a part. Quite obviously chafing under this presence from outside, Shawcross dropped his pretence of friendliness to him. He was planning and plotting to have the afternoon alone with Cynthia, who seemed half frightened, and herself aided the rescue party.

An offer to show her a place where they could look down on the famous cells of the monks in the Wadi Kelt—'You'd find it rather a pull in this weather, Miss Connett, unless you're *frightfully* keen, as Miss Cameron is'—was put by. Miss Cameron, it transpired, was not frightfully keen. She said she thought it too far.

This was baffling. He had expected the girl to play up to him. She was more than a bit of a fool, to

think the expedition was meant as more than a blind
for a much shorter walk.

Confronted by unwillingness, Shawcross was a dolt.
His manœuvres were too obvious for an opposition
now thoroughly awake. Cynthia's fluttering nerv-
ousness reinforced Martin's memory of Warren's
distress and were an added appeal to Valerie's
wishes, had any been needed. Martin developed an
unseeing obtuseness that brought him credit and
gratitude. Hints fell blunted from it.

On the way back Cynthia sat disquietingly silent.
She had been shown up as a school miss before an
older man whose admiration flattered her.

They had reached the Relief headquarters and
Martin had said good-bye, when Valerie ran back,
crying, 'Isn't that stupid of me! Martin, just a
minute! You've got my scarf in there. Half a second,
Cynthia!'

Cynthia, about to mount the steps, turned her head
wearily, then went on to the top.

Martin held the door while Valerie rummaged. As
she bent down she caught his arm and whispered,
'Listen, Martin! What are you doing on Saturday?'

'I'm playing cricket.'

'You can't. I want you to be in Cairo.' Her words
raced out. 'Cynthia's a little fool. Major Shawcross
has persuaded her to spend the week-end with him.
Oh, only a lark, Martin. Even he has the sense to
fool her by pretending to think she's straight, though
he doesn't believe any woman's straight. Martin,
you've got to engage a sleeping berth on the night
train back from Cairo. Any name you like but
Cynthia's—or mine. I can't explain now—Cynthia'll

be suspicious already. Only—I think that by then she'll have had enough of Major Shawcross, and if we have luck—you and I and Bunny—she'll be coming back on that train. Remember! I love Cynthia. And she's absolutely decent. Good-bye, Martin.'

At the top of the steps Cynthia confronted her. 'You took your time with Martin.'

'This wrap had got under the——'

'Got under what? What could it have got under? See here, Val. We're going to have this out.'

'All right. Not here, though. I'll come to your room.'

'Now,' said Cynthia, as she banged the door of her room. 'I don't choose to have a man tagging along in *my* private business. First you fetch Martin along where no one invited him——'

'*I* invited him,' said Valerie. 'And it was a good thing for you that I did. That man's one idea was to get you where you could make yourself cheap. I used Martin to see that he didn't.'

'You used Martin to see that he didn't! You used Martin to make a fool of himself and of you! Shall I tell you what Major Shawcross said about it?'

'No. I prefer that you keep his witticisms to yourself, the person for whom they were intended. I'm sure you agreed with them. There's nothing like letting a friend down, just because a third-rate man tells you you look like an angel, is there?'

'You're smart, Val, aren't you? As a matter of fact, I told him that if he was going to say mean things about my friends I was going to go right back. I thought you *were* a friend then.' Cynthia burst into a flood of tears, and flung herself along the arm of the chair in which she was sitting.

Valerie was vanquished, and tried to comfort her.

'Oh, I guess I'm just cheap, Val. Like you said. Cheap and mean.'

'No, you're not. And I didn't say you were. I said that man *wanted* to make you cheap. That's very different.'

'Well, he did—very nearly. Oh, Val, I'm frightened! Only——'

'Only what, Cynthia?'

'I wasn't going to let him think he could have me just where he liked.'

'But you've promised to go down to Cairo with him.'

Cynthia sat bolt upright.

'You know that, do you? Valerie Connett, I'm through with you as a friend. A girl who pries in on another girl's affairs——'

'I did nothing of the sort. It was your—gentleman,' said Valerie sarcastically, 'who gave you away. He said—and I couldn't help hearing: Martin couldn't help hearing—"If you'd let me have your hand, Miss Cameron, I could tell your fortune just as well as that fellow I'm going to show you inside the Great Pyramid." I knew you had a dentist's appointment this Saturday in Cairo. It was easy to guess the rest.'

A dental appointment was the one valid excuse accepted by the Relief Force authorities for going further afield than a three hours' motor trip would cover. At this date, the Force had not asked the British Army for services which later were very gladly given.

'He's a cheap skate,' said Cynthia to herself with sudden conviction. But she flared up afresh. 'If you think I'm going to stay friends with a girl who thinks of me what you are thinking you can think again.' She rose as she spoke.

'You are a little fool,' said Valerie. 'You've turned down a boy who was straight and decent, just for the sake of having the pleasure of turning the head of every middle-aged rotter who's lounging about behind the lines. It's girls like you that make me ashamed of being a woman. One minute first, though.' She had slipped between Cynthia and the door.

'Will you please let me go out of my own room?' screamed Cynthia. 'You've said in it words that I shall never forgive you for; and I intend to leave it until *you* have decided to leave it.'

'Cynthia, dear! listen! I'm sorry, honestly. I'm wretchedly sorry for talking to you like that. It's only because I can't bear to see you wasting yourself on a man who thinks that with a bit of patience and cunning he'll get you just where he wants. You were right when you said he was a cheap skate. Well? *You* were not meant to go about with cheap skates.'

'I've promised,' said Cynthia sullenly. 'And I can look after myself.'

'I know you can. But the point is, this man doesn't believe you can—doesn't believe any girl can, once she's alone with his blandishments. His attentions are an insult in themselves.'

'Oh, Val, cut out your preaching! I tell you, you're dull! You bore me and I hate you after what you've said. Are you going? Or shall I?'

'*I'm* going.' Then, 'If you find you've had enough
of Major Shawcross by Saturday evening—and he'd
make *me* tired in five minutes—remember, there's a
train back at eleven. I'd let *him* find himself the fool,
not me, if I were you.'

And Valerie went.

The next hour was one of little happiness for either
of them. Cynthia flung herself along the couch and
sobbed angrily. After that her determination set
hard and she swept away her hesitations. She would
show Val—and Major Shawcross, too—that she
could look after herself. In her own room Valerie
also wept, in a passion of reflection on friendship
lost.

XII

CYNTHIA HAD VERY FAR FROM THOUGHT OUT THE
implications of her promise. The A.R.F. trusted her;
her present escapade if discovered would mean
contemptuous dismissal back to America.

The unit had one or two women who used mean
subterfuge on occasion to cover disreputable ways
of amusing themselves with the riff-raff of the
British Army. But she and Val despised them, and
had carried themselves with an aloofness that
aroused resentment.

She had thoughtlessly let Major Shawcross know
of her coming trip to Cairo, which had been perfectly genuine and independent. He had immediately said that he would go down too, and take her
over the city and the Pyramids, and to a show at
night.

Self-respect and loyalty to her unit proved strong counsellors, even at this late hour.

They both, ostentatiously apart, caught the Friday afternoon train to Ludd, and changed there for the world's worst railway. Major Shawcross's first surprise came when he found he was not going to have her company while the train crawled from oasis to oasis. She refused to be with him except at meals. But after the break for the ferry at Kantara, at eight a.m., his insistence broke down her unwillingness, or rather, rudely ignored it, and she had him to herself all the way up to Cairo.

By the time they reached Cairo, his pose of elaborate admiring amusement, as from the strong experienced man to the graceful kitten-woman, had become a trying distinction. On his part, three hours exhausted his capacity for anything but lovemaking, his life's main recreation; and this capacity was growing fierce from frustration.

She kept her dental appointment; and they had the afternoon at the Pyramids. By this time she knew that she hated him. There is one monotony more wearisome than all others.

Alma Venus, setting the creation on fire, has loosed a wilder music than any poets have dreamed. But men and women have added to it subtlety. Cynthia had to the full the queer gift of combining flirt (which she undoubtedly was) with puritan (which her companion was savagely realising that she was) that has enabled the woman of the West to change the art of sexual relations from music to poetry.

The hotel at Cairo perplexed and terrified her. A gazelle of the lilied plains had strayed up into the

jungles, haunted by shapes of power in hiding. In
her cavalier's carriage anger appeared, and impatience. He was not inured to continual repulse.
As for Cynthia, she marvelled that she had ever
been the fool she saw herself.

The neat compartments of her life had collapsed.
Her own land was crowded and various, and knew
juxtaposition of race and colour, but everything
there was conveniently sorted out. Negroes provided
service, Italians oversaw that service; in the background, obsequious and watchful of his clients'
satisfaction, stood the Jew proprietor. She, the
American woman, apex to which civilisation has
painfully climbed, accepted and gathered into her
own small hands all these threads of obedience.

Here all was different. The hotel was sprinkled
with nationalities of every variety in Europe, a
grotesque opulence couched—no, rampant—in
escape from the destruction devastating its normal
haunts. Faces that in the States would have been
ruthlessly segregated as negro were allowed to preen
themselves in the open and call for food and drink.
There were British officers in all the War's gradations, from baby-cheeked subalterns flushed with
drink and self-conscious pride of their first sexual
adventure to middle-aged confidence conducting its
affairs in quiet assurance. Anzacs swaggered past,
with the insolence that must be pardoned to those
come from the earth's end to witch the nations
with a soldiership more efficient than time had
seen.

She was aware, and not now with exultation, of
glances that came her way. The diggers stared with

open admiration, the man from a more sophisticated *milieu* slanted appraisement from eyes that pretended to be straying elsewhere. It grew on her perception that she was 'placed' as here for one purpose, in this teeming laxity of the world War. Her job was to give pleasure to a man, the nature and extent of that service being measured solely by what his masterfulness could wring from her resistance. And good luck to him!

The War, among whose lesser results must be reckoned the weakening of the generous drinks that used to make glad the heart of man (so that for laager you had Japanese beer), had grimly compensated this loss by the abundance of the liqueurs it provided. You took your alcohol, like your life, in concentration. Other sexual adjuncts took on the same quality. In this Cairo hotel the music was not by any means 'yearning like a God in pain'. It was rising like a djinn in delirium, and tearing recklessly at any sanity the brain still kept. Between the tables a saturnalia was in progress. You could not (though the hotel proprietor did) call it dancing.

At the next table a group brought by Air Force officers were running a private show of their own. Why not? They had a gramophone playing a record which they did not bother to change. The music was an imbecile, maddening whine; the words strutted along to it like imps that you longed to be able to kick.

> '*Nevil* was a *devil*! a *perfect* little *devil*!
> He trotted after *any* thing with curls!'

A tall, superb-limbed man, with hard, clear lines
of face, paused at Cynthia's right. Eyes and cheeks
redder than their normal, he leant on the table
unsteadily.

'Will the lady'—he had to hesitate to collect
speech—'give me this dance?' he asked.

Her horror was too swift and overwhelming not to
carry its own message. 'Oh, no, no!' she said.

The man's own face grew ashamed, as he understood. 'Sorry,' he muttered. 'Beg pardon—my
mistake.'

As Shawcross coaxed him away, she heard him
still apologising. 'Most awfully sorry, my dear chap.
How was I to know lady was not a polly?'

'Why, of all people Cynthia Cameron!' said a
voice. 'Fancy seeing you here in Cairo, Cynthia!
Cynthia, let me present Jim Allardyce. Jim, this is
one of our girls.'

Cynthia, terror-frozen, felt that fate had trapped
her.

I have said that in Miss Cameron femininity
triumphed over the disadvantages of an absurd and
uncomely garb. It did this, however, by innate
unconscious merit. Mary Gordon's case was other.
Femininity was her profession. The lily was elaborately unsheathed. Shrugging mobile shoulders were
thrust out from the wraps that hung upon them;
eyebrows and gestures worked untiringly and to one
end, to draw attention to Miss Gordon's person.

Cynthia and Valerie, carrying themselves aloofly
and making a wider and deeper effect, had despised
Mary Gordon and her group. This schism, to
Cynthia's despair, was now closed.

'Isn't this simply great!' her discoverer shrilled
ecstatically. 'But where's your old beau, Cynthia?
You know, that Remfry boy.'

Cynthia hesitated, and the crimson rushed to her
brows.

> ('*Nevil* was a *devil*! a *perfect* little *devil*!
>   He's *busy* getting through the Dardanelles!
> And *harems* all *enraptured* are *waiting* to be *captured*!
>   For *Nevil's* such a *devil* with the *gels*!')

'He isn't here,' said Cynthia shortly.

Mary laughed excessively. She was at the stage
where life revealed its richness in humorous effects.
Cynthia disgustedly placed her as 'drunk'. But this
was an unduly austere decision.

'Why, of course he isn't here! We can all see that,
can't we? Oh, well, he always struck me as a bit
slow. What I call a handsome doll,' Miss Gordon
gratuitously explained to her company. She added
generously, 'But I never *thought* you'd stick to him
long—a girl like you, Cynth! Though I didn't realise
you were going to hand him the order of the
frozen mitt so soon. Come over to our table, you
two. It's more in the centre and there's more fun
there.'

Major Shawcross was vexed. Then he saw that luck
had sent him the ally he needed. 'Right-o,' he said
with enthusiasm, 'That'll be topping!'

Cynthia's brain leapt out for a way of escape.

'Just a sec., Mary,' she cried jovially. 'These
are not my best shoes if we're going to do any
dancing. Let me get them from my room.'

As she walked swiftly between the tables low

comments and laughter made her shrink as if they
were hands touching her flesh. Once actual fingers
caught at her dress. She turned in her inexperience
and faced a smiling group of Levantines.

She rang the bell of her room furiously. A French
half-caste chambermaid appeared. Cynthia ordered
a taxi at once.

The girl looked at her uncertainly.

Cynthia repeated the order. The maid whistled for
a messenger boy.

She was on her knees, packing, when a hand caress-
ing her hair startled her.

'Come to help you look for shoes,' said Major
Shawcross thickly.

She rocketted out of his grasp. 'Get out! get out
this minute!' she screamed.

He had filled up the interval of waiting for her,
which had been considerable, by more drinks, and
was not as steady in either walk or speech as he
had been. Though drunk, however, he was not so
drunk as to misunderstand the anger in her voice
and manner.

He made an attempt to put on a pose of admiring
disbelief. 'You look splendid!' he assured her. 'Real
sporting girl! Had to come—too long having to wait
for real sporting girl like you. Shoes—shoes—only
excuse. Must have kiss before I go—real sporting
splendid girl like you, Cynthia.'

Chambermaid and messenger appeared in the open
door behind him. Cynthia disregarded looks of
smirking understanding. 'This gentleman is wanting
the dining-room,' she said. 'Show him down at once.'

Temporarily immobilised by the new arrivals, the

major hesitated. Cynthia flung in the last of her things hugger-mugger and closed the box, handing it to the maid. In a whirlwind of vigour she gathered about her cloak and wraps and a festooning of oddments, and swept from the room. The major woke from his stupor and began moving after her.

Then first Odette, the chambermaid, understood. She was at a scene which appealed to the romantic element in her Latin blood. It was not as she had supposed, beauty acquiescent and conquered that had called her. It was beauty virtuous and resisting the beast—which, though rarer, is more exciting and like a story out of the lives of the saintly virgins who help you when in trouble. Noting the gentleman's lurch to follow the lady, Odette pulled the door to, and turned the key, which was outside from Cynthia's opening of the room. Major and messenger boy were behind it.

Odette's delighted little burst of laughter contracted into mock pity. '*Pauvre Jurji!*' ('George'), she said. "'E ees locked wiz zat man. And monsieur will be vair-y indignation, *ne c'est pas ?*'

To Cynthia, hurrying to the elevator, it seemed probable that monsieur would. She was not indulging in speculation now, however.

Odette grew motherly to this girl, whose fresh loveliness and absurd piteous helplessness and lack of sophistication touched her. Disposing Cynthia's things about her in the taxi, she said, 'Madame should not come here again. Eet ees no place for Madame. For military officers, yes. For other ladies, yes. But for Madame, no.'

Madame looked close to tears. Odette asked where she was going, and told the driver. Then her face

K

broke into merriment again. She leant towards the window, which was open for the heat, and said appreciatively, 'Monsieur is locked in Madame's room. But not wiz Madame!'

The joke was a good one, and all on Cynthia's side. But deep humiliation coursed through her body.

Fluttered and terrified, she began to look ahead. A night of petty vexations awaited her. Guards would enquire for her ticket, which she had not money enough to buy. Superior officials would be summoned; there would be conclaves and remonstrances and taking down of her name. The Canal ferry and train on the further side would both bring their quota of trouble. Next morning would be all trouble and annoyance, all the way up to Jerusalem. And afterwards correspondence; and explanations to her own unit. And dismissal home.

Distress began with paying of the taxi-driver. This genus reaches its worst in the Levant; and Egypt in this, as in other matters, drains into itself the dregs of what is lowest. Cynthia from her scanty funds overpaid him, a fact in itself provocation to extortion. But in any case no Cairo taxi-driver would have resisted the chance to bully a white lady without military or at least male escort, late at night and alone. Fighting a lost battle against insolence covered by darkness, Cynthia despairingly began to wonder if it were not better to let the cur snarling above her baggage keep it.

Out of the shadow stepped another figure, and her heart stopped. Then she saw that she was luckier than she deserved.

And insolence under cover of darkness turned to
cowardice doubled by that darkness. We have seen
that Captain Remfry in the matter of small nationalities was quite uninfected by the current senti-
mentalism, and on the Near Eastern nationalities in
particular held clear-cut and vigorous views. The
'Ayrabs', taking advantage of his preoccupation
with a ghastly campaign undertaken on their behalf,
had pinched for the sake of pinching things essential
to his peace of mind, to them valueless. Nothing
in their subsequent behaviour had seriously affected
the stain of this initial crime. The 'Gyppos' he
regarded with yet deeper disapproval, as a poisonous
semi-human scum exuding hate and funk and all
noisome qualities—effective only as thieves and
pimps and pandars and patriots. All this I set down
with a proper shame, remembering that it is 1932.
In the last dozen years the world has progressed far
towards universal brotherhood; to-day Captain
Remfry's clan and effendi and sub-effendi and Cairo
taxi-driver all rank equal in the scale of human
values. Warren and his bright associates have gone
into oblivion with the battles in which they went
down; and if we ever think about them at all we
see their abundant faults of education and outlook
and character. Also (thank God!) we now see the
abundant merits of the gentlemen who during the
world's madness did not perish and were never in
any danger of perishing. As a happy consequence
they are still present with us, to lead us on to better
and better (and even better) conceptions of man's
dignity, possibilities and rights.

But truth has 'an eternal title to our confession.'
And truth requires that I admit that Captain

Warren Remfry was not what a contemporary
thinker has called 'a great big-hearted democrat.'

He appeared out of the darkness; and the next five
minutes lived in Cynthia's mind as a pleasurable
dream.

'Has the blighter been paid? Or what?' asked
Remfry, inflexibly just in face of his deplorable
convictions.

Before Cynthia could reply, the taxi-driver himself
hastened to assure him that he had. And this, when
(or if) Warren Remfry's name ever comes up for
canonisation, is the first of his two miracles;
moreover, attested by the correct quorum of wit-
nesses (if the taxi-driver can be found).

'Yes, yes. *Plenty* paid. Quite—enough, sir.'

And the penitent driver, his arms crowded with
baggage, enquired eagerly, at a distance from
Remfry, 'Lady going this train? See, I take Lady
Langtry's things.'

The train was waiting. Warren opened a door into
a reserved sleeping compartment. The taxi-driver
piled Cynthia's luggage in, showing zeal to get his
voluntary service done and be gone.

Warren, watching him, was restive under some
feeling of duty neglected. He said longingly, 'Would
you think it wrong, Cynthia, if I slew this blighter
and chucked his body under the train?'

'Indeed I wouldn't. But please don't, Bunny.
Nothing matters now that you've come.'

And Bunny saw that this was so. Nevertheless,
conscience still made a protest, though now largely
as a matter of form.

'All right. Only it seems somehow wrong to let him

go, after he's been such a pukka scoundrel to you, without one good hefty boot that would make him realise that he was thoroughly alive and damned lucky to be.'

They wavered on this nice point of duty, and the moment for action passed irrevocably. The luggage had all been swiftly and conveniently disposed. The driver was half-way back to his taxi.

From the carriage's interior Cynthia beckoned.

'Bunny, come here! You darling!' she cried hysterically. 'You dear, dear, nice boy!'

Holding both his hands and with her head thrust into his shoulder, she sobbed, 'And I've been so mean to you!'

'You never have, Cynthia darling. It was all my fault.'

A few minutes later they were having their first lovers' quarrel.

'Listen, Cynthia sweetheart. It's hell——'

She put a hand across his mouth. 'You're not to say that, Bunny. Not now.'

'All right. But it's rotten having to leave you. Only, you know, you ought to turn in and get a bit of rest. I'll see that you wake up at Kantara.'

'And have you go, Bunny! Why ought I to turn in?'

'Well—suppose that someone's along presently trying to find you.'

She remembered, and was hurt. And Bunny could have bitten his tongue out.

'What's Valerie been telling you? It was Val that sent you down here!'

She stood away from him, sulking and humiliated. His eager coaxing failed.

'Oh, go away, Bunny! I know you and Val despise me.'

'We don't, sweetheart, honestly we don't. All that Val wanted was that there should be a man by whom you trusted and who knew how splendid you were.'

'Why had he got to be by?'

'Oh, well,' said Warren unhappily, 'you've only been with decent fellows, and you've never had any cause to know what utter rotters some chaps can be. And I knew—yes, I knew *this much*, Cynthia—that there was a bounder who was taking you over Cairo —and to the Pyramids and all that. And, Cynthia— Cynthia—my own sweetheart——' Half resistingly she let him take her hands again, and listened. 'It was this way, dear. It would have been all right— absolutely all right, if he had been a straight fellow. But you see, Val thought it just possible that you might want a friend who'd see things through for you. She thought,' Bunny floundered on, 'that a girl like you would probably get so sick to death of a second-rate man like this fellow that she'd simply walk away from him and leave him stranded.'

All of this was true, and neatly put. Cynthia's self-respect pushed up a timid head again. And so far relaxed its hold on her gratitude that this rushed out uncontrollably.

'Bunny, you dear dear boy! My *man!*' said Cynthia with immense satisfaction. 'You're a pal, Bunny, that's what you are, if ever any boy was.'

'Valerie's a pal too,' he said loyally.

'Never mind about Val!' Cynthia frowned. Valerie's case was remanded for further examin-ation. But Bunny was forgiven here and now and fully.

'And you see, sweetheart,' said Bunny, 'I'd wait all night, and for a thousand nights, as long as ever I was alive—wait anywhere and at any time if there was the least outside chance of a chance that you might be wanting me.'

The fire of his perfect manliness blazed up and enwrapped her, as impregnably as the bower of flames that enwrapped the Valkyr awaiting Sigurd. The platform was deserted; there was yet an hour before the train was to go; the whole easily locked compartment had been taken in one name. As he kissed her she knew that his veins were pulsing as madly as hers, and their wills were rushing together. Had he asked for surrender there would have been no resistance, there could have been no resistance; and in the moment of surrender she would have worshipped him as he worshipped her.

She saw the light in his eyes, and understood. And then—confronted by her look in which mingled passion, admiration, trust, apprehension, he hesitated, for no logic or reason at all, but unaccountably. And in that hesitation he set her apart, as still to be won, still to be guarded and served.

Under Syria's moon Astarte, ready to lie all Danae to the Hunter Boy, seeing him because of the holiness of the night stand back from lover and become comrade and adorer, learnt the value of herself and of what she had to give.

Time was put back on the plane of sense and reason. 'Suppose,' he said, white-faced, 'that cad came along now, though you've only just been getting your things into the compartment, and saw another fellow helping you——'

'I know, I know! He'd spread mean stories about me. And he'd think I'd left him not because——'

'Not because he was such an utter bounder that no decent girl could stand him——'

'But because—well, what *would* he think, Bunny? He'd think that—he'd think that——'

'I tell you what *I* think, sweetheart, which is much more important. *I* think that I'm just the luckiest man that ever lived, and that I've had the luck of my life in being here just now. And I think that you're going to shut this door and have a bit of a sleep until Kantara, And then I'll see you across the Canal and into the other train. And to-morrow we'll be having breakfast together.'

She held up her face to his. 'And *I* think that you're my own darling boy. It's the only thing I *can* think just now. Good night, Bunny!'

'Good night, Cynthia sweetheart! Until Kantara.'

'Good night, darling. My own dear dear splendid Bunnykins!'

Everything ends, even lovers' partings. Yet after this one had ended he reappeared.

'Sweetheart!'

'Darling!'

'I forgot to say—in case you are asked, your berth is taken in the name of Miss Falconbridge.

'Miss *Who*, darling?'

'Miss Falconbridge.' He went a deeper red. 'It was my mother's name.'

She tried to compose herself for rest, alone with a woman who awed her. This woman had not been

dimly imagined, far less born, a dozen hours ago.
She was a woman whose body two men had found
unbearably desirable. Yet one of them, for the sake
of winning her mind also, had put by the body when
it was his. Her mind? *That* immature childlike
thing? It had listened to so much twaddle pre-
tentiously presenting itself as the last wisdom of the
ages, had been so often 'thrilled', had found so
many bits of botched and second-hand information
'authentic', had been impressed by how many
cheapjacks of knowledge who had skipped through
'experiences' and 'established contacts' with the
latest 'dynamic personality' of foreign or home
production!

She looked back across long years of adoration,
from the first beginnings of memory. 'Don't you go
bothering your head too much, Cynth, about getting
highbrow!' her father had besought her when she
first went to Wellesley. 'You're plenty clever enough
for us now. And I guess you don't *need* that sort of
thing as some of those girls do.' She had had spells
of serious talking even with her boys, when she had
reasoned with them for being so frivolous and un-
conversant with the world's problems. Europe in
red ruin was surely a warning to their happier and
more civilised clime. True, the misfortunes of
savages are not likely ever to become our misfortunes; but the wise and cultivated mind will find
profit and pleasure in philosophic contemplation of
them. There is a moral to be found in everything,
there is always some thought in it that will build up
the four-square aesthetic and mental perfection of
our own spirits.

Celia Ward, of the American Relief Force, had

published a book on the folk-dancing of the Algon-
quin Indians and was on the Brynmawr Faculty.
Elizabeth Raekmer, also of the American Relief,
lectured on eurhythmics and soul culture and the
close connection between the two. Within the space
of one hour Cynthia had learnt that it was not her
intellect or the charm of her lively conversation
(heightened, no doubt—she had always been willing
to admit this—by the charm of her very perfect
person, but certainly not dependent on it) that had
won her so much more attention than fell to the lot
of Celia Ward or Elizabeth Raekmer. It was the
feminine in her, the flame whose dancing, ineffably
lovely clarity was from one source only, the body's
grace and poise and beauty. All her life in all its
moments had consciously or unconsciously been
lived in the overmastering fact that she was a very
glorious and darling girl whose presence gave
pleasure by its mere passing by.

But of course she had known this, the reader will
exclaim impatiently. It could not be a revelation at
any time. How could any girl be such a fool as not
to know it?

Yes, she had known it—after the fashion of so much
that we consider we know. But the only knowledge
that matters is the knowledge that is active, that has
come home to us in humiliation and danger, or in
ecstasy and victory. We are dreams to be forgotten
by the wakeful onward-sweeping careless life of
humanity; experiences that except for one ever-
shifting point lie submerged in the wash of un-
fathomed unlit ocean. We think of ourselves as
individuals; we have been told of one Eternal
Individual in relation to whom all live a never-dying

existence. But the knowledge is driven in upon us
that we are, first of all and last of all, vessels to be
used by the life-force as it moves endlessly on. Then
we are flung down, as the sapless leaves when
summer has died. In the shadow behind our lives
sit dim-seen impersonal powers.

And Cynthia, in the darkness of her carriage
as it rumbled through that dreary Egyptian land,
lay as in nightmare. Her proud virginity had
been smirched by lusty eyes upon it. Betrayed
by the physical perfection on which her strength of
assurance had rested, she knew now how she was
regarded. Life and Nature would have looked on,
whatever happened, grimly acquiescent. 'This was
the consummation for which we built those
limbs.'

'Those sworded figures in the backward gloom
    Sitting, thine ebbing fates and fortunes sway!
Nor will they spare, though thou should'st cry aloud!'

There came, however, other thoughts, imposing on
fear and humiliation a glow of awe and happiness
almost intolerable. That virginity had also been
worshipped as a holy thing. Another man who had
looked at her with hunger in his eyes had restored
her self-esteem. He had refused what her whole
being was crying out to give him, that it might come
with the gift of her mind unsnared and unbeguiled.
What he had refused was his without repentance,
for ever. She was exultant with the memory of that
sudden light of renunciation which had made her
his beyond recall.

At Kantara Bunny was at her door, knocking. She flew to it, and opened it.

"Don't hurry, sweetheart. We've time enough.'

'But I'm all ready, Bunny.'

Through the night's blackness and upon the deeper blackness of the Canal, across its glimmering lights and white trail of mirrored stars, they moved in their own world, hearing the voices of others as they came through their dream. Care and tenderness encompassed her.

'Where do we breakfast, Bunny? On the train?'

'No. At Ludd. We have an hour to wait there. Almost time enough to run out and see St. George's tomb at Ramleh.'

'St. George's tomb?'

'Yes. It was in this land that he killed his dragon, just as Perseus had killed one before him. It used to be a great place for dragons, sweetheart.'

'It's just *too* perfect, Bunny! Being with you!'

Her excited brain ended on this note of rest and security, and in her carriage on the Palestine side she fell asleep.

She woke once, at El Arish, and looked out, raising her head from the pillow. The sea was breaking on the sands, close to the train. She glanced at it once, and saw that wave and sky were friendly and aware of how well guarded she moved through these lands. On this coast Andromeda had faced the dragon emerging from that drowsy sea. But Andromeda had faced it with Bunny beside her, and what did a dragon matter anyway?

Yes, Andromeda had had Bunny beside her. Cynthia put her head down, and was again asleep.

She had the sweetness and freshness of the dawn to herself, before he came, an hour earlier than they were due to reach Ludd.

They steamed slowly through groves of olive and orange, and over pastoral spaces amid whose withered grasses towered an occasional plot of white lilies. Airs untrammelled and pure since the beginning of the world floated in at the windows and breathed about them. The miasma that was Cairo and the uncleanness that had arrogated to itself the name of the civilisation for which men were fighting had been blown away on this cold clear morning breeze. A boy's grace and eagerness were at her service. In a dream she gathered the hitherto unknown flowers of humility and found that they were also flowers of peace and stainless exaltation.

At Ludd they breakfasted, changing trains. The sand dunes by the station were one with the cleansing perfection of this mist-free sun and cloudless sky. Huge mulberry trees were fruiting. Scent of orange boughs was all about them. In the distance guns were thudding, a steady surf breaking far from this quiet fastness of green woods and comradeship. No doubt some part of that unceasing, wasteful, foolish bombardment did a momentary or trivial streak of damage. A deserted Arab house might have another beam dislodged; a line of mules might be stampeded by a shell falling noisily near one of a convoy; a life, even, might be spilt, though only at long intervals. All this was nothing. The mind hardly listened

before it withdrew into its own happiness with
dismissal of the harmless absurdity with which

> ' The kafirs also (whom God curse)
> Vex one another night and day.'

But suddenly she remembered.

'Sweetheart, I hate them! I hate it all!'

'What do you hate, dearest?'

'Those guns.'

'Ah, they're not doing much damage to anyone.
You see, the Turco gunners, like our own, have a
certain amount of ammunition allotted to them
which they are expected to shoot off. It's just to
keep them in practice.'

'Do you mean, they simply shoot it off?'

'Oh no, not quite. They *say* they are aiming at
something, of course. One of their observers reports
that he sees a bit of dust somewhere, which *may* be a
British working party. So Jacko has a pot at it.'

'And kills men!'

'Oh, only once in a blue moon, darling. Very likely
the dust was only a few sheep, or nothing at all. And
if by any chance it *is* a working party, why they just
down tools and skedaddle to whatever cover there
is.'

'Oh, Bunny, I'm so unhappy!'

'But why, sweetheart? I never knew before what
happiness is.' He was puzzled as well as troubled.

'It's so silly. So hateful. Can't you Europeans *see*
how we feel? You laugh at our not wanting to come
into the War.'

'Why, darling, we never did.'

'Yes, you did. You do. You laugh because you have heard about our singing "I didn't raise my son to be a soldier." Now, Bunny, you're laughing now!'

'I wasn't, honestly.'

'You were.'

'Sweetheart, I'm so absurdly happy that I can't help smiling.'

'You were smiling *at what I said.*'

'Well—it *is* a bit funny—I mean, the idea of a lot of people singing *that.*'

'It isn't funny.'

'No, of course not.'

'Not the idea behind it, Bunny. When I think of what may happen—of you, Bunny——'

'Oh, but that won't happen, darling. Not now that I've got you. Besides, there isn't going to be much more fighting on this front. There isn't really. We've got all we want, having captured Jerusalem. And Jacko knows he can't get Jerusalem back. He jolly well learnt that last Christmas. We shall simply both sit tight in our lines while they settle up the scrap in France.'

'Do you really think so, Bunny?'

'Of course. What else *could* happen? Any attack by us would be madness, especially now that we've sent so many of our white troops to France. We've only untrained divisions on this front, half of them mostly made up of Indians only just recruited. Allenby isn't an absolutely crazy fool—you'll grant me that. He isn't going to try a sheer gamble with nothing in his hand!'

'You and Martin told me that the April shows were both gambles.'

This was awkward. She had never given the impression of over-close attention when he and

Martin embarked on military exposition. However
his tolerance extended to his own judgments; h
dismissed them now magnanimously.

'Oh, well. . . . Anyway, we shan't have an
more. Those shows proved to us exactly how muc
we could do on this Front, and that we had alread
done it. And as for Jacko, he asks nothing bette
than to be left alone—which is what we are goin
to do.'

She was not satisfied.

They were in the Jerusalem train, slowly climbin
up into the region of rocky cistus-bushy ravines
when she hid her face in his coat. The guns could n
longer be heard.

'Listen, Bunny!' Her voice was so low and breath
less, he hardly caught it. 'If I ever have a son
sweetheart, I'm not going to risk him going to an
war, no matter how just and fine everyone says it is
I'm not going to let there be any chance of hi
father's eyes and limbs being smashed by this hatefu
silly wicked thing that you men think so grand!'

She submitted to the passion of tenderness in hi
caresses, but she had not finished. 'You don't see—
you can't see, you men are so stupid!'

'Of course,' he said gravely, 'I know that what i
happening is awfully hard on the women who hav
to lose the men they care about.'

This is the correct conventional thing, which w
shall go on saying to the end. But Cynthia ha
broken out of convention into reality.

'The women! the women!' she cried. 'You mak
us the excuse for everything you do wrong, jus
because you never think—because you never feel—

as we do, because you don't even begin to understand how we feel!' She clutched at his coat convulsively, and buried her head against it to hide the
fact that she was crying. He tried to comfort her and
to understand her distress.

'I was like you, Bunny, a week ago, and just as big
a fool. You know Mrs. Sanderson, the Englishwoman
who's running your Jerusalem canteen? Her
husband was a British officer who was killed three
years ago in France and she has a son fighting. I was
talking to her about what's happening now, and—
and—I was just a *fool*, Bunny, a *fool*'—she said
passionately—'because I knew nothing, I could see
nothing—I could only say the kind of thing we
always say without thinking—because we *can't* think
—that it must be very terrible for the women of
England. And she said wearily, "Oh, the women,
the women! *They* don't matter. It's the men that we
are losing." And she laughed in a way that was so
bitter that I thought she must be half insane. But
I know what she meant now.'

'Yes. It's rotten,' he said.

'When Martin told us about his friend whom he
had to leave to die, Val and I thought it an *awfully*
sad and terrible story, and we were dreadfully sorry
for Martin. But we didn't realise that it had actually
happened. I didn't see it then—as *you*, Bunny! It was
only someone who belonged to someone else—whom
I didn't know, whom I never should know!'

She had wakened memory, that had lain asleep in
paradisal groves ever since the boy had first seen
her beauty's perfection and cast aside all sorrow as
a dream beside this the reality. Now he was far

L

back from the present, even with her beside him; he was living over again half-forgotten friendship with faces that were clay. Terror, kindness, laughter, courage, and dying were with him.

Then his hand straying over her hair brought him back to delight, she felt his love quicken with knowledge of her in his arms; and her own quickened with impulsive dread and revulsion from fate that inexorably takes away

> ' Our youth, our age, our all we have,
>   And pays us but with earth and dust.'

'You see,' she said, 'you won't understand, you can't understand. You have been brought up to think that it is men's job to worship women, to see that they are lovely and charming and all that. But I've seen *you*, Bunny, my own darling, darling boy. And although I want *you*—just *you*, whatever happens —I can't bear losing the Bunny that I first saw, who is such a perfect, dear boy. And I thought—sweetheart, you don't know how shocking it is for me to be talking like this to a man, but I'm going to get it said, and then you'll know that I've given *all* my chances of happiness and self-respect into your hands and that you can kill me with wretchedness if you want to, for I've kept nothing back. But there's going to be a time when I shall have not only you, but my own first sweetheart—you as you are *now*, Bunny— with just the eyes and the way of talking and walking that you have now. And he's not going to be sent out to any war anywhere to be just killed as if he were nothing!'

He said no word in reply.

XIII

I

WARREN REACHED HIS BATTALION, AND FOUND himself in the midst of confusion. He stopped a man of his own Company.

'What's up, Henderson?'

'Battalion's to move, sir. Orders just come this morning.'

Barrett, his own former Company Commander, hailed him. 'We're moving, Bunny my boy. The Brentfords to the Front! Better begin rubbing up your parlezvousing.'

'Rubbing up what?'

'Thy French, O Bunnyrabbit! We're for the bloody wars again. France!'

He learnt that seven battalions of the London Division, the Brentfords among them, were to leave immediately for the Western Front. Moloch had eaten up his abounding rations and was demanding more. His glance had swept round the globe and fallen on this obscure corner of Palestine.

Somewhere, doubtless, sun and stars kept on their wonted way, and the seasons urged forward. But Remfry himself stood alone and unmoving, in a sudden trance that foresaw the end.

It is vain to analyse men's minds in this new alignment of their lives. That day has gone, and its emotions are done with. And yet—there is a historical interest in noting how men, our own flesh and blood,

felt in such sudden recalls from quietude to war.
Barrett, Remfry knew, was vexed and peevish—the
middle-aged man who had long outlived his genuine
patriotic fervour and now desired merely to get the
folly adequately finished and to return to the saner
dullness of peace. In the battalion were diverse cur-
rents of response. There was excitement at knowledge
of being moved nearer England, with possibilities
of leave and of seeing home and friends and girls
and music-halls again. But not much even of this
except in the most unthinking and unimaginative
stratum of the Brentfords. The Brentfords were for
the most part cockneys, clerks and warehousemen
and small shopkeepers, shrewd and realist. A faintly
irritated acceptance was dominant. But as I said
before—what does it matter? If the Great War
taught us anything at all, it was that individual men
and women are nothing, they have hardly even the
substantiality of the dreams to which pessimists of
former ages have compared them. For a dream can
leave a memory of discomfort or delight. But men
and women are born and live, and die to be forgotten. Humanity sweeps on, a gesticulating shadow
that has no form or substance and can remember
nothing of the millions of its former gesticulations.

Warren woke up with a start and began to get his
jobs done. He telephoned first to Martin.

'Yes, I know, Bunny. I mean, I'd just heard. I'm
ever so sorry.'

'Oh, rot, Martin! The business has got to be gone
through with.'

'I'm going to get back to the battalion.'

'Why should you?'

'Do you think I'm going to stay out here on a cushy job, while you fellows are for it again?'

'We'll talk about that when we meet. I'm coming in Wednesday early, to see about C Company's train accommodation. I'll get up to your billet somehow. But don't be an ass about trying to go with the battalion. As I told you before, you've earned your reprieve, if any chap ever did.'

Two days later Authority sent round to all units a severely worded circular on the misuse of the telephone. It gave examples of 'frivolous and unnecessary use of a public service for private ends.' One was the text of the conversation that I have given above.

Decision was hard; but Martin made it on the unthinking principle that there was only one decent thing to do:

> ' I could not love thee, dear, so much,
>   Loved I not honour more.'

There may be sense to an old song sometimes.

He went to Major Austin-Gary, and said, 'My old crowd, the Brentfords, are ordered to France, sir.'

'Rough luck, after all they've been through! Things look pretty bad, don't they? We'll have to put in our last man before the Hun's properly licked.'

Austin-Gary looked at him absent-mindedly. He was drawing up a team to play the Tenth Division; a number of players were ill or engaged otherwise, and on the piece of paper before him he had pressed into service not only that tried and favourite athlete,

Mr. A. N. Other, but his less-known compeers, Messrs. A. R. Abbit, A. R. Otter, A. R. Ascal, A. R. Uffian, A. R. Obber.

'I want to go with them, sir. Will you help me to work it?'

'What's that, Chapman?' He drew his pencil lightly through Mr. A. R. Uffian's name, and wrote in above it tentatively, with a query mark after it, 'Caleb Wenyon.' 'Do you think you could get Wenyon to turn out against the Tenth Division? He used to play when he was up at the Varsity, I know. Otherwise, it looks as if we'll have to scratch. You can't take the field with half a dozen men.'

'But why?' he asked, genuinely amazed, when Martin had managed to collect his attention. 'What's the sense, Chapman? Those fellows are in for a rotten thin time, if I can guess anything.'

'That's just it. They're my crowd, the crowd I trained with. I'll look a fair rotter if I stay on here and let them go.'

'Caleb warned me you'd be coming with this idea,' Austin-Gary ruminated. 'Look here, Chapman. Turn up your right arm a minute, will you?'

Martin, mystified, did so. 'There's nothing wrong, is there, Major?'

'I want to look at it a moment. What's this?' he continued, indicating two gold streaks. 'Two wound stripes. You've been hit twice. Don't you think you've done your bit? Mind you, if you were a fellow who'd had a soft job all along, I'd be the first to agree that you damn well *ought* to go, though in that case you wouldn't have any special keenness to go, and it would probably not be possible to get you sent!'

'It's rotten seeing fellows you know being sent back again.'

'It's perfectly bloody,' Austin-Gary agreed sympathetically. 'Sheerly, absolutely, foully *bloody*! I know how you feel. But I say to myself that I had my dose in Gallipoli, to say nothing of First Gaza afterwards. You've had your dose, too, Chapman.'

'So have a lot of the fellows who have to go back, Major.'

Austin-Gary tried another line, the rallying line. 'We've got through only half our cricket programme; and Corps H.Q. hasn't a whole crowd of chaps to pick from, as the Divisions have. You were a find, Chapman, a natural first-wicket batsman. And you've done distinctly useful work as a change bowler more than once, with those slow leg breaks of yours. As skipper of the Corps team I forbid your going.'

In the end he said, 'All right. If you *will* be obstinate and go against what your friends think best for you, try your luck. I warn you, I think (as well as hope) that you'll find it damn poor! They're swinging these fellows across with a speed unparalleled in modern war. They're wanted jolly badly, the first moment they can be got to France. You'll only get handsomely told off if you butt in with the plea that one man extra be included when the whole thing has been fixed up and practically finished. Besides, it will mean getting another fellow here for your job—it'll mean a whole heap of annoyance to make the change—the change of *one* man, Chapman! They'll not think you worth it and they'll strafe you to hell!'

They did strafe him to hell. Martin 'phoned through to his old colonel—who was away at divisional headquarters and never heard of his desire, which was mislaid in the rush of really urgent messages coming in. He got on to his brigadier and was snubbed; on to the divisional general and *was* told to go to hell (this, by a person strictly literal-minded, might have been interpreted as permission to join the division in France). There was nothing doing. No one was going to bother about an individual, whether to keep him or send him away. War does not recognise individuals.

If the change had been made at normal notice he would have been called back to his battalion almost automatically. But this was a speed dictated by dread necessity. Regiments were being pitchforked across to France without time to collect outlying straws.

II

On Wednesday morning Martin met Valerie as he was entering the Damascus Gate. She asked him, 'Have you seen Bunny? He's in Jerusalem, you know.'

Martin answered, 'No. I knew he was coming in. But I didn't know when.'

'You know that his Company are going on the evening train?'

'No. I know nothing.'

'Well, they are. He and Cynthia are lunching together, and I know he's going to manage to see you afterwards.'

'See me where, Val?'

'At your own place. He told me he was going to jump a lorry to the Mount of Olives. He's at the station now, I expect, looking after accommodation for his Company.'

Martin made his way to the station, where he found Warren occupied as Valerie predicted.

'Hullo, old chap! Just look at this! We're expected to sleep in these cattle-trucks, which are about half as many as we need.'

'You didn't let me know you were going to-day, Bunny.'

'How *could* I let you know? This is another hush-hush business, of the sort the War's been full of. The whole thing is to be kept secret from Jacko, who is to go on lying squat in terrified belief that the Brentfords are still opposite him. My God! what a set of Napoleons we have on top! I mustn't tell a pal over the military telephone what a whole cityful of mitching, sneaking, watchful Ayrabs see going on under their noses. However!' He proceeded to rag the Railway Transport Officer, a second lieutenant, with good-natured severity.

'You expect me to get a hundred and fifty men into less than a dozen open trucks! What was your job when you were in real life? Sardine-packing?'

'You can get twenty men into each one of them, sir—at a pinch.'

'At a *nip*, you mean! What about my outsize cannon-fodder? I've a quartermaster-sergeant-major who weighs fifteen stone and fills three chairs.'

'He could travel with the driver, sir.'

'I see! Have a place to himself, and sit on the coal supply! And do you expect my fellows to *sleep* to-night? Am I to run a rope round them, so that they can drowse off standing and support one another without falling out on the track?'

'It's the best I can do,' said the R.T.O., who being only a second-lieutenant could not quell his tormentor.

'Meanwhile,' summed up Remfry with real savagery to Martin, 'G.H.Q., and every shabby little imitation headquarters throughout this bloody army, is simply lousy with cars, one to every man who can put up a tab of any sort. Oh, well! never tell me this War hasn't been worth while *as an education*! It's jolly well taught the infantryman *his place*. I hope he'll remember the lesson when he's demobbed, and will for all time continue to demean himself lowly and humbly before his betters.'

The job was finished so far as circumstances permitted. Time drew on towards noon. Warren turned, and confronted his friend with a strange irresolution in his manner.

Before he could speak, Martin said, '*I'm* one of these soft-job merchants with a car, and it's here at your disposal. And to-day I fetched a fellow down to drive it and if need be look after it while I left it. It's outside now.'

'Splendid!' said Warren listlessly, his attention drawn off to a lorry arriving with kit from the Brentfords. 'Half a second, Martin! I say, Corporal! Can *you* take over now and see that stuff shoved in? I want to spend a bit of time with Captain Chapman.'

'I can see to everything, sir. And if I might, sir, I'd like to say good-bye to Captain Chapman. I used to be in his platoon before Gaza, sir.'

'Damn it, Isaacs,' said the unhappy Martin, 'I ought to be going with you fellows, and I'm not. Look here, Corporal,' as he thrust out his hand, 'you men have taught me what comradeship is. I shall never know it again, no matter how long I live.'

'May I say a word, sir—frankly, sir?'

'Of course, Corporal.'

'Then, sir, some of us were talking over old times the other day, and if you'll excuse the expression sir, Sergeant Hawkins said, "Those two"—meaning you and Captain Remfry, sir—"were not only like brothers to each other, they were more like brothers than officers to us as well." If I might be so bold, sir, I think we London chaps have been lucky in our officers. And it isn't every regiment as can say that, sir. And I'm sure, sir, that every man that's ever served under you or known about you, wishes you the best of luck, sir.' He spoke breathlessly, half-frightened of his eloquence.

'We shan't forget Captain Chapman, shall we, Isaacs?' said Remfry.

'I should say not, sir.'

'And that,' said Remfry, as they left the station, 'is Whitechapel Jewry. And its other names, in this case, are pluck and decency and loyalty and humble acceptance of a rotten and low place in the general lordly scheme of things.'

'Do you mind,' he said, while the car was whirring up the steeply winding road from the station to the City, 'stopping your bus where that path goes down under Aceldama?'

The car was left in the driver's charge. Bunny, without speaking, led the way until they came to the inward twist of the track, and could look out over the Valley of Hinnom.

Then he turned to Martin, again with that irresolution of manner.

'Look here, old man, I'm afraid I can't come up to see you at your place this afternoon, as I'd intended.'

'That's absolutely all right, Bunny.'

'Will you see us off? Can you manage it? About six-thirty to-night.'

'Of course, I'll see you off.'

'Then—Martin—Martin, I'm afraid this is good-bye.'

He went on, 'I mean, we shall see you at the station, of course, and all that. But that isn't what I wanted. Will you look my people up if anything happens? That's their address.' He handed him an envelope.

Martin took it. 'I'll keep this, and I'll look you up after the War finishes.'

'Rather! But see my people in any case, won't you? I want you to. They've heard about you.'

'Of course I will, Bunny.'

Again that queer uncharacteristic irresolution. Then, 'I seem to be treating you pretty shabbily.'

'Not a bit. I understand, Bunny—absolutely.'

'Of course you do. Of course you would, Martin. You'd understand if no other fellow in the world did. And now, old chap—just sit down a sec., I want to say something.'

Warren sat down on a boulder, and Martin followed his example. Warren continued, talking gaily and nervously. 'We two have heard the chimes at midnight, as Billy Wagstaff wittily puts it—meaning thereby, in our case, that we've both endured Jacko's oppressions and the slings and arrows of outrageous fortune and an outrageous higher command. Remember, Martin,' he went on soberly and slowly, 'when we were first rookies at Shoreham? Gosh! but those were the days, weren't they?'

'Those were the days,' Martin agreed.

'Remember how patriotic we all were—out to win the war that was to end all war—to share the quick sharp tussle that would bring in the millennium for everybody, even for a defeated and rightly penitent Germany?'

Martin remembered. How will any ever forget the perfect dawn which shone over youth preparing to enter Death's halls as if they were a gymnasium?

After a pause, Remfry added quietly, 'Whatever happens—and Martin, I feel as if you and I were looking a very long way ahead—we've had these four years together. And they've been the years of my life! I wouldn't have given them up even for the years that I thought I was going to have, when the War came. We've been pals, Martin; and we've been friends with a whole lot of fine fellows who've gone west. It's meant everything to me, Martin— being with you, I mean. I—I wanted to tell you, Martin, so that you would know it always. That's all. I say, isn't that a perfectly ripping view, all down the valley?'

'Ripping,' Martin said.

Warren, picking up a stone, flung it out far. It described its semi-circle, and sank into oblivion again, in the wilderness of thorns and scrub and other stones.

XIV

I

THE FACES OF HIS OLD COMPANIONS LOOKING OUT FROM
the compartments, roaring songs or ribald jests at
the Arab woman who swept the station waiting-
rooms, began to fade out in Martin's mind. A month
passed, joining the other months through which,
while Allies and Central Powers were locked in the
long-drawn death-grapple, the Palestine armies
watched each other quietly across the stretches of
sun-burnt grass.

There had, of course, been breaches of the peace,
violent while they lasted. The fierce and bloody
fighting of April, on the coast as well as east of
Jordan, had been broken off by the peril which,
then (as well as later) drew away so many troops to
Flanders. It was renewed in May, and again in
June, when the Seventh Indian Division pushed the
Turk down on to the malarial swamps beyond
Arsuf. At intervals after that raids occurred; as the
summer passed to its close the Indians, in particular,
developed a superiority consciousness that often
found jaunty manifestation.

One day in mid-July, at dinner Wenyon tossed
down a note.

'Read that, boys—a chit from an old pal who's
D.A. & Q.M.G. of the Seventh Division.'

The note was exultant. 'Jacko grows jumpy. The

other day, his nerves were so upset that he bom-
barded us furiously for four hours on end, merely
because the 53rd Sikhs paid him a purely friendly
and informal visit in the morning, just to see how he
was getting on and if there was anything we could
do for him. It's true they had similarly walked
across, a couple of days before, and collected a
matter of two hundred prisoners or so. But this time
they weren't up to anything in the least unkind. But
he misjudged us and let fly at the landscape in
general and nothing in particular.'

The warriors of Gallipoli and Ctesiphon and a
hundred hill fights in Judæa had abundant reason
for beginning to cower where once they had stood
aggressive.

'The poor devils are starved,' said Austin-Gary.
One thought leads to its kindred thought. 'I believe
the Bull will decide to eat them up this autumn,
after all. It would be a mercy to put them out of
their misery.'

The haven of calm on Olivet had remained
untroubled. There had been one change only:
Major Blundell had mysteriously disappeared,
though where he could be usefully set no one could
guess. He was alleged to be experimenting in the
possibility of making petrol out of the Jordan Valley
shale. He had been seen, like the Scholar Gipsy, at
long intervals, but had not troubled his old mess.
No one who had glimpsed his figure, unmistakable
at whatever distance, had pressed up for conversation. Conversation is exhausting when you know
you cannot say consecutive sentences without one
at least being an egregious blunder. 'You are wrong.

And I'll tell you why.' The Major's old comrades had remained contentedly in their peace; and every Saturday Martin and Austin-Gary had played cricket, on Olivet or on some divisional ground.

Excitement returned, when on the 13th the growing wrath of Turk against German came to explosion. The Turkish command had insisted that their handful of allies did something besides criticise and try to over-rule, so a savage attempt was made to break through and annihilate the British posts that kept the Jordan bridges. From river to coast a heavy bombardment was put down, under cover of which some hundreds of German infantry overwhelmed advanced pickets, but in the end were slain or captured. The Palestine war had stirred in its sleep.

The evening of the second Sunday after this news, Martin was asked to supper with the Frobishers. The Captain was taking a 5 o'clock service at the Y.M.C.A., and meeting Martin in the city had issued the invitation and then apologetically (as to a British officer) suggested that he might care to go with Mrs. Frobisher to the service. His past revived in Martin; it was many a day since he had attended any religious service, and it came over him that it would do him good to listen to an honest man like Frobisher.

'Thanks awfully. I'd like to come.'

When he called for the Frobishers, he met Cynthia in the corridor of the Relief headquarters.

'Why, *Martin*! if it isn't good to see you again! Mrs. Frobisher has asked Val and me in to supper to-night. She told us you were coming. We're awfully glad. I haven't seen you since Bunny went.'

'I'm waiting to take Mrs. Frobisher along to the service that Frobisher's holding,' said Martin.

'May Val and I come with you? Just wait while I get her?'

The hall was packed out with Australians, magnificent men, superbly vigorous in all they did, such thews and frames as Mars not twice in a millennium gets the chance to mangle. Frobisher invited them to choose their own hymns; and by acclamation they chose for a start, 'Tell Mother I'll be there':

> ' Tell Mother I'll be there,
>   In answer to her prayer!
>   O tell my darling Mother I'll be there!
>   Tell Mother to prepare
>   Heaven's joys with me to share!
>   O tell my darling Mother I'll be there!'

The amazing scene was fairyland, undoubtedly fairyland. The maudlin words and tune were being sung with immensely enjoyed remorse; tears were flowing down the cheeks of the husky trooper next but one to Martin. Martin had trembled for Frobisher, when he realised that the audience had clamoured for such a beginning. Had it been British soldiers who had chosen it, he would have been sure of mitching mallecho. Even now his cheeks grew hot with amusement and annoyance whenever he remembered how as orderly officer he had once been told off to take a parade of Brentfords to listen to a local cleric—not an army chaplain (an authorised plague) but a Jerusalem missionary—

M

who had asked if he might hold a service. Th
padre had made part amends for having formulated
such a demand, by desiring the men to be at thei
ease, 'quite at your ease, men' (this request had
been granted in full,) and had asked them to pick
the hymns. The battalion wag, unfortunately pre
sent, had called for 'Count your blessings.' Th
orderly officer had been forced to listen to th
bawled injunction:

> ' Count your rations, count them one by one!
> Count your rations! see how you've been done!
> Count your rations, count them one by one,
> *And* it will surprise you what the quarterbloke ha
> done!'

To Wenyon, after Frobisher's service, Martin said
'But there wasn't the twitch of a muscle! Those
huge toughs were genuinely moved, shaken to their
depths. Some of them were sobbing.'

'Yes,' said Wenyon. 'And only the previous even
ing, as like as not, they were painting some quarte
of a pagan village red. They are certainly the mos
wonderful people that even this War has drawn
into its scope. Has the world ever seen such soldiers
Or ever seen such astounding birds? They'll chuck
pianos out of upper storey windows and generall
sack a respectable-sized town belonging to ou
nominal allies of Egypt; and the next day they'll b
beseeching Mother—what was it you said the hymn
advised Mother to do, Chapman?—to prepare—
prepare——'

> ' " Tell Mother to prepare,
> Heaven's joys with me to share," '

said Chapman.

'Ah! and the old lady might well prepare! They
do right to warn her! I'd ask for some chance of
preparation myself if I knew any considerable squad
of Aussies was likely to invade Heaven.'

At supper afterwards, Mrs. Frobisher said, 'Isn't
the news from France simply great! Don't you think
so, Captain Chapman? You must be so *happy!*'
Martin, though his job now was soft enough and
set in idyllic peace, kept the soldier's anger at what
seemed to him facile optimism. He said, more
irritably than was consistent with politeness, 'Oh,
yes! Great for us who merely have to read about it!'
'Now, Captain Chapman'—she was stooping over
a spirit stove; and turned to look him in the face—
'you know that no one here would use "great" in
that sense. It's simply that it looks as if the wicked
business would really finish this year. You can't
imagine what that thought means to me!'
'I'm sorry, Mrs. Frobisher,' he apologised. 'Yes,
it *is* great, if that's what is happening. But can we
be sure that it is?'
'Well,' she said, straightening, 'we've only got
what your official people tell us, of course.'
'Yes. And unfortunately, we know what that can
mean sometimes.'

Martin was not one of the minority of neurotics
who have furnished war-novelists with their officer
heroes, nor of the majority of crude (yet vaguely
unhappy) beasts who are now supposed to have
composed the rank and file of the warring armies.
Nevertheless, long before 1918 the War had become
mainly vexation to those engaged in it. It had

gathered to itself such a prospect of eternity, it had proved over and over so futile and tremendous. Allied offensives had won so many smashing victories and taken towns of such immense importance; yet all had been swung back after a while. Italy—Roumania—America—had all come in, each entry making swift overthrow a certainty for the overmatched enemy. He had survived, and seemed rather to thrive on additions to his adversaries. Moloch asked a fantastic sum for his favour, demanding a life—many lives—for every yard of trench. The folly of hoping ever to meet his price was apparent to all except the professional patriots.

Martin caught Cynthia's glance. It deepened into a kindness that was like a sudden overflow of light from behind a cloud. Something was for his own sake, as well as Bunny's. There were thoughts and fears that they now shared in common.

'Martin Chapman, Englishman!' she said, and raised her cup of coffee. 'Cheerio, Martin!'

'Cheerio, Cynthia!'

'Are you two just going to drink to each other?' asked Frobisher.

'Not at all!' said Martin. 'We're all friends here.'

'I should say we are!' said Cynthia.

And all in the room laid themselves out to spoil Martin.

'Do you know what I think you English have to teach the rest of the world, Captain Chapman?' asked Mrs. Frobisher.

'I suppose,' he said unconvinced and unconvincingly, 'the usual things that people mention—you

know, sportmanship, fairness, law and respect for
order.'

'No, not at all. Of course,' she conceded, for Martin
was their guest, 'you *have* those qualities. But what
I was thinking of was something that Cynthia said
to me, coming back from Wilbur's service just now.
Cynthia'd better tell you herself.'

Martin turned to Cynthia.

'It's like this, Martin. I thought we knew all about
friendship in the States. I guess we do, when it's a
matter of friendship between boys and girls. Your
boys don't *understand*. They're either just too stupid
and *dull* for words, or else they want to make love.
But I hand it to you that you know better than any
people on earth what friendship between men is.
You and Bunny have taught me that.'

There was something bottled up in Cynthia that
had to be poured out. She rose from her seat
opposite Martin, and came across impulsively. The
chair beside him, as the result of manœuvring in
which Mrs. Frobisher had been his accomplice, was
occupied by Valerie.

'You change places with me, Val. You don't
appreciate Martin as I do. Don't look so distressed
when a girl makes up to you, Martin! I don't
wonder that Bunny calls you Martin Puzzlewit!
Now, Val!' said tactless Cynthia. Val vacated her
chair. 'I want to get Martin to *talk*, Mrs. Frobisher.
Tell us everything, Martin. Do you know, we
Americans are getting to see that you British are
human! Tell us about what it was like when you
first joined up—about meeting Bunny and you two
boys becoming friends—about France—about what's

happened to you since you came here. Please, Martin!'

'If Captain Chapman,' Mrs. Frobisher began.

'Martin, please, Mrs. Frobisher,' he said.

'If Martin'll do that it'll be fine. Won't it, Val?'

'Yes. It will be very interesting,' said Val.

Martin did not find it easy, but he did it.

II

When the party broke up, it was within an hour and a half of midnight. Two nights previously, July 23rd, had been full moon. Martin now, standing outside the Relief headquarters in shadow of a towering cypress, stretched his arms to make sure that he himself was not a shadow. In that suffused mist of half-light everything looked wraithlike. And the overflowing kindness which he had just left was something he could not reconcile with the reality of his place in the World War.

The dream deepened. Valerie stood beside him.

'Martin!'

'Yes?'

'Have you got your automobile here?'

'No. I walked in, across the Valley. I wanted to walk back, since it was only two nights after full moon.'

'Are you in any hurry to get back?'

'Rather not! Why, Val?'

'I want myself to walk over Olivet in this heavenly night. And I wondered—you remember, you asked me to come with you, two months ago, and I said——'

'You said I shouldn't understand, Valerie. But will you trust me to understand now? May I come with you?'

'Please, Martin!'

'Do you think it will go all right with Bunny?' she asked, when at length they rested.

'Oh, yes, I should think so. After all, the whole show appears to be finishing, doesn't it?'

'That's just the question, Does it? Or *doesn't* it?'

He did not reply.

'Martin, what do you yourself honestly think?'

'If you want to know, Val, I'm no end worried.'

'You think he won't come back?'

'Unless the show really does finish within about a month of his getting into it, he won't come back,' he said in his slow grave way. 'I don't see how he *can* come back, knowing the man he is as I do. He *might* get wounded, of course. But he's had that kind of luck so often that I'm superstitious that it won't come his way again.'

'How often has he been wounded, Martin?'

'Four times, I think, though he only counts it as three times.'

'And you call that luck!'

'Luck such as comes to only one fellow in a thousand. If you knew him as I do, you'd marvel that it came to him.'

'Do you know what I think? I think that we've nothing to learn in stupidity or cruelty from savages, sending men back when they've suffered once and— by luck, as you call it—been only wounded.'

'That's what our Indian soldiers think.'

'*Nothing*,' said Valerie angrily, 'to learn of cruelty or stupidity.'

'Call it necessity, Val. We've got to keep going on with the men we have, until we've won the things we went into the War for.'

'Until you've won the things you went into the War for! Do you still talk like that, Martin? You? After all you've gone through? Do you for one minute suppose that you'll ever win "the things you went into the War for?" You'll come out a nation that has chucked away all the things it had that mattered——'

'No,' he interrupted her. 'We shall have kept those.'

'What do you mean? You know that you were fooled and bullied into entering the War, as we were, by propaganda.'

'No,' he said firmly. 'We weren't, Val. I know nothing about what happened in the States—you had more time to decide than we had. But I do know that *we* were taken clean by surprise. You won't believe it?'

He saw that she did not believe it. But he continued, 'Anyone can see what's going to happen. We shall get back, those of us who do get back, too tired to argue and suspicious that perhaps, because we were in the thick of it, we didn't understand as well as the fellows who never went to it. But there's one lie that won't prevail, so long as one of us is left alive to know in his soul how damnably and utterly untrue it is.'

'What lie's that, Martin?'

'The lie that you can see growing up already,

now that the War looks as if it might be finishing.
The legend that every nation planned and plotted
deliberately until war came. It's not true, Val;
and it hurts that you half think it.'

'Oh, Martin, of course I can never think it of
boys like you and Bunny.'

'But it's not true of our nation, either. War was
the last thing we were thinking of, four years ago.
I played cricket the day before it was declared;
and I wondered if I should be chosen to play for
the London Banks at the end of the season, against
the Stock Exchange. A week later, I was one
of the first hundred thousand enlisted, but even
then, Val, not sure if I hadn't done the wrong
thing. For I'd reckoned myself a Socialist and a
Pacifist.'

'Not a Socialist, Martin!'

'Ah, it doesn't mean anything so dreadful with us
as it does with you. In the States, don't you
rather frighten yourselves with names?'

'Maybe.'

'We don't, except when we get an extra panicky
election. And, Val, you don't *know* how keen my
generation were—the serious ones, I mean—on
peace and friendship between the nations and no
more war. And on getting rid of poverty and rotten
conditions in our own midst. All this devilry came
clean out of the blue.'

'Yet your people *chose* to go into it.'

'Yes. We chose,' he said proudly. 'We weren't
hounded or dragooned or cajoled into it. It was an
act of will. And that's why it's the only war we've
ever been in, that our children need never be
ashamed of.'

'Weren't you jealous of Germany's trade and afraid of her fleet?'

'No. We were keeping our word to Belgium. And because we kept it we saved what mattered most.'

'You did not!' she cried. 'You have lost what mattered most. Do you think any beast has ever been as silly as man? Sending boys like Bunny where they'll be smashed and killed or blinded or terrified! Martin, do you know that if anything happens to him it'll just about finish Cynthia!'

'I know,' he said. 'But you've got to get this right about us, Valerie. And you've got to get it right about my generation. I want you to understand us. Will you listen, Val?'

'Of course I'll listen.'

'I told you that I thought I was a Pacifist and a Socialist, and all that. What I thought I was, my younger brother was—in fact. And he wasn't going to join up, and he didn't—for a long while. He put up with the questions that meddling old gentlemen asked him. "My boy, why aren't you in khaki?"'

'How old was he?'

'Seventeen and three-quarters when he joined up in 1915.'

'I should have thought *that* was answer enough!'

'Well, it wasn't. Either for them or for the girls who considered they were doing very fine, patriotic service in offering white feathers to any boy they thought was of age to be shot at. And it wasn't funk, I tell you. It was just honest conviction that the whole thing was wrong and foul that kept him back. This was until the first Zepp raid over London. That night he—my mother and sister and he—stood outside and watched the searchlights focusing

on the Zepp and heard the bombs exploding. When
he was dead, my sister wrote that it was a very
white-faced boy that went home with them afterwards, saying nothing. Next morning at breakfast
he said, "Mother, I'm joining up." He had two
months in France—longer than the average second-
lieutenant gets—and he was killed in the first
week of the Somme. He never for a moment thought
—countless thousands of our fellows never thought—
of himself as going off to kill Germans. He only
knew that men had to die, and that he could not
stay away from what was happening.'

Martin ended, and sat silent, looking out toward
the city. The moon had swung triumphantly into
the dome of night and the Temple area shone
softly and clearly. There was no sound or sign of
man stirring on the surface of these eternities.
'Martin?'
He turned his head.
'Will you forgive me?'
'What for, Valerie?'
'For being so mean to you. And such a fool.'
'You never have.'
'Yes, I have. I've cut you all these weeks, except
when I wanted to make use of you.'
'You'll never know how proud I shall always be
that you realised I was here to be made use of.'
'I know, Martin. And it meant that I trusted you.
But I was a fool, not to have known that I wanted
and needed your friendship. I was afraid you'd
think I wanted something else.'
Martin made no reply.
'Will you listen to *me* now, Martin? I've placed

you as "Britisher", till I found you were—well, Martin Chapman. You've placed me as "American".'

'No, by God!' he said. 'I have never done that, and never could. I know why you've asked me to be with you, and I know that I must not say the only thing I want to say—the thing you said I was bound to want to say. And I'll play the game. But I'm never going to admit that I placed you as "American". You placed yourself that day I first saw you, though I didn't know it then. But you did it; and you know where it was that you placed yourself!'

She rose. 'Let's go on again.'

Reaching Olivet's crest they rambled on to a wilderness of borage-covered boulders from which the Valley lay in prospect. The Pride of Jordan, its dark core of woodland, was a huddle of blackness. The gracious charity of midnight and the all-surveying moon flooded the hills and blue still sea. Only by an effort of memory could Martin recall the vivid moments of vexation or fear and hours of tediousness that he had passed on those hollows and heights. Crag and brook and wrinkling dust, the slopes where he and Bunny and Henry had lain exposed, and the roughening of earth's texture that had given respite from the searching fire of machine-gun and shell-splinter, all had died to one undistinguished peace.

It was because his thought had been recalled to Bunny and what was happening in France that he remembered so stabbingly the battle of last April. The moon seemed to concentrate into a lantern held by some invisible hand and turned full on to a

pit in which lay a hummock of weather-blanched
bones. Under the skull was the outline of a hand
supporting it. The gesture was despair, resignation,
reproach. That crevice in the hills, so long forgotten,
imagination had plucked out of darkness.

'Martin,' she said, 'I was angry with you because
I thought you were talking the old patriotism stuff
and forgetting what's really happening in Europe.
I'm sorry, really, Martin. I guess women will never
understand how men's minds work.'

'You're the first woman I ever knew put it that
way. I've always heard it that men didn't understand the way women's minds work.'

'Well, that's true too. But you're right, we do
forget that there's more than one way of misunderstanding. I'll own up, I *did* fetch to Jerusalem a
whole lot of silly notions about—well, about your
people in particular. I daresay I've got some of them
still. But they seem somehow dead and done for.
All I think—and all that Cynthia thinks—is that
you and Bunny are two boys too good for the use
that you've been put to. And in return, since I've
said such a handsome thing about you, sir, will you
overhaul your way of thinking about us—about
me? Oh, I know, I know, Martin—you'll say it
needs no overhauling. Please,' she said, 'don't be
hurt or misunderstand. Please don't think I don't
care! I guess we were badly made, we women.
When a girl likes a man as much as I like you, she
is ashamed of herself for feeling pleasure that he
thinks he cares about her, but she can't altogether
help feeling it. The world was made by someone
of the masculine gender all right, for he made it for
men! He gave you a hundred ways of caring for one

another, but only one way of caring for a woman.
I'd rather—a thousand times rather—talk to a man
with brains—I mean real brains, with some
character behind them and honesty and modesty;
I don't mean some conceited, objectionable boy—
than to all the women in our Relief Force. But I
know *you* would never waste your time talking to
me unless you thought I was nice *as a woman.*'

'No, no,' he protested.

'But it's true! You are not talking to Valerie
Connett, as you might be talking to some man,
because you think she's got intellect or has had an
exceptional experience that interests you. You are
talking to her because you think you care about her
as a woman.'

'Oh, for God's sake, Valerie, don't talk such utter
rot to me! I'm sorry! But you know perfectly well
that you are wrong. I'm not a man who thinks of
nothing but girls. But you can't prevent my *seeing*
what you are! If a fact's *there* you can't get rid of it
by being angry with it, Val!'

'I'm not angry with it. But I know it's *not* there.'

'All right. I know it *is*, and I know it every hour
that I'm alive.'

'Well, I'm going to give this heavenly moonlight
and mountain the credit that belongs to them!
But I don't forget Cynthia, even in moonlight on
Olivet. If I were fool enough to believe you, there'd
be Cynthia to remind me of what a really lovely
girl looks like, when I got back to her—without
any moonlight or Olivet!'

'Cynthia's a picture,' he said. 'She's a darling. I
could love Cynthia. I do love her. But not this
way, Val. I never think of her except as the jolliest

of pals when I'm with her. She really is the sweetest pluckiest girl I ever met. But she's just that.

She was climbing over rocks; and she reached a hand to him, that he might steady her as she jumped down. 'Now we've got it. It's as you think of Cynthia that I want you to think of me. I want your friendship, Martin. I want to have it always.'

'You've got it always, Val. There's just one thing that has happened in my life,' he said simply. 'That's getting to know you.'

'Oh, but you haven't got to know me, Martin. And I *want* you to know me. That's why I asked you to come with me to-night. I felt I simply must do this shocking thing, after I'd heard you talk as you did about Bunny. I'm glad Cynthia's going to marry Bunny, because I want him to be my friend too, as long as I live, and you don't know how I care about Cynthia.'

'I do. You feel about Cynthia as I feel about Bunny. He never had to go through the things I've had to go through—until the War came. And I sometimes feel as if it were just too foul and rotten for words, that a boy like Bunny should ever have found out the things he *has* found out. You don't know Bunny, Val. You know what he *looks* like— some young god who had stepped out of a patch of summer heather beside the Mediterranean. He plays games as if he did it just to show people what beauty is. But it isn't just looks. It's manliness, and pluck, and decency. He's been spoiled, except that nothing could spoil him. He doesn't care about himself, honestly. He'd throw his life away with just the same swing of his body as he walks to the wicket with, to save the most ordinary chap that he has in his company.'

She laughed half-nervously. 'You've never shown much curiosity about anything that belongs to me—about anything but me. Cynthia and Bunny knew all about one another almost at once. Where do you think I live?'

'I know you are American.'

She laughed again. 'American! And Cynthia is another American! And American girls are known to be very pretty and fresh, aren't they? I suppose it adds nothing to your knowledge when I say I come from Virginia and Cynthia comes from Pennsylvania?'

'I've heard about Virginia, of course.'

'You've heard about Virginia! That gets us on. There's a tradition of chivalry where I live. Do you suppose any girl in Virginia is allowed to grow up under the impression that she's homely? That's what you call plain. If the War hadn't come, do you think Dad would ever have let me be educated?'

'Were you educated, Val? I never thought about it.'

'Yes. I went to an expensive school for two years. But Dad thought the best education was having me around in Virginia. And I don't think he was so very mistaken. When the War came to us, though, we all got patriotic, and I took a six months' course in First Aid and The Care of Children. That's why I'm in charge of an orphanage now.'

'I know something about war,' she continued. 'My father's generation grew up in its shadow. They had no education except hatred and bitterness. Dad will never till his dying day quite forgive "the Yankees". He'd think it an aberration, my being such friends with Cynthia, if he saw it. In a way, an Englishman is more respectable than a Yankee girl from Pennsylvania.'

'How am I more respectable?'

'You come from a land that has an aristocratic tradition.'

'Yes. But my class don't share in it—except by permission to admire from afar.'

'You admire, anyway. And admire openly. Whereas the Yankees think they despise. And your people don't *really* believe in democracy, any more than we do. You and Dad would get on together, Martin. He'd find something satisfying in your craggy mournfulness. Dad's a dear,' she said. 'But I *know*, for I was brought up in its shadow, what carrying resentment forward from defeat means. The Civil War didn't touch Cynthia's people. It ruined mine, for long enough. We keep a kind of perpetual minor Hallowe'en for an uncle that was killed, and goodness knows how many friends and neighbours. One of our farmhouses was burnt, and the Yankees looted even the musket that Richard Connett carried at the Battle of the Brandywine. I was taught to believe that all Yankees were grasping and hypocritical. We almost hate them worse than ever now, when we see them coming down into Virginia and buying estates that we can't afford to keep, and using them just for less than half a dozen weeks in a year. We fought for States' rights and the North fought for the right to interfere with us. We both lost. They *daren't* and can't touch us ever again,' she said fiercely, 'whatever we do. But we've lost the sovereign freedom of Virginia,

the soul that kept her apart and unique—those are
the States' rights we should have cared about.
They can swamp us with their automobiles and
their advertisements and their wealth and their
patronage. And neither of us know that we have
lost the united strong America that would have
grown up without the war, and have grown up
without hatred and violence and boastfulness. And
Virginia lost a whole generation of her youth!'

They were above the narrow lane down to
Gethsemane—at the point where a tablet notes
'*Hic Dominus Flevit*'. A drowsy confusion of hoofs
floated up to them, a mist of sound drifting with
the dust that clouded all the road from Jericho.
In shadow of Gethsemane walls and cypresses a line
of Australian troopers were riding up the last
weary stage from the Valley. By the way they
moved men and horses conveyed that they were
dead beat.

This frieze wrought on the stuff of moonlit darkness fascinated them into stillness and they watched.
Then Martin spoke.

'Those fellows have got to go through it soon,'
he said.

They were onlookers, it seemed to them, at yet
unfolded time. This human river flowing muffled
up from the depths was history coming to vision
ere it came to deed. The war was starting anew;
and these men were its doers and victims, moving
there in all the close sleepy irritation of weariness,
the fires of consciousness damped down to the limits
necessary for attainment of their billets and rest.

'I've seen it coming,' said Martin. 'When they

took away another lot of our white troops—Bunny's
lot, you know—I thought we should just sit tight
this autumn and hold the line while they tried to
end things in France. And then I saw new stirrings
on this Front. It was first one thing, then another.
One day I met the First Seaforths marching somewhere between Ramleh and Jerusalem. They're
in the Seventh Indian Division, who are *miles* away
from there, beyond Jaffa. I know their colonel
quite a bit, and he started to see me. Came and
spoke to me for a few seconds, but seemed somehow
uncomfortable. All he would say was that they
were doing a route march. Well, they weren't—
not there—though I'm hanged if I know what
they *were* doing. But they are moving troops all
over this Front, night and day.'

'What's the point of all these Aussies coming up
from Jericho now so that no one can see them?'

'But they *have* been seen.'

'By us?'

'Yes. And by a dozen pairs of skulking eyes at
odd points along their course. And remember,
Val, they were marched *down* to Jericho in full
daylight this morning. At any rate, *some* Aussie
regiments were. *I* don't know what's happening,
but something is. And my belief is, they are being
brought up now in order that they *may* be seen, and
reports get back to Jacko. Jacko'll think he's going
to be attacked near here, perhaps just beyond
Ramallah, because his spies have reported Aussie
troopers marching stealthily up from Jordan.
And he'll mass in the wrong place, to find that
we're going to smash through somewhere else.'

'Oh, Martin! I feel as if someone just ought to

stop the whole thing, before it begins—before those men and before the men in France get killed! It's like watching murder done before your eyes and being unable to do a thing to prevent it. I've had a dream like this once—when I knew a child was going to be killed and I was held down by invisible hands and my throat was gagged so that I could not cry out to warn people of what was going to happen.'

'There's nothing we can do, Val. The business has got to be gone through.'

There was at last a gap in the marching troopers. They rose and returned to the city.

XV

AUGUST BROUGHT IN QUICK SUCCESSION, THE EARLIER one having been held up by the Censor, letters from Bunny. Ten days after reaching Taranto, the Brentfords were about to be sent into the line.

' Much the same scenery, and you wouldn't feel you'd been two years away. Not the same dead cow that we had as mess neighbour in 1916, but another of the same kind. Same old rats, only more of them. But we are leaving them very shortly.

'As I guess you have gathered, things are moving. The signs are that we've been fetched over in good time to finish the bloody War—not swearing, Martin; a technical phrase—in a way that will give a bit of style to it. Haig would never be such a fool as to have grand troops like us and not use us. I'll tell you more *après la guerre.*

'Mother writes, "your father and I want you to

bring Martin Chapman here when peace comes."
You'll come, won't you? They'll like you, I'll pledge
my word for that. You'll like them.

'Things go finely with me.'

The War was quickening on the Palestine Front
also. A fortnight after his Olivet walk with Valerie,
Martin had to run out to his old division now
reconstituted out of recognition with untrained
Indian troops in place of those who had gone to
France. He lunched with an artillery unit whose
major lent him a horse and gave him directions
where to find Sellar, formerly of the Brentfords, but
made divisional general's orderly officer some time
before they went, and left behind.

Sellar rode out with Martin to one or two other
nooks where survivals from the Brentfords still
haunted their old home. There was a cheery exchange of greetings and gossip.

On the way back Martin asked Sellar, 'Is there
going to be anything special doing on this Front?'

'No,' said Sellar vigorously.

'You honestly think that?'

'Rather. How could we do anything? We've lost
half our best troops, shipped off to France. We've
only crocks and Indians left, barring the Aussies,
who are cavalry. And we know that cavalry are
finished, so far as modern war is concerned.'

'They why have they kept the Aussies here?'

'God only knows!' said Sellar fervently. 'To
terrorise the civilian population, I expect, and stop
them from rising against us when they see how few
and untrained our infantry are. Anyway, there's
nothing doing—nothing whatever.'

But Martin caught his face as it fell—Sellar was a poor orderly officer—and he said, 'Liar, Sellar!'

So Sellar suddenly looked all round him on the open upland, then said, 'For God's sake don't go spreading it, but something *is* going to happen. You can't have helped noticing that for yourself,' he added and paused.

'Yes. I've noticed it. But I want to know if it's mostly bluff, or if it's going to be anything considerable.'

'From all that I can see—it's going to be something very big indeed—bigger than any of us imagine even now or than we ever thought would be possible on this Front. And now let's drop that matter. Have you heard from Bunny, barring what you told me at first?'

'No. Just the two letters I told you of.'

A week passed; then he saw another portent. Exploring Jerusalem with Wenyon in the afternoon, they found the street leading out to the Jaffa Gate blocked. The Palestinian Jews were being enlisted to join in the fight for liberty and the millennium. A line of unwarlike-looking youths, long-haired and long-trousered, was forging its difficult way to the station. As Wenyon said, it looked extraordinarily like an American major football match, so slowly did it surge forward and with such noise. A yard would be made; and there would be a shout. 'Yakob!' 'Isaak!' A tearful woman, or several tearful women, would rush from the crowd and fling arms round a recruit's neck. The warrior himself would lift up his voice in sympathy. Zion's heights after silent centuries again resounded with the lamentation of an army in distress.

The remarkable scene attracted their attention, as well it might.

'What's up?' asked Chapman.

'Recruiting for the Jordan Highlanders, for the Jewsiliers.'

'Oh, of course! Ass that I was to ask!'

Wenyon whistled, then repeated the current jests as to the new battalion's slogans. 'For skin and country! No advance without security!' He looked quizzically at his comrade. 'It's a queer, mad world, Chapman—mad and bad and sad. I wish I could line up against this, for the sake of artistic contrast, the average tommy's or second-loot's farewells. "Nah then, old girl! don't you take on about nothing!" "Cheerio, Dad!"'

Martin's younger brother, going out to what they both knew was his death, had said only, to his mother, 'We've been chums, haven't we?'

Wenyon continued to philosophise. 'You'd think these beggars were all off to the butcher. Whereas all that will happen is a fat feeding time in Alex or Cairo, a certain amount of alleged training which they will do very badly, thereby causing British casualties by sergeants dead of a broken heart and broken voice, a disbursal of shekels for alleged service, and a return to Jerusalem *après la guerre est fini.*'

'What's the idea?'

'Search me! The cost of the War must have been dropping badly since the Huns mopped up so many of our guns and fellows, so some way of keeping it up has had to be found. We're spending eight millions a day, Chapman, eight millions a day, my boy! Doesn't that send cold shivers down the spine of our Disbursing Officer? *And we could have had a perfectly good war—good enough for you and me, anyhow— for a couple of millions a day.*'

This seemed to Chapman undeniable, and he brooded over it for a minute.

'I suppose we *shall* have to pay for it.'

'Sure thing. You and I will be paying as long as we live, you may bet your boots on that. I've long ceased to care a damn about what happens to the War, so long as they don't ask *me* to go back to the bloody thing. But I'm beginning to get afraid of the Peace—when it comes!'

A wilder wail than ordinary, a fiercer and more despairing rush of more women and more girls at a red-headed man with pinky eyes, arrested them.

Martin said, 'It makes you sorry for these poor devils. If they feel this way about it, obviously it *is* this way for them.'

'If I understand that oracular pronouncement aright, I'm afraid I disagree with it. You wouldn't say that those who *say* nothing *feel* nothing?'

'I suppose not.'

'All right. Call it a difference of technique, if you like. I'm afraid I prefer ours.'

'All the same, I'm sorry for these poor fish. A goodly percentage of my old crowd were sheenies, and they weren't like this. This is what Christendom has made of the best stuff the world ever had.'

Wenyon whistled again. '*Why* Christendom? It was Johnny Turk that had the say here.'

'It was Christendom that sent all its rotten prejudices beating round this city. I'm going from now on to take folk as I find them. And I found White-chapel Jewry a pretty decent thing when I was in a tight place.'

But Wenyon remained unrepentant. 'No advance without security,' he repeated; and seemed to get great satisfaction from the repetition.

'I'm going to forget all this nonsense,' Martin said impulsively, 'and every other kind of nonsense. Come along with me, and I'll see if I can get a couple of absolutely topping girls I know to have tea with us.'

As luck would have it, near the Relief Headquarters, Martin saw Cynthia before she saw him. She was wearing a pith helmet far too large for her; it flung a wide shadow over her face. Caught unawares and off her guard she looked worn and troubled.

Wenyon thought, seeing the undisguised happiness that flashed into this beautiful girl's eyes, that Chapman had not been spending his time to bad purpose.

Martin introduced him, and said, 'Cynthia, fetch Val out, won't you? You two come and have tea with us, after we've had a bit of a stroll somewhere.'

'I'll try, Martin. But Val's so *busy* these days—you know they've shut up the Mount Scopus orphanage and turned the children all over to her?'

Martin did not know. But he renewed his request.

So they went along to Valerie's office, and brought her out. And after she had said that she really could not spare the time, and given excellent reasons for the statement, she weakened and decided that she would come.

'We've heard about you from Martin,' she told Wenyon.

'I've been wondering,' replied Wenyon, 'as to when Martin was going to do the neighbourly and decent thing and introduce me to you two. He wouldn't have done it to-day if he hadn't got so absolutely bored with life in general and me in particular that he was prepared to do anything.'

'I'm sorry you didn't tell us that before,' said Cynthia.

'Why,' said the scandalised Martin, 'it's a whopping lie, Cynthia. Ask him to repeat it, and see him blush.'

Wenyon, confronted by questioning faces, blushed undeniably, and Martin was exonerated.

Wenyon laid himself out to induce cheerfulness in the company, and in Cynthia in especial. At tea he gave them a brief graphic description of the 'Jordan Highlanders' recruiting party. He concluded with his just-coined epigram, which gave him much pleasure. 'And that's one of the reasons why we're paying eight million pounds a day for a War that would be dear at two millions!'

'I'd say it was dear at five cents!' cried Cynthia. She had not yet tumbled to the Englishman's habit of jesting with uncrumpled face and ironic understatement.

Wenyon, the ex-Wadham don, had spent a year at Princeton with a travelling fellowship. The girls rushed at him with questions, and he was very happy.

He foretold a gloomy future for the University of Oxford.

'We shall have to cede it to the States when the War finishes.'

He was asked to be explicit.

'It will be *practical* cession. What's the £ worth now?'

'Well,' said Cynthia, 'we get quite a lot for our dollars. Getting on for nearly twice what we should have got before the War, Miss Ohlsen told me. That's because the rupee and the piastre are tied to the pound.'

'You'll always, from now on, get a lot of pounds for your dollars, Miss Cameron. The result will be that Englishmen after the War won't be able to afford to go to Oxford. But for Americans it will be so cheap that the best people will stay at their own places of instruction; we shall get only those who want the cheapest education they can find. And they'll turn Oxford into a real varsity on the best up-to-date models.'

Valerie soon subsided; and Martin said little while Wenyon made conversation. It was Cynthia, the most actively troubled, who tried to meet her new acquaintance midway. All understood that his purpose was kind. He felt the shadow of some cloud he could not see, and wanted to disperse it.

Valerie wanted nothing but a cup of tea. But having got it, she asked Martin for a cigarette. She had to ask, because she had always refused one when offered. Smoking was still something that 'nice women' did with a considerable degree of awareness of their boldness. But to nerves and energies as tired as hers it was a sedative.

It served another purpose, not consciously admitted. Her 'smoking' was nominal; it was, how-

ever, excuse for ravishing turns outward of the
delicate wrist and fingers, as she knocked off the
slowly accumulated ash in her saucer. Grace and
poise were holding court.

They were not holding it for Martin. Beauty is a
spirit rejoicing in its own existence and clear, sweet
rhythms. Yet she knew that he was watching her
and nothing else in the wide world. She was glad
that she had consented to leave her work and come
to this respite. She found herself sickened of her
routine of ordering meals, overseeing servants and
hearing complaints, looking to this and that orphan's
sickness or clothes, trying to enforce American
standards of cleanliness and decency.

'I'd trust my life with old Puzzlewit!' She had had
glimpses (which imagination, more instructed now,
was beginning to fill out not altogether inadequately)
of some of the experiences that had tested Bunny's
enthusiastic confidence and proved it solid fact. In
the maelstrom where lives were spinning down, and
woman's love was a commodity as cheap as man's
courage, your job could be terrifyingly insubstantial
without knowledge of one person who reversed the
sane and usual order, and set *you*, your happiness
and safety, first, and the ruin of nations in a very
secondary position.

Of course she had no thought of marrying Martin;
so well established was this conclusion, that the
suggestion if it dared to raise its head was discouraged immediately and dismissed without discussion. But she had let herself slip into the way of
accepting his loyalty as the background of her life
and job in Jerusalem.

Martin, meeting her eyes, was rewarded with a

smile of utter sweetness, such as comes only when it comes involuntarily, out of thoughts that are making for rest and peace. He certainly was a darling; and that smile was personal to himself, recognition that he was a friend.

He was given another reward, this time deliberately. For him alone, those beautiful fingers with all the grace that care and languor could give the action, tipped the last ash away from her absurdly smoked cigarette. Then, 'Let me have another, Martin! Please!'

'But what will happen to all the Greek and Latin that they teach at Oxford?' asked Cynthia.

'They'll be dropped, along with dull stupid games like cricket and rugby football, and we shall adopt baseball and real American football. Of course we've no salaries to pay for decent coaches in these games, but we shall amalgamate the stipends of all the outworn subjects that we get rid of, so as to be able to engage at least one tiptop baseball coach and one football trainer. Oxford will never see another Regius Professor of Greek after Gilbert Murray. *He'll* probably be allowed to last out his time, as an interesting survival and because Americans like to see him when they come over. But we shall want his pay, and that of the Professors of all the other dead languages, towards establishing a President Wilson Professorship of Physical Culture.'

Cynthia was serious and puzzled. 'Why, Captain Wenyon! Oxford wouldn't be like Oxford at all, but just like one of our punk universities out West!'

Pennsylvania is "East"; and can look out grimly

and with pursed lips of disapproval, towards the wildness that is "West."

She grew suspicious. 'Did you say you'd *been* to America?'

'Surest thing you know.'

'If you had, you wouldn't think that "surest thing you know" was talking as we do.'

'Honour bright, Miss Cameron!'

'Captain Wenyon,' said Cynthia earnestly, 'do you know a *single* thing as a result, except the bunk you can pick up from English books and newspapers without going to America?'

'Rather. For example, I learnt what is the real bond of union between the different States.'

'Which is, Captain Wenyon?' asked Valerie. Coming from Virginia, she disapproved on principle of being treated with levity, but he might as well be encouraged to lay himself open to the discomfiture he deserved.

'Dislike of Boston,' he said triumphantly. 'For the sheer fun of it I used to quote Boston, East, West, South and North, and was always promptly told that Boston wasn't the States, though it durn well thought it was—that Boston was *not* anything whatsoever that the real America was—that——'

'He's passed, Cynthia. He's been to the States.'

'No,' said an authoritative voice. 'You're wrong. And I'll tell you why.'

'Mere dislike, Wenyon,' Major Blundell explained, 'could not serve as bond of union to any political entity whatever. For dislike is negative, and by its very nature is necessarily disruptive. This was very clearly shown in the quarrel between the Union and the Confederacy. There was dislike there'—he paused to look round on his auditors.

'There certainly was,' said Cynthia, though it was Valerie who thought it.

'Dislike,' repeated the lecturer, 'which had been steadily growing during many years. It began with entirely diverse and often opposed economic and commercial interests, and it was exacerbated by what the South held to be unjustified and uncon-stitutional interference with their mode of life. We have already, you will be interested to hear, the beginnings—*at least* the beginnings; in my judgment, very considerable beginnings—of a centrifugal disposition of sentiment in my own country. In Australia, *already*, Wenyon—please note that I have said *already* and with deliberate emphasis; I am not merely peering into the future, I am inviting your attention to what is actually in being—we have *already* a schism of feeling between New South Wales, the richest and most populous State, and other States, particularly Victoria. It is a matter that in my judgment should be closely watched—very, very closely watched indeed, for it is full of menace for our dreams of a united Australasian Commonwealth. And,' he rose to a climax, indignation giving wings and volume to his voice, 'you, Wenyon, you, who in happier times would be instructing the youth of England in political philosophy and doctrine, *you* maintain that dislike, whose dangerously fissive tendencies I have plainly set out, is a bond of union!'

'Oh, Lord!' said Wenyon.

'I beg of you, do not interrupt. Whatever you have to urge in defence of your singular theory you can state presently. There is a most unfortunate habit which I have noticed among our would-be scholars of the younger school, to turn everything upside down.'

He glared at a waiter, who winced with dread of some unsuspected remissness and hurried up to their table.

'I'm awfully sorry, sir,' said Chapman, remembering. 'I never asked if we could have some fresh tea fetched for you, sir.'

'Thank you, Chapman. Very weak, please. In my judgment—and I am not glancing solely, or even principally, at the British Army when I say this, for the practice of our own Australians is, if anything even worse—tea is made far too strong when it is served in canteens and messes. What was I saying?'

'Why, Major,' said Cynthia maliciously, 'you were saying that Captain Wenyon turned things upside down.'

'Oh, yes. Yes. Our would-be scholars of the younger school turn everything upside down, for the sake of showing their superiority to the wisdom of the ages. Dislike, which is what we were discussing, is a blending of psychological elements that even to a prima facie examination cannot hold any mutual attraction. Let us carefully consider the nature and origins of dislike . . . .'

XVI

WHEN AT LENGTH THEY ESCAPED, CYNTHIA took Martin ahead. As they went to Relief Headquarters she talked in low tones.

'Dad's written about my engagement, Martin. He doesn't understand. He thinks it's just another boy I've met. And he doesn't like the boy being British. He thinks Bunny'll meet some other girl and let me down. Or that it'll mean my living away from Pennsylvania and not seeing him and Mother again. Or my not being happy. What can I say to him, Martin?'

'You can't say anything. You see, he doesn't know Bunny, as you and I know him. It'll be all right, the moment he meets Bunny. Tell him that.'

'I should just say it *would* be all right! Who wouldn't see what an old sweetheart Bunny is? But Dad's all right. He says—and mother says it too—that he trusts me, and knows that whatever I decide is right.'

Her manner, vivacious and swift all through the long boring interlude that had followed tea until they had shaken off the Major, had drooped instantaneously as they left the hotel. Martin, startled, looked into her eyes now, which he had been half afraid to meet. They looked (it suddenly came to him) as if they were used to tears these days. In their shadows was growing up what had never been there before—the image of a watchful, frightened courage, that saw and dreaded a day that was coming. Those shadows also were new.

'Martin, will you do something for me—just as a friend? I was your friend first, you know—I mean, I saw before Val did that we simply had to have you as a pal.'

'But, Cynthia, of course! We *are* friends, you and I, we always shall be friends. There's Bunny, you see——'

o

'Yes,' she said humbly. 'It's because you're Bunny'<
friend that I feel I can ask you to be mine. Bunny
told me that whatever came into my mind I was to
tell you. You haven't any idea how Bunny used to
talk about you, Martin. Will you do something to
help me?'

'I should just think I will.'

'Even if it should make Val mad with you?'

'Of course.'

'Be quiet, Martin! and keep your voice low, unless
you want to be made to pay for it afterwards when
you next try to make up to Val! Do you think it'<
any use pretending to me that you haven't fallen
for Val? And she won't make up her mind what she
wants to do with you or if she wants you at all. But
she jolly well isn't going to let you walk off with an
other girl while she's letting things think themselves
out!'

'But it would be different with you, Cynthia.'

'Well—yes and no. Different up to a point—and
Val would allow it. But I wouldn't assume that
point was so very far, Martin—if that's any comfort
to you.'

It was a great deal of comfort, and Cynthia saw
it in his face.

'Now I've helped you,' she continued, 'which is
why I'm asking you to do something for me. If
you turn me down you can probably get Val to
yourself instead. I know she doesn't want to go in
yet. She hasn't admitted it herself—I know my
Val—but she's got a half-idea of getting you to go
with her while she potters round for another hour
or so. But it's I who need you, Martin. I want your
help. Will you just let me be with you? I can't tell

you why, but it's to-day that I want help more than I can say.'

She had learnt a good deal, and part of it had been to accept a lower estimate of herself. Martin, thrown off his guard by her revelation of what to his obtuseness was a clasped book, Valerie's mind, hovered irresolutely for a moment.

'*Please*, Martin. I'll make it right for you with Val, afterwards. Trust me, Martin.'

'Why, rather! *Of course*, Cynthia! I'd love to come with you. I—I—I was just thinking of what you said about Bunny.'

'Martin, I believe that's the very first lie you ever told. And you've told it to me, which means that I'm a bad influence for you!'

'But, Cynthia, I'd simply love it!'

'Yes. You *might*—*if* you hadn't been told by me that Val had mentally earmarked Martin Chapman to spend this last hour before the sun sets, strolling with her round Jerusalem battlements! But she's only wanting a companion. I'm wanting a friend who'll keep me from being alone with myself. Martin, I just can't stand going in now, to my room where those letters are, letters from Dad who doesn't understand and letters from Bunny who thinks he can keep *me* from understanding. I know I'm booked to go out of my wits one of these days soon. But I'm keeping it from me, Martin, every minute I can.'

'Of course I'll come, Cynthia.'

Wenyon took leave. He had no choice, for the war was swiftly stirring to plunge forward again. This was almost certainly the last day that even Martin, whose job was less exacting than his own, could

take all the hours of afternoon and early evening off.
Confidential papers were coming now, not in
single spies but in battalions; and these really were
confidential, and not a mere waste of time and paper.

Wenyon looked at Martin uncertainly.

'I'll be along at dinner,' said Martin.

Wenyon thought he understood, and went.

Valerie also halted uncertainly, outside her rooms.
Cynthia settled her purpose for her.

'I'm taking Martin with me, Val. My case is the
opposite of that fellow's who let another fellow have
his glass of water. Martin's my glass of water for
to-night, Val; and "My need's greater than thine".'

Valerie coloured up. Then she said with dignity:

'I'm sure I don't want to bother Martin. I hope
you'll both enjoy your walk.'

She went indoors.

'Now, Martin, you're fussing,' said Cynthia, as
she drew his reluctant steps back to the city.

'I don't like Val being annoyed.'

'If you had any sense you'd know that her being
mad with you was the nicest thing that has ever
happened to you. You've seen Val Connett mad
with you, Martin Chapman, because you never
gave her the chance of being magnanimous over
the disposal of your services as escort, but let yourself
be stolen by a vamp like me. You've scored,
Martin.'

Martin did not seem to draw any deep satisfaction
from this assurance. After all, the return move rested
with the stronger player, and he had no reason to
anticipate that it would be played mercifully.

Cynthia laughed merrily. 'To think that I've been
turning down offers of cars and lunches and evening

strolls from pretty well all the commissioned ranks of the British Army! Shall I run over the list of generals and colonels, Martin, that are anxious to be pals with me—we won't bother about anything below a colonel? And then I pick on a mere captain, and he looks wretched!'

'No, I'm not, honestly. Of course I'm not, Cynthia you goose! I only just don't like Val being hurt.'

'Why *shouldn't* she be hurt? She never even suggested to you that you could offer to take her around this evening. She kept rubbing it in when we asked her to come out for tea that she could hardly spare even this bit of time that she *has* spared, and that she must—MUST with big capitals—get back to her orphans' evening meal. But I'll fix everything up, since it was I who "tore things". Honest Injun, Martin! Cross my heart and hope I may die if I'm not being a good girl while I'm saying this to you!'

The Temple area was at peace. The old grey mistletoe-crammed olives gathered into themselves handfuls of the darkness about to cover the world. The ground was still hot from the summer heats; the shrubby herbage was merely sprinkled with flowers. Over Olivet a cloud loomed up and made itself a heart of red smouldering.

They were not tourists, so they could ignore the buildings and speak with the spirit.

'It's what I told you, Martin. I feel I daren't go in to my room and the rooms where we meet and have our meals. The news I know is coming seems to be waiting for me there. It's like the feeling I used to have as a child, when I was left alone in the dark. There's a ghost that's unfriendly there.'

'But that's nonsense, Cynthia, really.'

'It's bound to *seem* nonsense, Martin. I know that. But I *know*, I've got this presentiment, that Bunny's going to be killed. I know it as clearly as if he had told me.'

'Listen, Cynthia. Do you know, every chap who has to go through it gets presentiments? And in nine cases out of ten they come to nothing. I was dead sure before Gaza that my number was up. Well? It wasn't. Bunny's had presentiments himself, though he's not a chap who'll talk about what he thinks, still less about what he fears. But I *know* that before Nebi Samwil he was certain he was going west. He even went so far as to want to divide up his money and things among his platoon, the night before, because he said he'd not want them again. There!'

Hope returned half-heartedly. She listened.

Then, 'What did he actually *do*, though, Martin? He didn't really give everything away as you have said?'

'No. He didn't. But that was only because I told him to stow that nonsense.'

'And nothing happened?'

'Not quite nothing. He stopped one, as it happened. But it was only a flesh wound, in his arm.'

She shuddered, 'And you men talk like that—about things that when the world was sane would have made everyone who knew you be horrified!'

'Well—the world isn't sane any longer. There's no other way to talk, Cynthia.'

'So all I've got to hope for is that Bunny'll be wounded! And I shan't be with him!'

'Cynthia, why should he be wounded? Anyone can see that the whole show is finishing.'

Shadows crept up from the Valley. They rose to go. Passing the Holy Sepulchre, ten minutes later, she said, 'Martin, I just want one last look at this. Do you mind?'

'Why should it be a last look, Cynthia?'

'Because I used to come here with Bunny; he used to say that he liked the place for the very reasons that most people sniff at it, because it is full of all kinds of ragamuffinly ragged dirty superstitious people. He had a fondness for dirty, ragged people. He liked even the fact that Christians quarrelled about it. He said he was sick of the pious peacefulness and good will towards everybody, including those we know are utter skunks, which is considered to be Christian doctrine now.'

'He was a heathen, was Bunny. I did my best for him, Cynthia, but it was no good.'

'You're rather much of a heathen yourself, Martin, aren't you? That's what Bunny used to say about you—"the thing I like about old Puzzlewit is that he's damned good without being in the least Christian." If I were an ordinary girl, I'd have been jealous, the way my boy used to talk about you.'

'Well, *I* used to get jealous, the way you carried him off. Do you realise how precious little you let me see of Bunny all this summer, Cynthia?'

'I know. It was a shame.'

'This place,' she added, 'is mine and Bunny's. After to-night I'll never come here again—because I used to come here with him.'

The building was in a twilight of sound as well as sight; two or three voices came hushed from recesses. Candles were being lit.

They moved round silently, watching the half-dozen worshippers kissing sites where the cross had been, where Our Lord's body had been set down, where Adam's skull had been touched to life again.

A Russian peasant woman, a leper, was dragging her painful way up the steps of Calvary. She was sobbing, as she pulled her limbs one after another, kissing the steps in an ecstasy of devotion.

It was here that Cynthia broke down. 'Martin!' she said, gripping his arm as she cried convulsively and angrily, 'What has God done all these centuries, to deserve the love He gets from men and women? What has He ever *done?* Oh, Martin! *Martin!*'

She recovered as quickly and suddenly as she had given way. 'When I saw that poor ragged wretch of a woman—who hasn't had a single thing out of life except the right to serve others and to suffer—I was mad. I felt as if God were a fraud and a humbug! He takes things He has no *right* to take, and He takes them in such a lordly way. He doesn't care!'

When she left Martin she was mindful of her promise. 'I'll make things right for you with Val.'

He lingered uncertainly.

'No. Don't try to see her now, Martin. Trust me, that I understand a girl better than you do. She'll be all right to-morrow, even if at first she should pretend that she isn't. Good night, Martin. You've been a brick to me.'

'Good night, Cynthia.'

Val, enthroned on one of the ridges of Zion in her new orphanage, had her meals alone, except that Cynthia almost more often than not used to come in to share them. It was after supper that Cynthia came this evening.

She swept straight to the attack. 'Val, you're treating Martin pretty meanly.'

It was Valerie's turn to open eyes widely. 'Oh!' she said coldly.

'Now don't get high hat to me about it! You once called me down about Bunny, and you were right. So I'm calling you down about Martin.'

'So *that* was why you and he went off together!'

'No. It wasn't.'

'You went, anyway.'

'Yes. And why should *you* worry? You haven't ever bothered to make up your mind about him, whereas I made up mine long ago, that I want him as a pal.'

'Well——' (uncertainly) 'I like him as a pal too. There's a lot that's very nice about Martin.'

'Then think about that a bit longer, till you make up your mind. For *I* can have him as a pal but you can't.'

'Why can't I have him as a pal—if you can?'

'You know why, Valerie Connett. He's yours body and soul, and you know it, which is why you treat him as you do.'

'I like Martin' said Valerie thoughtfully. 'I think he's a darling, in his slow, honest way.'

'He's not so slow. Bunny used to say, "I call him Puzzlewit and the name's stuck. But there's nothing puzzlewitted about him. You saw him play cricket, Cynthia." And I said, "Stow cricket, Bunny. I don't understand cricket." And he said, "All right. All I know is, I've had to take over the company twice in the midst of really bad shows, because of casualties up top. And each time it hasn't been one of our clever little boys that I've picked for a bit of nasty work, it's had to be Martin".'

'That's very interesting. But you see, Cynthia, I'm not in love with Martin.'

'Then let me tell you, you're being jolly mean. If you're not in love with him you ought to stop being pals with him.'

'Do *you* intend to stop?'

'I should say not. But we're different. Martin's going to be my pal for life, if I have any say in it. But *you* ought to tell him that you're through with him.'

'I suppose some people might think I ought.'

'But you aren't going to?'

'I really think this is *my* business, and no one else's.'

'Shall I tell you what's wrong with you, Val?'

'I'm afraid I'm not interested.'

'Val, you old sweetheart, don't get mad with me! I like Martin and I'd trust my life with him,' she said, echoing Bunny's words. 'And you know I've been just crazy about you ever since we met.'

'That's all right, Cynthia. You know that I'm just as fond of you as I could be. But I don't see why I should marry Martin because I like *you!*'

'I never said you should. I only said that you have no right to like Martin and to keep him miserable. You think I've been spoiled. I expect I have. But haven't *you* been a bit spoiled too? I suppose every Virginny girl thinks she ought to be wooed by a lover who's a General Stuart, all feathers and fine moustache and prancing round and round all kinds of bewildered Yankees!'

It was here that Val made her mistake. 'I don't know what my people would think of Martin,' she said questioningly to herself.

'Val!' said Cynthia, scandalised. 'You *shabby*—
little—cat! Martin's not twenty-three, and he's been
through things that make anything that's happened
in our time in America seem a picnic! You've got a
boy crazy about you and ready to worship the
ground you walk on, a boy who's had simply *blazed*
into him all the pluck and experience and sense that
doesn't come to one man in a thousand in his *whole
life!* And he's got fire and keenness and absolute
straightness and loyalty and—and—every decent
thing a man could have. He hasn't got the adorable
boyishness of my own man, I grant you that. But I
never met another but Bunny who had. Besides,
Martin is older than Bunny—he's lots older. But
he's got a swing that Bunny says told him Martin was
a crackerjack at games, the moment he met him.
He says that that first night when they met together
as recruits in England he picked out this fellow
because he looked so like a man, every inch a man.
Have you noticed the way his eyes wrinkle up with
laughing, when Bunny's ragging him and he's trying
to pretend not to see?'

Valerie *had* noticed it. But she chose not to confess
this.

'Your people—by the way, what are your people?'
asked Cynthia, who knew very well.

'They are an old Virginian family,' said Valerie
with dignity.

'Great democrats, aren't they? I suppose Patrick
Henry was an ancestor of yours? Also George
Washington? And the rest of the great Virginian
democrats? They made their money out of planta-
tions, didn't they? Or was it out of slaves? So Martin
Chapman, who isn't one of the idle swell British

fox-hunting class, but is merely a boy who has gone through four years of hell and made no fuss about it, isn't good enough for them to look at!'

Val got really angry. As she stood up ready to blaze back, though uncertain what she could say, it was a different Cynthia who confronted her.

'Val, you darling thing, I've made you mad again! And I never meant to! It's only—only that I seem to see things now that *you* can't see—things that I never dreamed existed. Anyway, all I meant to do was to tell you not to be mad with Martin because I took him off with me to-day. I told him I'd make it right for him with you.'

'Oh! you told him that, did you?'

'Why, Val! I simply *had* to have him to talk to! You see—oh, Val, you know what's happening in France.' And Cynthia, overwrought by her own suppressed wretchedness and by the sight of Valerie's anger now, burst into tears. Valerie, melted in a moment, threw her arms round her and cried too.

'Anyway,' sobbed Cynthia, persistent, 'are you going to do the straight thing by Martin and send him away?'

'No,' said Valerie. 'Leave me alone, Cynthia.'

XVII

I

MEANWHILE, ON OLIVET'S SUMMIT MARTIN, TOO, WAS receiving ghostly counsel. The day had been one of change and shuffling. The calm sea of war as it lay in this sheltered nook was indubitably being agitated and shaken. No one in Martin's mess felt certain that his place would be here, twenty-four hours hence. The cricket match against the Third Indian Division on Saturday was scratched. This was an omen, for the Division's commanding officer was keen on his team and on their playing.

After dinner Wenyon took Martin off to his den. He offered him a cheroot. 'Have one while you can. This may be our last smoke together on Olivet.'

'Why?'

'Why? Listen, Martin! You shall hear Caleb Wenyon prophesy. There's a damned big show coming.'

'I know. Allenby's going to try another push across Jordan.'

'Allenby's going to—*what?*'

Martin repeated, this time less certainly.

'Allenby is *not*. The Bull'—a soubriquet of the Palestinian commander, deserved both by voice and by thrusting dogged qualities—'ran into trouble enough the two other times to remember it. No, Martin my boy. The push is going to be in the right place. Up the coast. And you'll be in it.'

'I wish to God I thought I should, Wenyon.'

Wenyon looked at him hard. 'Forgive me for being intrusive and personal and all that. But why this pessimism and thirst for sudden extinction, in one so young? I'd rather had the idea that you had been having an uncommon good time with us.'

'Rather! It's been frightfully jolly. You fellows are the cheeriest crowd I've struck.'

'Not so much to make us *un*cheery, is there? War's not so bad when it's waged on Olivet. But what I meant was—I rather thought, Martin, that you had struck pleasant company in Jerusalem?'

Martin went very red. 'You mean, those girls I introduced you to?'

'Yes. I thought them the most charming I'd met for many a long day. I'm an old bachelor, Martin. But you know, I often think I've been an old fool as well! Let me give you a bit of advice, and you won't take offence, will you?'

'Of course I won't. Especially from you. I don't know what I'd have done without you since I came here, Wenyon.'

'Pretty much what you've done *with* me,' said Wenyon, who naturally overestimated the time Martin had managed to get with Valerie. 'Martin, why don't you make that girl promise to marry you?'

'I wish I could.'

'You mean you've asked her?'

Martin nodded. 'She's no use for me.'

'If you ask me, I think she's got a great deal of use for you. Though she mayn't have discovered it herself yet.'

Martin was silent. Then, 'I've *practically* asked her, I mean.'

'Practically be damned! Ask her outright—actually and factually, outrageously, overbearingly. Ask her, you idiot! Tell her she's *got* to do it.'

'She won't let me, Caleb.'

'What! How can she stop you?'

'She says it'll spoil our friendship and end it for good.'

'She's as American as all that, is she? Take my advice, and spoil your friendship and end it for good. You do like her, don't you?'

'I worship her,' said Martin simply.

'Forgive me. I asked a silly question. Naturally anyone would *like* her. It wouldn't be necessary to *see* her even. She's got a voice that's the nearest thing to music outside a forest of nightingales—or a tumble of brooks in midsummer. You see how poetic she makes even an Oxford don! But you were the fellow who found her first, worse luck! Go in and win!'

'She sometimes pretends to be apologetic about her American accent—as if there were the least things she need be apologetic about!' said Martin, kindling with the knowledge that he need not hide his praise.

'There's no such thing as "an American accent", Martin Chapman. There are twenty different American accents, just as there are twenty different British accents. And some of them are the vilest and cruellest cacophony, and the world's going to be hounded crazy with them. But *there are others*!'

'I should say there are!'

'Others, Martin, that are wandering music which you wish might never finish and might move more slowly still. And your girl's got one of the loveliest sorts. Why don't you do as I say?'

'I've told you. It would end our friendship.'

'Speaking at a venture,' said Wenyon slowly, 'I'd say that was bluff, and I'd call it.'

'Suppose it isn't? I'd lose her.'

'If it isn't, you're going to lose her for good some day. And it'll be all the worse when you do lose her, if you let things go on and on, and allow her to think you're contented to be just pals. You haven't worried her enough. She doesn't think you're desperate. You've let her do all the bowling. Try a turn yourself.'

'You know,' said Martin, suddenly confidential, 'she came over Olivet with me in moonlight, and it was then that I learnt what a pal she could be. No man could have talked better than she did—it wasn't just sentimental stuff about the mountain and about the things fellows generally get from girls.'

'Yes,' said Wenyon dryly.

'Well—you know what I mean.'

'I know that, on your admission, she went over Olivet with you in moonlight—just as a mere pal, of course! She did *that*! Went over this glorious mountain with a promoted foot-slogger like you—like myself! An oread familiarly with an ordinary British infantry captain!'

'That's just the trouble! I'm a bit *too* ordinary for a girl like that!'

'Ass!'

'It's true, Wenyon.'

'An ex-don can't tell you properly what an ass you are. I wish your charming friend Remfry were here! The case calls for one of the brutal and licentious, one of the free in speech and morals. I'm now a sober staff-walla.'

'But, Caleb!'

'But, Martin! But, Chapman! Don't you know that a girl like yours—yes, I'm going to speak of her as yours—doesn't make up her mind about a fellow *by himself*? She isn't going to hand herself over to a chap simply because of his *looks*? He's got to come with some poetry about him.'

'And where the devil am I going to get that?'

'You've got it! To the end of time you're the man who went over Olivet with her in moonlight.'

'She was an angel!' said Martin to himself.

'Quite so. But you—you were the man who was with the angel. The man the angel trusted. The man she knew wouldn't spoil even Olivet in moonlight for her. Do you know, Martin, I think I've gone crazy about this country! I believe I'd be an out-and-out Zionist, saying that it belonged, just as a woman does, to the one who cares most for it, and that the Jews ought to have it since they've kept it as their dream for all these ages of years—if only the Zionists wanted it for decent purposes! But they merely want it as so much soil for intensive kitchen gardening. Jordan isn't Jordan to them—not Jordan the Descender, the rushing two hundred miles of paradisal river, racing from snowy Hermon and coming from Galilee—my God! what a passage for a few million gallons of ordinary mortal water! They don't care a damn about that divine valley with its steel-blue sea! The Dead Sea to them is nitrates, the Jordan is electric power for their damned factories, Haifa and Carmel are to be the pipe-line finish and rows of fat houses for fat, objectionable folk. If they could, they'd wipe out the river and sea altogether, and send the Mediterranean up the Leontes and down the Valley all the way to the Red Sea. Have you read the impious proposals they've been making? I'm glad I shall never see Palestine again after this War ends. It'll be my Yarrow Unvisited to the end of this incarnation. I'd hand the land over like a shot if it meant handing it over to Isaiahs and New Testament fishermen. But—oh, my God! Chapman, you know what it does mean! Let's forget it.'

'It's not a thing one *can* forget.'

'No. It isn't. Worse luck! I tell you what, Chapman,

P

you and I in some ways are the luckiest generation
that ever lived—in other ways the unluckiest. We
were old enough to know what the earth was like
before the machine had actually finished it for bad
and all; and we were young enough to have a share
in the finest and bravest adventure that men were
ever in. I wouldn't swap *our* Men of Marathon—
that's you and I, Chapman, among some few
millions of others—for the Athenian Men of Marathon. We were *in it*. And in this new damnable
detestable post-War world that I foresee and hate
already we shall feel like men who wish they had
died! Do you remember your Latin?'

'Not very much, I'm afraid.'

'What did you read? Virgil, of course?'

'I liked Virgil.'

'Remember that passage in the very first book of
the *Æneid*, when Juno arranges for that storm and we
get *Æneas's* lament that he had been allowed to
survive when all his pals—better men than himself
—had been allowed to go west?'

Martin did remember. It had struck him at the
time as showing something of 'a yellow streak' (all
that fuss for so little!) and yet as magnificent in its
eloquence of grief.

'Its poignancy comes home to me many and many
a time, when I'm looking forward—as one may begin
to do now, at last—to taking up the life of peace
again.' And Wenyon quoted, rising to go as he spoke:

' *Ubi tot Simois correpta sub undis*
scuta virum galeasque et fortia corpora volvit.

Diomed, first of Greeks in fray
Why pressed I not the plain that day—

that day when you or I were in the tight corner,
Martin, when we never expected to get out and yet
did get out, though better fellows got done in. Listen!

> " *Why* pressed I not the plain that day,
>   Yielding my life to thee?
> Where, strewn beneath a Phrygian sky,
> Fierce Hector, tall Sarpedon lie——"

Good Lord!'—looking at his wrist watch—'I ought
to have fled long ago! I began this excellent lecture
with the remark that this would be our last smoke
together on Olivet. I predict that within twenty-four
hours you'll be sent back to the sphere where you
so greatly distinguished yourself before, and will
get just about a fortnight in command of a company
in the line before the big push comes. Anyone can do
your present alleged job. But they're very short of
experienced infantry officers. By the way, how's your
Arabic been getting on?'

'Not too brilliantly, I'm afraid.'

'I—see. Other engagements. But you could order a
drink, at a pinch? Or tell a noble Arab to *imshi*[1]
damn quick? Austin-Gary was asking me, and I told
him I was sure you could do that much; and he said
it was all that would be needed. Listen. How far
do you imagine the Bull's going to try to get
this time?'

'Haifa? Nablus perhaps?'

'Damascus, Martin.'

'Gosh!'

'Don't bother me with meaningless interjections,
but " *Think*, Abib (*dost* thou think?) "! That'll mean

[1] Clear off.

a whole lot of new occupied enemy territory, for
which they'll need politicals. General Money's told
Austin-Gary pretty much the place where he'll be
sent if all goes according to plan. Austin-Gary will
need a deputy, and means to wangle it that a certain
promising Arabic scholar with a distinguished
career in the fighting ranks and considerable athletic
prowess shall be that deputy. He's told Money that
you are a whale at Arabic.'

'May he be forgiven! But Austin-Gary's a brick!'

'You don't even now seem to have tumbled to the
implications of what I've been laboriously telling
you. What was it your charming young barbarian
friend used to call you?'

'Martin Puzzlewit.'

'The name was nicely chosen. Don't you see, O
Martin Puzzlewit, that out of our temporary politicals—the good young subalterns who have learned
the lingo understanded of the noble Arab—they'll
have to make afterwards a permanent political
service for this divine country? You can stay on
here—you can ride through the orange-groves dis-
pensing justice between noble Arabs and noble
Hebrews. You can take that heavenly girl with you.
You can go partridge-shooting. You can slaughter
roe-deer and gazelles. And you'll be a happy
splendid English gentleman, Martin Puzzlewit. And
when your boys have gone through their excellent
prep. school and excellent public school, send them
up to excellent Wadham. There'll be a stooping old
dominie there who'll bore them with blather about
the time when he was young with their father in the
Holy Land.'

Martin's batman entered.

'Message from Signals, sir. For Captain Chapman, sir.'

Martin read with the numb despair with which one reads of poignant sorrow that is ancient history. No one could have supposed it could be otherwise. 'Remfry killed attack eighth deepest regret whole regiment—Barrett.'

II

He had one last service of friendship to render. By that cable the Head asked him to do it.

'I've got to see Miss Cameron,' he said, handing the telegram across. 'It's a rotten show for her.'

'You'll not drive yourself, Martin.'

'Yes,' said Martin. He was not thinking.

'I'll send my batman with you. He's a good driver.'

'Mine's all right. I've often taken Bennett with me. Get the car out, Bennett, will you,' he said.

'Very good, sir.'

When he had gone out, Wenyon spoke.

'Martin!'

Martin looked up.

'There's nothing to say—except that it's rotten and that I know what this means for you.'

'No. That's right. Many thanks, Wenyon. It's rottenest for her.'

'You're wise to go and see her now. She'll have a night to begin to get it over.'

'She won't get it over, Wenyon.'

He drove first to Valerie's place. It was late, close on ten o'clock, but she would probably still be up. She came out looking startled. Yet not altogether surprised. One glance, however, told her that her thought was mistaken. For once Martin, looking at her, was not thinking of her.

'Bunny's killed,' he said. 'Will you help me tell Cynthia?'

She put on a wrap and hurried out. They drove to the Relief headquarters.

She came out, ten minutes later, and told him. 'Cynthia says she won't see you now, Martin. She wants me to thank you. Her actual words were, "Tell Martin that I thank him—for *everything*". She says, will you see her to-morrow—whatever time suits you best. I'm going to spend the night here. Good night. And thank you very much.'

That was all.

At the end of Herod's later wall, on its way to Mount Scopus the road twists sharply left and dips into the Valley's upper end. Martin stopped the car.

'You go on alone, Bennett. I'm going to walk back across the Valley.'

'Very good, sir.'

'My best pal's just been killed in France, Bennett.'

'Yes, sir. Captain Wenyon told me, sir. I'm sorry, sir.'

'He was engaged to the girl that lady and I called on. It's a bad business for her.'

'It's the way it happens. It's been a rotten thing, this War, sir.'

This seems an inadequate summary. Yet Martin knew and understood its eloquence. There was nothing you could say except this, that it was *rotten*. There was no soundness in it anywhere.

'I want to keep moving, not sit still and think. Good night, Bennett.'

In the Valley's heart he halted in a ring of old olive-trees. It was a dark night, but he was surrounded by glow-worms. It deepened his loneliness, to be in the midst of these ghostly lamps.

It came to him that this—and not the garden which the monks have walled in and keep (a very lovely garden, with its balsams and verbenas and hollyhocks, and rosemary for remembrance)—was the true Gethsemane. The aboriginal olives were here, lonely in their spine-clambered rocks.

He had never thought of glow-worms and Gethsemane together.

A lykewake was being held, with those glassy green candles round the dead past of two boys who had been friends.

Either side towered, blacker shadows in the dimness, the grandest city Time has seen or shall see, the holiest hill on earth. Midnight had found between them a quiet place of glow-worms and gray-leaved bushes.

Christ used to spend such nights here. This was the Garden of the Agony.

'Dear Jesus Christ,' prayed Martin, 'my friend, my friend Warren Remfry, who was the bravest and most decent and lovely fellow that ever lived, is dead. And he'll be all that, wherever he is, death can't have made any difference to him. But'—and a gush of tears came blindingly—'it's the damnedest shame that ever happened. It's rotten and foul and *filthy* —it's just damnable, and there's no other word for it. Please help Cynthia and Bunny's people at home. And oh God! it's a hateful thing to have happened. There was Henry went, in that rotten way beyond Jordan, where we simply had to leave him to die —I *had* to leave him, because there was nothing else that I could do. And now Bunny's gone, just when everyone can see that the War is finishing. If it had been me it wouldn't have made any difference except to about three people. But I've been having a soft time on Olivet, and Bunny's had to die.'

He did not know why he had been talking aloud, except that here he felt not out on the wide hillside but in a shut circle of spirits that listened and understood. It helped him to have spoken. There was sympathy somewhere; his words had been approved.

The glow-worms shone on steadily. His glance suddenly fell on a queer semi-circle, a half-moon of insects shining about a tiny mound. He stooped to the mound, curious; handled and lifted it; and found it was the cricket ball that they had lost, when Bunny had swung his muscles far out and superbly towards the Valley. This silent witness had been waiting here, hidden and secret, until this hour when it should testify to his friend! The absurd chance awed him as nothing had ever done. The passing into dust and oblivion of that lovely, eager body had not been blind accident, it had been foreseen, an event set and registered even on that happy afternoon on Olivet, when he and Valerie and Bunny and Cynthia had first made friends.

The day came back with all its vivid, laughing memories, He saw again the divinely nonchalant swing and tiny swagger of Bunny going to the place where his bowler's run began, the easy, swift, purposeful racing back and the arm coming over while the whole body released from that deed grew instantaneously watchful for another. He saw him pulling on sweater and blazer, when his glorious stay at the wickets was ended; and thrusting hands deep into pockets to look as aggressively stocky and commonplace as possible—their ridiculously boyish Bunny! He was back in that delighted admiring group—the decent old buffer of a brigadier was congratulating them both, they were both looking as modest as only the true Olympians can, Cynthia was purring her ecstatic pleasure, Valerie——

No one would see that group again, as no one would again, though the world go on for ever, see Bunny taking up the ball and placing his field, and then sending in those superb in-swingers that came with his arm; or see him making that rattling shot of his that raced through the covers as if it came from a gun, not from a bat. The mould was broken. There are a thousand ways in which athletic youth creates out of dust and time's dying the illusion of living beauty, as there are a thousand ways in which the same dear illusion incarnates itself in a girl's celestial grace. No two ways are the same or remotely resembling. He picked up the ball and took it back.

It was past midnight when he reached his billet, to find another message from Signals. Captain Chapman was to report within twenty-four hours to a battalion in the 54th Division, which was serving against the central mountain massif of Ephraim. He was to be in the big push, as Wenyon had predicted. His days on Olivet were over.

XVIII

His car could be kept for one last service, taking him to his new unit, the Colchesters. Austin-Gary readily lent a driver to bring it back.

He hurried through breakfast, left his batman to pack his kit, motored into Jerusalem; and saw the girls together. Then he told them he was going.

'They've posted me to the 54th Division, to the Colchesters. They're in the line, nearer the coast.'

Cynthia held up no longer. Tears returned, in a burst of indignation and agony. 'Then there is going to be fighting again, as everyone says!'

'I want to be in it. I don't care about stopping on Olivet any longer. I'd rather have something to do that will give me a chance of being a man and not have any time for thinking.'

The accidental cynicism passed unnoticed by any of them.

'Your going's the end of our life here, Martin.'

'I suppose so, Cynthia.'

'I want you to go. I want everything to break up. You and Bunny came to us together. That doesn't mean that I don't want to see you again, dear Martin. I shall always want to see you, as long as I live. You'll always be in my memory as the nicest bravest boy I ever met, except—except——'

Her tears were flowing again. He said hastily, 'I know, I know, Cynthia. And I'll always think of you in the same way, you know that.'

'Of course I know it. You'll let me write to you,
Martin. And when I come to England, I want to
see you. I hope you'll have—luck, Martin.'

They were in a sequestered quadrangle shaded
with pepper trees; steps went up into the Relief
Force building. Her impulsive affection taking him
by surprise, she kissed him, and took his hand and
pressed it to her breast. 'There, Martin, you darling
pal! Good-bye. And remember, we're *friends*!' She
ran swiftly up the steps and into the house. He heard
that she was crying.

Val and he were alone. She had been present
through a scene where she had not counted, had
hardly been noticed.

He looked at her with wretchedness and pity in his
face. 'It's been a rotten business, Val.'

'Too rotten for words.'

Valerie, unseeing, imaginative, wrapped up in
her own world and dreams, for the first time saw
into his mind. Startled, she *knew* that if Bunny had
not been killed he would have come to her now as
her lover. She knew, too, that he was not going to
say one word of that.

He stood there, this queer, serious Martin, watching
with his whole soul, as Martin did. He was weighing
her worth, not as that absurd verb might imply,
but as a worshipper, and for once she felt slight and
trivial enough, although—no, because—she saw,
beyond all chance of question, how perfect she was
in his eyes. It was like a scene out of old-world
poetry—not Martin Chapman whom she had half-
feared her folk might find laughable in his more
than New England earnestness and rigid goodness,

but a knight of the antique time turning from the lady of his devotion. 'I love thee purely—as men turn from praise': the line of that woman who knew how such men as Martin feel and act flashed through thought. He was not going to say how deeply, dearly he loved her, because of his friends, the dead boy and Cynthia. She read deeper yet, to the thought that had come without thinking. He was going to make no claim on her, because he was 'going to the wars', not to wars that were half frolic but to wars where men died.

In that moment she knew that if he had asked her to marry him she was nearer to the necessity of accepting him than she had ever thought she would be. She knew also, even had he known this (as he did not) he would not have spoken. If you want to analyse this obstinacy you will find no name for its reason except a word that will not serve, it is so stained with man's conventions, whereas the thing it expresses is the freest, most spontaneous feeling in the world—delicacy. Martin would not take her if the manner of the taking lost any the least portion of the love and respect of his friends—the dead boy and Cynthia. Valerie, too, in the pang with which she saw that now, when she might (she was not certain) have listened, he was going to leave without speaking, was exultantly glad. If he had seized his chance, it would have been not Martin but another man usurping his opportunity, and she would have lost Martin for ever.

His voice came, after what seemed ages. 'Good-bye, Val. It's been the most wonderful thing that ever happened, this friendship between Cynthia and you and us.'

'Good-bye, Martin. And good luck! Don't think it hasn't mattered to us, to have been friends with you.'

Why did this moonlit dream swim up, of tired men on tired horses slowly filing past Gethsemane? She and Martin had looked on, awed and detached, as at some sorrow so fixed by fate that in all but the technicality of very deed it had already happened. Those men, Martin had said, were to go through it; they were riding there as if in vision, who were appointed to die on some Palestine meadow. That vision was no longer a frieze; Martin was passing into it.

Thought changed sharply, instantaneously. She wanted to fling wide her arms to Martin and ask him to speak and to say what lived in the core of his mind all his moments. She could not let him go thus—he was going to his death, as Bunny had gone! And he was going, thinking her indifferent.

But it was Martin who spoke.

'Good-bye, Val. I'll be seeing you again, you and Cynthia, wherever you are in Palestine. I'll wangle leave enough for that.'

She wanted to ask him to 'be careful', as a mother asks a child who is off on a fishing expedition. She saw the absurdity of the impulse. 'Good luck again, Martin.'

'I shall get it,' he said confidently. 'I always do. Cheerio, Val.'

'Cheerio.'

XIX

HE WAS WITH HIS NEW UNIT FIRST IN THE PERIOD O
intense concentration with which Allenby prepared
his smashing blow. He came to it as a stranger to a
group of intimates, and lived in the inevitable
isolation of the man who has come to a group of
comrades. He came as a company commander
and found it queer to be 'sir' to so many of his own
age, as well as to young men who were older.

Rarely have troops fought on a front so loosely
strung as this one. In Mesopotamia you had the one
communication, by way of Tigris; six months in
the country, and you seemed to have met everyone,
if not up the line then at Ashar Barracks Mess in
Busra or on a P-boat (there never was such comradeship elsewhere as in Mesopotamia, cemented
by such grim humour). In France, movement
and thoughts alike were related to England. But
in Palestine you were merely part of a fan flung
widely open. You had no cross communication
and no central home.

So in these three weeks when the hammer-blow
were prepared experience was of many kinds
according to where you were. Left in Jerusalem
you became a limpet, stranded by war's sudden ebb
which had simply shrunk away from you, you had no
idea where.

The crash was said to be gathering in the Jordan
Valley, an uncomfortable thought if you were in it
Everyone knew that the real Army (the Anzac
excepted) had been switched across to France, so

that the attack would have to be made with inadequate forces.   Allenby would descend without
warning—troops would be moved quickly down that
ghastly track to Jericho—we should climb the
embattled hills beyond. This did not explain why
Allenby was fooling and fussing so now in the Valley
with this business—yes, it was 'business' in the low
comedy sense; the word was inspired—of making
half a dozen chaps drive low sledges drawn by mules
and create the dust of a vast cavalry movement,
bringing down on them angry bombardments. This,
one saw, was bluff. But bluff for what? There were
other preparations that could not be bluff—raids
that cost lives, registration of guns, elaborate and
vindictive shooing of civilians and especially Arabs
to a distance from the Valley. Undoubtedly a push
was coming against those impossible crags, and you
would be in a forlorn hope, sacrificed to help the
men in Flanders!

Along the mountain line of Palestine proper, from
Jerusalem to the Sea, a happier excitement lived.
By God! but something was up, though the Bull
was not letting on precisely what. Day was elaborately   filled   with   marches,   time-wasting   and
pompously brief: night, with swift workmanlike
countermarches back, twice as far as you had come
by night. Troops were hidden in groves of orange
and olive, all through the blazing hours lying as
close as a lion that does not want to be disturbed.

Merrow, the Colchesters' Adjutant, impressed on
Martin the need to see to 'morale'. There was an
idea that the new company commander from Corps
H.Q. was a novice in war. It was quickly found

that he was not. His men found it out the first day,
and settled down under an officer quietly efficient
and at the same time aware that the private is a
person with feelings, possibly capable even of thought
and of self-respect. The citizen soldier made himself
feared under Cromwell. He was of some use in the
Great War also. Martin was the citizen soldier, who
is no soldier except when fighting is forward. His
former service, like his present, was with a territorial
battalion.

That a storm was beating up the enemy could
no longer doubt. Its beginnings blinded him.

When Martin joined his unit, Turkish planes still
ventured timidly across our lines. But British planes
swept up arrogantly and in whelming force, struck
them down and drove them helter-skelter back.
Every appearance of a Turkish plane was the signal
for a fury of concentration against it. In the last
fortnight before the Battles of Sharon and Ephraim
opened, only four enemy planes appeared. In that
fortnight the woods and coppices, pressed into
service, were cover to the stealthy creeping forward
of the lion about to spring.

Martin saw the very last Turkish feat in the air.
A drove of four planes miraculously appeared and
made for the foremost of two kite balloons. Every
archie was set upon them, a fleet of planes swung up
to engage them. When the whole sight and strength
of opposing Mars was occupied this one way, out of
the unseen heaven, no one knew from what dizzy
altitude, pounced nose head-long a fifth enemy plane,
that righted itself and raced pitilessly at the balloon.
Its machine gun spat, the balloon went up in flames.
Still racing onward, it repeated destruction with the

second balloon. Then in sight of four watching
British divisions the victor lifted himself out of sight
and returned to safety. From miles of Palestine hillside cheers resounded, gladness that so gallant a foe
had escaped after working our harm so cleverly.
No one (so unjust is the mind of man, preferring to
watch skill and valour than mere misfortune) did
more than note two observers falling under para-
chutes through the air, one to break a leg, the other
to crash on a tall oak and lose an eye.

The world was waking from its numbness. After
years of communiqués assuring you that 'our infantry
yesterday raided the enemy successfully, taking
prisoners' or that 'the Italians advanced on a front
of fifty yards south of Gorizia'(again taking prisoners)
—after the torment of the spring during which the
German thrust had smashed armies and captured
guns by the many hundred and men by the hundred
thousand—came at last news of victories, real
victories and unbelievable advance.

Then your eyes, gazing tear-filled at sunrise in the
West, were caught elsewhere. We had lost Gallipoli;
we had failed before Salonika; Serbia and Roumania
had been broken. Without warning came this word
of Bulgaria defeated and suing for armistice. You
clamoured for more news sheets, every hour of every
day of this wonderful week which no one who lived
through it can forget. We *lived* then. And no one
knows what is in this word *lived*, unless he endured
the death-in-life which preceded it.

The British-Indian-Anzac Army in the Holy Land
stood to, men's minds waiting for zero hour. Officers
appeared at the Fast and Grand Hotels in Jerusalem,

Ω

unceremoniously turned adrift guests and servants
commandeered the accommodation ostentatiously
'for General Allenby and his Staff.' Spies fleeing
ghostlike over the haunted hills and up the dangerou
rift of Jordan carried the news to the enemy. H
also stood to, his eyes on his defences of the river and
the crags that kept apart British and Arabs. He wait
ed for the dawn to show him his foes once more
striking at the desolate hills where their assault had
already twice been shattered.

Martin's brigade had orders to attack at 4.45 on
the morning of September 19. Canteens of tea would
be up at 3.30 a.m. C Company's three-weeks
experienced commander went round his lines, seeing
that the hinges of his diminutive section of the Wa
were oiled and smoothly working.

It was ten o'clock, and his Company had turned in
for such sleep as they could get. There had been the
usual desultory shooting; a muffled explosion in the
hills over there; an arc of flaming light followed
quickly by another and a third; a Very star going
up and turning over and scattering into sparks
No, there had not been quite this usual desultor
shooting. That was the queer, disquieting thing
there had been much less than usual. Mars had no
been at his uneasy grumbled muttering in sleep; th
creature was so still that if you were awake you fel
that he was awake also and brooding mischief.

To Martin's right crashed out what he knew wa
the beginning. The Welshmen of the 53rd Division
moved to the assault. All through the darkness the
were storming the heights that overlook Jordan
The eyes of the enemy, tense with anxious straining

lifted and were turned this way. It was the start of that thrust beyond Jordan that he was sure was coming! His energies and his fears were focused.

Martin did the natural thing. He had been lying down in a trench; he rose and peered to where the arcs of flame were jumping and vanishing. And the impulse stirred to comment on it to Bunny. 'The taffies are off the mark on time,' he said aloud.

The reality of his friend beside him, as he had been on so many eves of battle such as this, had been overpowering. He had been so sure of that warm, friendly, laughing presence, so vivid when death was threatening (the high disdain of the English scorning to give the monster the tribute of any notice except derision), that he had spoken without thinking. No question had come. Question came now. To whom had he been speaking?

This boy not yet twenty-three had more friends among the dead than he would ever have among the living, though he should die full of years. He had shared in four years of such comradeship as men will never know again. Five months ago he had been a subaltern among friends, his worth known and approved, his respect and affection valued. Now he was a company commander among men with whom he had shared no perils to speak of; a stranger in a battalion where men had already formed their alliances.

A deeper loneliness rushed over his spirit.

He wondered, in this pause before action, if there were the least hint of sense or meaning in all that happens. In the incredibly distant years before the

War he had been deeply religious after the manner of England's austerely puritan tradition. He had been one with the splendid wave of effort and enthusiasm which the War overwhelmed for ever. No doubt his generation had been unsophisticated and crude and uninstructed, ridiculous in its belief that there were things worth doing, and that righteousness and beauty might both be saved for the age that was to follow them. But they had not been disillusioned and nerveless and unhappy, as the generation into which he had to move forward.

Henry had belonged to that defeated and finished time; and had kept his faith, as Martin had not, up to the very end. Bunny, too, had belonged to that generation. He had not shared its earnestness, as we have seen. Yet Martin wondered, he was not sure, as he remembered how straight and rigidly keen on the decent thing Bunny had been beneath all his gaiety. All he knew was, this boy had exchanged with him companionship and eager friendly affection.

> ' Diomed, first of Greeks in fray,
>   Why pressed I not the plain that day,
>   Yielding my life to thee?
>   Where, strewn beneath a Phrygian sky,
>   Fierce Hector, tall Sarpedon lie?'

He did not sleep, but from time to time glanced at the illuminated dial of his wrist-watch. He saw his comrades stirring uneasily in chilly discomfort of mind and body, strewn at intervals along the trench; he sat up and handled his revolver, to make sure (though he was abundantly sure) that it was ready.

At 3.30 figures began to move dimly. The tea was up, and with it thick slices of buttered bread. Men arose silently, and ate and drank.

At 4 the battalion moved forward two hundred yards.

The hillside had plenty of scrub, tall cistus or taller terebinth and mastick plumps. After a progression almost on all fours and sometimes actual full length, they lay down. The enemy first line was less than two hundred yards away. They waited—in that almost intolerable tension which absorbed mind and ear expectant of the coming terror. The minutes were running out.

At 4.15 the bombardment crashed along its fifty-mile length.

For nearly thirty minutes they lay flat in twilight that should have come seeping in, but arrived quivering and expanding in glare and explosion. They could hear nothing but the noise of their world being blown to pieces. An occasional shell burst devastatingly short, and a volcanic whirlwind enveloped them. A cirque of rocks was shattered; the air filled with missiles. Fragments of stone and iron spinning back from the barrage stunned one man, wounded three others.

As the storm quickened to its appalling fulfilment, the battalion rose and moved up, hugging the curtain of shell-bursts. The barrage lifted; and they were into the Turkish front line, which was mopped up. No prisoners could be taken yet.

As dawn came glowingly up, the darker cloud that crowned the hill revealed itself as an oakwood. The Colchesters tried to rush it in sections, one half company advancing while the other half put in rapid fire. Cover and slant together proved too much. They were held up and had to lie close again.

It was at this stage that casualties would have to be paid; no one supposed that the Turkish front would be smashed without initial hand-to-hand fighting.

D Company, Martin's, was on the extreme right. For a matter of seconds he stood up, scanning the ground with field glasses. Three snipers tried their luck. Two bullets chipped the boulder that had sheltered him before he rose; the third flattened itself against the middle one of his captain's pips.

He had seen that the wood and summit overhung a steepish dip that had only low scrub. To right of this dip, to right of Martin and the battalion, was another hill, with a longer slope and at its crest overlooking and commanding the hill they were trying to storm.

A man squirmed through the heath, from battalion headquarters. The colonel required the attendance of the company commanders. Meanwhile no further advance was to be attempted.

They spread out their rough maps under a rocky ledge.

'Six ak emma,' said Colonel Pollock. 'We've been held up almost an hour by this damned wood. The Hampshires colonel has sent word that his crowd are pushing on by line A K B as per schedule, and want us to support them vigorously while they do the next bit after they reach B, which will be in about fifteen minutes. There's nothing we can do, that *I* see, except blaze away like Hell. There's

no sense in our all getting scuppered. When the
Hampshires are through we ought to be able to push
on. Any one of you noticed anything?'

Martin told of the opening to his own extreme
right, which was the battalion's extreme right.

'But what good's that, Chapman? It doesn't give
us the wood. We've got to get the wood somehow.'

'If you could let C company support us, sir, I
think we could take the hill I mentioned. It strikes
me as not strongly held. The Turk obviously thought
that his wood covered it sufficiently. We could then
enfilade the wood from the top.'

'It's worth trying, sir,' said Drake, the senior
captain. 'The battalion's been in shows like this
before and knows how to use every blade of cover.
As a matter of fact we could practically chuck the
frontal attack we're doing now and send five-sixths
of our fellows up where Chapman suggests.'

'Supposing the Turco counter-attacked in front?
——' the Adjutant, Merrow, began. He did not
finish, for he saw that the supposition was negligible.
When the whole line was advancing, from Jordan
to the sea, the enemy would not be such a fool as to
thrust out a salient, especially one that sloped
down hill.

The risk was good enough. A half company was
left in front, to put down the heaviest fire it could,
individual not massed. The rest of the battalion
swung to the right.

It took an hour to capture not only the hill that
slightly commanded the wood but the wood itself.
In pushing their way up the former Martin's
Company took an outlying section of the wood. He
ventured the risk of exploiting his success, sending

back word to Drake, whose Company, C, was supporting D. 'Captain Chapman's message, sir. I can take the wood with support of one Company. I propose to attack half left, instead of up the other hill.'

Drake approved, and in his turn sent the message on to battalion headquarters. He put in his own men, supporting Martin's. Two companies fought for the entrance to the wood.

The barrage of shells had moved up to the summit. The crash and splinter of oaks ripped up and sent spinning made even in the heavier noises of ravage and explosion a sound as of sylvan giants busy in woodcutting. A strip of heavenly Palestine hillside was being blackened and shattered. The dead and wounded subsided into pockets of the violated copse.

Martin had to halt a good hundred yards short of his objective, the hill-top, to send back word that the barrage of shells, and of machine-gun fire from the Hampshires to the Colchesters' left, was keeping him back. When these nuisances had abated somewhat, D company went in with the bayonet. It was a nasty bit of work that Martin preferred to forget at once. It would later on flash upon that inward eye which can be so many things besides the bliss of solitude. Anyway, the hill was taken.

The summit was an ancient high place. Across the top of a platform of rough-hewn stones, where the oil of sacrifice used to be poured, lay a dead soldier, his head huddled forward. Beside him was another, not yet dead but dying fast; his arms were stretched

out at full length, he was beyond consciousness and
his breath was sobbing away.

Martin had too much experience to halt on an
exposed point. D company went swiftly over, and
waited a hundred and fifty yards beyond. A Turkish
gun began to shell the summit.

He saw that C company had swerved to the right.
In this pause Drake and he saw each other and
walked to a momentary meeting. 'Damn good,
Chapman. It was you who took that hill.'

They were no great distance from the sea, and
could watch as they went forward the edge of this
far-flung battle. The Navy was flinging in its strength
and from ships that floated on the still Mediterranean
came the repeated flashing of guns and puff away
of white smoke. The hills were thundering and
smoking; vast reverberations shook the ground over
which they walked.

For the enemy every element harboured his des-
troyers.

To Martin's schooldays' picture of the world of
Greek mythology had come a richer splendour,
finding it in Palestine to be fact and truth. Oleander
concealed running brooks that came as if from
Paradise. Cyclamen shone on the dust-bothered
hills, the brightest star in their sudden garland of
glory when the gentle mitigation of spring followed
a winter in itself half spring.

He had never supposed a pang could be added to
that which he felt from the sight of man's inhumanity
to man. He found it could. His first thought, when
he looked back to the summit, a wood no longer but
a stack of charred and leaning poles, was, illogically,

shame for what he and his fellows had done to a dream and the shining inhabitants of a dream.

He saw the nymphs in twilight shade of shattered thickets bewildered by the ravage pouring through the hills. Fighting in the sands before Gaza or in unwooded Judæa had done little harm. But now they were going forward into the divine coppice that covered Palestine's northern half, away from the scrub that another season renews, however it be hurt. They had left 'Christian' Palestine for ever and were entering pagan territory.

He was one of the very last persons to see a wild hunting leopard in Samaria. It sprang out of a styrax spinney and found itself cornered. Man, its enemy, was all round it; grace and swift litheness stood helpless in a ring of weapons. With a shout a Colchester rushed to bayonet it.

His captain knocked his bayonet aside. 'Let the poor brute go!' he said.

It vanished into a waving of cistus, and presently its trail was lost altogether.

Between 8 and 10 they halted, a space of deceptive stillness in the eddy and race of war. They were allowed to eat half their iron ration.

There was another gathering of company commanders with headquarters.

'We've got to wait,' said the colonel, 'until our fellows have taken these places.' He indicated them on the map.

'Wonder what sort of a time they've been having on Ferkoh Ridge,' said Captain Heathcot, of A company. 'They told me at Corps H.Q. that that was the real Turco position that held the rest together.'

At 10.15 they moved forward again. It was for a time disquietingly easy. There were plenty of bullets, true, but the fire was ill directed and ill sustained. The enemy had, clearly, scuttled back to some new point of concentration.

They came up against it in twenty minutes.

It was another wooded hill held by a desperate garrison, who died in their tracks.

There is no point in lingering over the three-quarters of an hour of costly step-by-step fighting that followed. What happened was happening over fifty miles; in some places were worse 'shows' than this one. The last machine-guns had been rushed, and the gunners bayoneted, when Martin, conscious of physical exhaustion from the pace and steepness, wondered at the wetness of his arm-pit, and found that he was wounded. It was nothing; a furrow from a bullet. One of his men bound a field-dressing on to it, and later in the day he got the doctor to iodine it. His left side felt a stiffness for a week.

What made the day's steady fighting and advance memorable was the speed with which they worked their way up to the Turkish machine-guns, capturing them before they could be taken away or damaged, and their ammunition with them. By noon Martin's Company alone was using four captured machine-guns vigorously and effectively. They had taken twice as many when the day ended; and overtaken and left behind six field guns.

The terrain of this Palestine war is easy to understand, easy to see. The enemy held an island of rugged mountain territory, with ditches on three

sides of it; westward was the Plain of Sharon, northward the Plain of Esdraelon, eastward the Valley
of Jordan. From the mountain territory Carmel
thrust up north-westward, planting his footsteps in
the Mediterranean. The Vale of Dothan ran between
Carmel's south-eastern end and the central mountains, and connected Sharon and Esdraelon.

Eastward of Jordan were the even steeper hills of
Gilead, and the high plateau of the Hauran leading
up to Damascus. These for the present were left
alone, except for Lawrence and his Arabs raiding
the railway.

The enemy was pinned to his mountain fastnesses
in Central Palestine. Over miles of tossed-up boulder
troops from almost every race that the Empire
holds fought against an army that grew hourly more
despairingly aware that its day was finished yet
exacted its price for departure. We have been with
Martin's comrades pushing stiffly forward; to their
right an Irish division struggled in similar country,
and beyond the Irish division was a Welsh division,
whose flanks were strengthened by a West Indian
battalion and a coloured contingent from South
Africa, the Cape Corps Rifles. All these were fighting
the Battle of Ephraim.

However bravely the enemy resisted here, if he
lost the plain of Sharon he lost everything, for he
had been fooled into massing his forces in the mountain heart of Ephraim and especially where it overlooked Jordan. Once his tenuous Sharon defences
were swept away, a tide of war would burst up the
coastal plain and, swirling through the vale of
Dothan, would occupy Esdraelon in his rear.

The Battle of Sharon was fought by Indian divisions

in whose ranks were Manchesters, Leicestershires,
Seaforths, Black Watch, Sikhs, Punjabis, Gurkhas,
and Pathans from the Frontier. Behind them was
the terrible concentration of Anzacs and Yeomanry
and Indian cavalry, ready to rush through the first
gap.

XX

WHEN MARTIN AND HIS FELLOWS MOVED FIRST TO
their positions for the attack, the darkness hummed
with the rising of what seemed innumerable bees.
Just on midnight the Air Force had already jarred
the enemy's nerves, working havoc on the railway
station and aerodrome at Afuleh. Now it swung up
into the most appalling and perfect feat of destruction ever wrought from the skies.

Throughout the Battle of Ephraim the Turkish
planes cowered unable to rise, partridges in stubble
hawk-patrolled aloft. When the bombardment's
shattering explosion burst all along the line of the
central hills, wings were already hovering above the
enemy's main aerodrome, at Jenin, in the beginnings
of Esdraelon. Henceforward without intermission two
British planes kept the air here, every three minutes
relieved by another two. Each plane carried four
bombs. At a sign of movement on the earth below
—the whirring of wings anxious to rise, the running
of a man to a hangar—a plane swooped to within
aiming distance and released a bomb. And every
plane, when its relief arrived, threw itself joyfully
downward, like a demoniac schoolboy engaged in
cruel mischief, and poured bullets into the hangars
before going.

The enemy fought blinded and baffled, under supervision of insolent wings that sent their messages to the hunters pressing up behind them. Not a single Turkish plane appeared, to strive with them for the mastery of vision.

It was stiff fighting in Ephraim; troops were hurled back here, were checked there, before the advance was made all along the line. But where the hills softened into the amenity of long grassy slopes overlooking the Mediterranean victory came instantaneously. The Battle of Sharon was won with swift triumphant strokes. The Seventh Indian Division rose from the trenches they had held for six months in the lush marguerites and many-flowered turf, and swept away the Turkish lines before the malaria-haunted marshes of the Falik. This Falik, it had been understood, was a stream needing engineers and pontoons. By 7.30 it was reached; the talk and thought of engineers and pontoons became so much mirthfulness as the horses clattered across a ' ford ' six inches deep, and were galloping northward to the next river.

The infantry made the breach and the cavalry burst through it. A spate of racing war flooded the long plain that fringes the sea. In their wake followed the guns, swiftly limbered up, and the ammunition wagons and the transport to feed men and beasts. The infantry could halt to cheer as the army of a vision thundered by, in the horses' wake squadrons of swaying camels, mincing mules, plodding donkeys.

''Struth! if we haven't turned the blinking Zoological Gardens loose after Jacko!'

'Jacko's going to have a fair treat. We're giving

him a circus, we are! We're being bloody kind to
him.'

'He'll be thinking he's been drinking too much,
when he sees camels a-chasing him up and down
the Holy Land!'

In a forty-mile skelter the cavalry took only nine
hundred prisoners. Once the lines of trenches were
taken, the plain was almost unguarded—so completely had the Turk been fooled into crowding his
troops inland, to be ready to rush to defence of the
Jordan crossings and the Gilead mountains.

The eyes of the world fell and have remained on
this superb sweep and sickle of war, thrusting upward
and curving round by Dothan into Esdraelon behind
the Turk fighting for dear life in the Ephraim
mountains. And no wonder! Within twelve days
Damascus, unbelievably, had fallen, at a cost of
4,026 casualties from first to last. The Turkish dead
will never be known, but 75,000 prisoners were in
our hands. All his machines and material of war
were wrecked or taken—guns, aeroplanes and aero-
dromes, horses and transport.

Four thousand casualties—the victory was cheaply
bought, war seems a playful pastime. Of the four
thousand, three thousand fell in the opening two
days, when a struggling foe sullenly clung to the
mountain defences he had made.

When night fell on the 19th, the men fighting in
Ephraim were without word of the stupendous
success that had fallen to their comrades in Sharon,
and which hour by hour was expanding to more and
more. They were excessively tired, and glad that

the weather was dry. They lay where they found
themselves, on the heath of cistus. Their blankets
could not be got up to them, and cold became a
discomfort towards dawn. But they slept.

They did not know, I say, of the great thing that
had happened on the coast. But they knew this,
that they themselves had made such progress as
they never hoped to make against that foe and that
terrain, both alike stiff and surly. Obviously the
battle had gone supremely well elsewhere. The check
would probably come on the morrow. It had shown
no signs of coming as yet.

Martin had had pleasant words of congratulation
from his colonel and adjutant; he knew that his
men liked and trusted him, and that his reputation
for courage stood high with them. He did not think
it was courage. It was merely habit, and part of that
habit a wise refusal to think while a job had to be
done.

The 20th was the Colchesters' last day of fighting.
It was hardly worth calling fighting; they moved
forward and occupied a new line. In the beginning
of their advance a few shells fell; and two men were
wounded, both by bullets.

For them, as for the rest of the infantry, plenty of
work remained in the days that followed. They
had to clean up the unimaginable débris that the
whirlwind of disaster had blown over the hills of
Ephraim and Samaria and the long gentle slopes
down to Esdraleon. Roads had to be cleared of
shattered carts that blocked them, of baggage and
garbage. Holes made by explosion had to be smooth-
ed over. Carcasses of men and beasts in thousands

awaited burial. Fires had to be lit to consume all combustible rubbish. Carrying fatigues were incessant. Prisoners had to be collected and sent in. The desolation harboured queer, maddened, starving scarecrows who had been soldiers but now were gleanings that Death had negligently let fall while making his mighty harvest.

It is idle to deny that in war there is a 'thrill,' often of the most crazing, exalting kind. Never has this come in richer fuller measure than in this most triumphant sweep forward that came to the British in 1918. But the thrill belonged, as it always does belong, to the mounted pursuer, it does not come to the plodding infantryman. For him there came at long last—not exultation, but—the 'lift' of relief and release. Jacko had run 'clean off the map'; the War had vanished far over any horizon that the soldier could see. So far as the infantry of Palestine were concerned, the War had ended. From now on they were onlookers, with body and mind and spirit daily drawing in breaths of cool sweet life and air.

Presently, when their jobs in the backward area were finished, they would no doubt trudge forward.

News from now on came freely, all of it exciting. At dawn of the 20th a man ran through Nazareth streets in pyjamas, waving an electric torch and shouting in German for his car and chauffeur. It was Marshal Liman von Sanders Pasha, whose 'Lightning Army' had dissolved into terrified masses, blocked in ravines where hostile aircraft hung above them like fiends in some medieval picture of the Judgment or of Hell's kettle of Torment. Ragged

R

men were fleeing, they had no notion whither.
Horses with bloodshot eyes and failing limbs were
being scourged on by lunatic drivers.

The Marshal managed to dress and to destroy
some papers. Then he, too, fled from the wrath that
possessed the hills and passes and occupied the
spaces of uncharted heaven. Australians were
clattering up the stony ways from Esdraelon.

Another cavalry squadron, English, appeared out
of the vale of Dothan, where it enters Esdraelon.
They loomed up above a Turkish battalion sick
with flight and fears, at Lejjun, which in the Hebrew
tongue was called Armageddon. There was no
pause in which the mind might reason with its
shrinking infirmity. The lances drank deep of
blood.

That morning the enemy, still entangled in the
hills of Ephraim, struck back at the Welshmen, in
insane hope to turn our flank on the heights that
overlook Jordan. He drove us back, but only for an
hour. The return swing came, with troops from
English county regiments, Welshmen, Indians, and
the Cape Corps Battalion, and he was pressed hard
on to his breaking centre.

From the coast striking inland, after winning their
part of the Battle of Sharon, the Seventh Indian
Division all through the night moved over a country
growing furlong by furlong more rugged. The
tracks were such that nothing wheeled could go over
them. In a bewilderment of crags that each resembled
the other the brigade that should have made the
next attack got lost; the Seaforths found themselves
confronted by a village commanding the Nablus road

which must be seized. Success had made commanders casual and hurried. Jacko was keen only on his going and reckless as to the order of his going. Our guns were far behind; but one swift blow with these superb troops and he would scuttle!

So the Seaforths were flung at the castellated hill, crowned with houses before which were perfect fences of cactus. In this last fight of all that the First Seaforths waged in the Great War nine officers died, among them the gallant and dearly loved 'Tim' Mackay, the best hockey player in the Division and the most unselfish comrade. With them died the noblest blood of Scotland—shepherds and fishers of the Isles, with the clear-sighted eyes that the townsman never possesses and with the thoughtful friendly manner of those whose bodies and minds are free. It was a bad finish to so much valour and glory. The battalion had endured days whose names are a trumpet-blast—Festubert and Neuve Chapelle and Ypres, Sheikh Saad and Sannaiyat and Ista-bulat—to be broken on a trumpery hamlet in Palestine.

> ' In some chance battle on Cithaeron side
>   The nursling of the Mighty Mother died.'

The survivors clung to such shelter as vines and rocks gave on the terraced slope, until artillery arrived in the afternoon, and 'a few whiffs of grapeshot' shelled the enemy off the summit.

Meanwhile the horsemen galloping far up Esdraelon eastward began to seize the crossings of Jordan by the Sea of Galilee. West of the river no retreat remained to the Turk.

In Jordan's Valley we had waited hitherto. But on the morning of the 21st movement began. The West Indian Regiment—'the Black Anzacs' men proudly called them—stormed spurs to northward, and held them under a tornado of fire. The New Zealanders flowed forward, spearhead of the grimmest and finest cavalry the world has ever seen. Destruction was to swing his net widely over Gilead, no less than over Ephraim and Sharon and Esdraelon.

The Turk, his front in Ephraim inextricably gripped by his tenacious foes while arms were closing in on him from east and west and were being extended in his rear, turned wholeheartedly to flight. He thrust, fiercely, unreasoningly as insects or birds in their great migration, all his forces one way. Instinct supplanted mind, and instinct was tortured into raving madness.

The Wadi Farah, the steep way that leads to Jordan where it is midway between its two great lakes, became a place of agony such as even war has hardly known. The British planes, flying swiftly as hawks to a drove of lemmings seeking outlet to the sea, hovered at the pass's ends, then dived to a hundred feet from ground and dropped their bombs. Below no thoughts survived but those of escape; but these narrows were not built for escape. An army was on the wheel, securely fastened down while the hammer-blows that broke it fell. Between hills precipitously inhospitable was a wagon's space; and from plane to plane, as the executioners arrived and went off to return with more death, was but a three minutes' respite. The one that had dropped its quota of bombs would perceive its relief already

humming thither; it would swoop lower yet and
inward along the pass; its machine-gun would whip
through the columns stampeding behind the terror
in their front and catch the fugitives sobbing among
the rocks.

After the puny and painful growth of millenniums
Mars had reached adult stature at last. He had
found a use for both extremes of age: the man too
old to fight was no longer useless, as in former wars,
he could work where gases and miasmas that poison
were prepared; the boy too young for campaigning
rigours could do this job which is for youth alone,
he could climb into the air and recklessly toss his
life from height to height, he could swoop hawklike
down, he could scud swiftly over a hillside and
scatter death. Youth was aloft, living days hysterical
in their excitement and sudden tremors; below was
crashing and screaming, brute madness of mules
and horses and camels, anguish of men demented
or in physical ruin. The transport piled steadily up,
as the planes worked their way down from the exits
of the passes. Guns were dragged by their teams
into the trivial brooks by the way; men already
maimed were pinned and crushed beneath over-
turning carts. An army was held in steel jaws until
the infantry could draw up and complete the
butchery. Fires blazed at intervals, and the flames
lit up the ashy distorted faces of the dead and dying.
This was the most triumphant chord in the vast
orchestral music that the God of Death was playing
—a crescendo that seemed almost at once to reach
unbearable heights of terror yet waxed and swelled
from hour to hour and did not cease by day or

night. By noon of the 21st, ninety guns and a thous-
and wagons of all sorts lay abandoned and broken in
the Wadi Farah alone.

XXI

BACK IN JERUSALEM NEWS FILTERED IN OFTEN BUT
bewilderingly. No one was bothering about Jerusalem now. On the 20th Valerie heard that not
Martin only, but the whole of Corps H.Q. had left
Olivet; rumour spoke of three to four thousand
prisoners,'mostly Jaffa way.' The 3rd Indian Division
—or was it the 53rd Welsh Division?—was expected
to take Nablus to-day. The cavalry would be in
Nazareth by nightfall.

At breakfast on the 21st, which she took with the
rest of the Relief Force, a dozen people had news.
They were growing wise, these Americans, in British
units and their location. The front was no longer
one general blur of 'British' (in which Australian
of course was included). Some were confident that
the Anzacs were about to launch a tremendous
offensive across Gilead, to link up with that *magna
nominis umbra*, Colonel Lawrence. Frobisher had been
told that it was the 7th Indian Division that had
made the gap by the coast. Transport-Commandant
Gleeson had had word with a colonel at Corps
H.Q., the solitary swallow left after the flocks had
flown; 6,000 prisoners had been taken, 100 guns,
camel trains by the dozen. Thirty planes were
bombing Turkish transport, every time registering
direct hits.

Colonel Francks, Lawrence's German counterpart, had come (said Rumour) swinging up from Jericho to Jerusalem, in a crazily desperate effort to get news. If he found this part of the front slackly held, then the enemy would counter-attack against it, they would try to take Jerusalem back. The British could never afford to lose Jerusalem, it would be such a blow to prestige that it would more than offset their victories elsewhere, even if the rest of the world should then continue to believe in those victories. Unfortunately (for everyone admired the brave fellow) Francks had been too far, too venture-some this time. He had overdone the insolent Aussie, and an irate British colonel of the Army Service Corps (greatly daring! even in the world's orgy of courage he should be singled out for some out-standing decoration) had arrested him, despite his emu feathers and felt hat. He had been searched (owing to *one* mispronunciation), found to be a spy, and would be shot next morning. It was a wretched ending to a gallant career. Allenby, amused by such impudence in the British hour of triumph, had said 'Damn the fellow! I won't shoot him. He had a Devonshire mother. And the Hun's a man, any-way, whatever his crimes.' But the Provost-Marshal had urged that in that case they could not shoot *any* spy, and presently the British forces would be loosely flung over new country where every peasant would be tempted to convey information to the enemy. So he was going to be shot, after all.

Every day muffled firing had come down the sounding-board of the mountains. This was particu-larly heavy on the morning of the 20th. Through the rest of the day it died away gradually, and by

evening only at long intervals a faint explosion
came through. Store-Major Schwartz heard a canteen
sergeant report that 'Jacko had cut and run right
out of Palestine.'

Cynthia's quietness in her farewell interview with
Martin threw Valerie off her guard. When he had
gone physical collapse came, and she was ill.

We need not go over the weary round with her
distressed brain. We have been over it ourselves,
and know that it is endurable only because of time's
mercy and the exhaustion which the machine inflicts
upon itself at last. There were hours when she
sobbed with an abandonment of bitterness that she
had not known since childhood's days: and hours
when she lay rebellious and angry and worn out
to the semblance of indifference. Over all was the
tormenting obsession that the whole event was so
unnecessary, so due to man's imbecility and so
against the course of nature, that it simply could
not be true. Old men had to die, and men whose
bodies were diseased. But not gaiety, youth, easy-
moving vigour. Why must fools put a bullet through
that?

It happened; and we know how often it happened;
and we know how we felt.

Decency and courage kept her mind sweet. She
knew that in the commonness and triviality of death
she could not look for any deep or real sympathy
from anyone except Val. No one credited her with
a heart that could suffer greatly; and Bunny was
merely a boy, probably one of many boys, who had
amused her. She held to her friendship with Val,
and fought her way back to endurance of life.

The steps of that painful way back, and the arguments by which they were won, no one guessed but Valerie, and they were known even to her only in part.

After four days she insisted on taking up her work again. Her unit were shocked at the change in her appearance; but the ordinary restoratives that are prescribed for the wealthy—a sea-voyage, a sojourn in some bracing climate—were not available, and the patient refused merely to rest.

It was just a fortnight after Martin had gone that she went to Miss Ohlsen, who was the head of the Red Cross women's contingent, and said, 'Miss Ohlsen, there's going to be a big British attack in a few days.'

'That is what is generally believed, Miss Cameron. But it's been expected so often, you know, and it hasn't come off. I think myself that it's more likely that General Allenby'll do nothing but just wait. After all, what *can* the British do? They've sent their best infantry all off to France.'

'No. It's coming, I'm sure, Miss Ohlsen.'

'Perhaps so. But it can't make any difference to our work.'

'I think it can, Miss Ohlsen. And I think it ought to.'

'The United States is neutral as regards Turkey,' Miss Ohlsen reminded her.

'I'm not neutral. And I'm not going to be.' And Cynthia threw her head on her arms and cried.

Miss Ohlsen had heard something. A British boy that Cynthia liked had been sent to France and was killed. She did not suppose that a girl like Cynthia would be left unconsoled for long. She was far too pretty not to draw admirers. It was just as well that these entanglements with British young officers should come to nothing, though Miss Ohlsen was sorry that it should be by their death. There was no sense in war anyway.

Cynthia checked her tears fiercely, and spoke fast. 'My work isn't all that important, Miss Ohlsen— not now, when men are dying. Nothing matters now except doing what we can to help them.'

'But we have to be neutral,' Miss Ohlsen reminded her again.

'We haven't got to be so neutral as all that. I want permission—so does Val—to visit the British hospitals. We can make plenty of spare time, without letting down our work here. We may be neutral against the Turk, but these boys are dying for us, though we don't know it.' Tears surged up again, almost irresistibly, like a flood of anger and despair. But she had iron in her will, and her sorrow was to herself alone. These others should not see it.

Miss Ohlsen thought, 'This is a pretty girl's romantic feeling. She wants to go round comforting wounded officers and feeling that it's very, very nice for them to see her telling them how brave they've been. Well, of course it's natural for a girl like Miss Cameron.'

She did not set Cynthia's emotion very deep; she thought it was her instinct of giving and receiving pleasure from masculine admiration. She knew perfectly well which of the ladies under her had attracted service and homage from the alien armies that occupied Jerusalem. And of course (she acknowledged to herself) the girl wanted to be kind

and felt genuine pity. She had noticed that there
was no real harm in Miss Cameron, who had always
been friendly and willing to please.

'The wounded won't stay in Jerusalem long,' she
assured her. 'Colonel——' She hesitated; she also
had friends in the British forces. 'You know that
what they have here is only a Clearing Station.
They keep the wounded, unless they are cases too
bad to be moved, only twenty-four hours, and then
send them down the line.'

'Please!' begged Cynthia. 'I want to see what
wounded come through. No, it isn't what you think,
Miss Ohlsen. That's finished. My boy is dead. Oh!'
She turned aside; then after a moment continued
passionately, 'If you won't get permission for us to
see the wounded when we have time I'll go myself
to the British authorities. They *can't* mind our doing
that, just Val and I going when we have time.'

So permission was given.

The first two days of the push, only a few wounded
reached the Jerusalem casualty clearing stations. But
a rush came on the 21st and following days. They
were a hilariously happy crowd, from whose demeanour the splendour of the conquest was apparent.

Cynthia saw the shattered heroes of the Cape Corps
Battalion received from their baptism of fire; and
by sheer luck was present again later, when Allenby
himself, a huge figure of cheerfulness and strength,
paid a flying visit. 'You fellows did magnificently,' he
told them. 'Well done, Cape Corps! You were like
veterans in your very first battle. I'm proud of you.'

Happily inspired, he added the word of magic.
'*England* is proud of you, Cape Corps boys!'

He stayed—a moment—to scatter news from his overflowing cornucopia of triumph.

'The Arabs have reached Derea. The Huns started bombing them. So Lawrence flew over and asked us for help. We sent three planes back with him, and the moment they arrived four Huns came over, and our fellows went up and drove two of them down. The Arabs and Anzacs are pressing on to Damascus.'

Nearest the door was a man whom Cynthia thought a negro, being unaware of the gradations that elsewhere replace the convenient simplicity of her own land. His legs were both uplifted in splints: one arm was in another splint. She stopped to talk to him.

His face was radiant. 'We boys stood the test well,' he assured her.

Her heart overflowed in gratitude—for what? Why, merely for this, that human nature can be so magnificent, that the Life Force takes no unduly scrupulous note of the signs that to us are all-important but lavishes pluck and valour on 'lesser breeds without the law' that Nordic England and America have set up for mankind. This dark-skinned warrior's courage made him a comrade.

'We *boys*,' he repeated, dwelling with pride on the word, on every word—and surely the sentence was all compact of eloquence!—'stood the test well. General Allenby has said that we stood the test well. *We boys*—stood the *test*—*well*.' He had found a thought that would feed and uphold his mind until he died.

Her experience had made her, American of the Americans, draw closer to the British, the ogrish

race who had done unparalleled things to them
during the Revolution and who now were fountains
of oppression all over the world, than she had ever
dreamed was possible. In these days of forward-
leaping triumph, when the British Army was visibly
Wordsworth's Happy Warrior,

> ' happy as a lover, and inspired
> With sudden brightness, like a man inspired,'

she identified herself with Bunny's comrades, with
Martin's comrades. Their people were her people
henceforth, though nothing ever would or could
change her deep Americanism. They were a good
people, kind and gay and valiant and merciful.
Yet——

Tears were close to her all through these days, so
full of pity and triumph. The very triumph made the
pity often an unbearable thing; her heart seemed as
if it would break when she found herself alone. It
was seeing these wounded that saved her.

Tears came now, a rush to her eyes that she dabbed
hastily away. It was indignation mingled with
admiration. As she had felt at the Holy Sepulchre,
seeing that miserable Russian leper woman dragging
her way up the steps and weeping in love's ecstasy
all the while, 'What has God *done* to deserve all this
devotion?' so now she felt, 'What has the British
Empire done to deserve all this service and admiration and loyalty? What has it *done*? Has it given
freedom and equality and justice? Has it made a
man secure of his right, whatever his race or colour
or land? Made it certain that if God Himself were
to come again in a Buddha in India or to send

genius of imagination or brain or character in some negro, he would be treated for what he was and not for what he looked?' No, she did not actually *think* all this, but it was *in* the one blazing thought that she did have: 'What has England done to deserve such loyalty—men of subject and coloured races giving their bodies to be smashed like this, *proud* that she accepts such service?'

On the 21st she heard there were wounded in from the 54th Division. She asked eagerly if there were any Colchesters among them. There were. She asked her way to their ward.

She asked the first man if he knew Captain Chapman—who had come to them recently from Jerusalem. No, he wasn't in Captain Chapman's company, but had heard of him. He believed Captain Chapman was all right. He hadn't heard that he had been hit.

A man three beds away caught the name and raised himself on his elbow. 'I'm in Captain Chapman's company, Miss.'

Cynthia went to him immediately. 'There was a lady enquiring after Captain Chapman yesterday, Miss, when we first came in.'

So Valerie was not so casually indifferent as she chose to pretend to be.

Captain Chapman had been all right when these men left the front. He was a good fellow, the best company commander they had ever had. Yes, the battalion was still fighting.

XXII

I

SINCE HISTORY BEGAN, ESDRAELON, THE PLAIN OF
battles, has seen hosts fleeing to where the land fissures
down below Beisan to Jordan's fords and the forest-
fledged uplifted land of Bashan beyond. We may
suppose it full of watching ghosts, seeing their own
faded passion endured afresh with deeper, wilder
horror. From the sickle-sweep of Gilboa where
Israel's glory was slain on her high places—to
Tabor's wooded tower against whose summit
encampment so many armies have surged—men
might look over waving prairie fed by Kishon's
pulsing springs and see only the glint of lilied, many-
coloured pasture that conceals the wild gazelles, and
the red-roofed settlements of Jewish farmers beyond.
But the plain has known assault and frenzy of
Canaanite and Egyptian and Assyrian and Hebrew
and Philistine, of Roman and Jew, of Arab and
Christian, Saracen and Crusader, Frank and Turk.
No other soil on earth's surface, except Flanders
only, has drunk of blood more often or more
deeply.

The last drove of fugitives huddled together, a
confusion of infantry and gunners, of guns, machine
-guns, transport. If fight were shown, it was fight
which could have but one ending.

As the shapeless mass was pushed closer to the
crumbling edge that breaks away to Jordan, the

Hants battery galloped over the open plain and set its guns in action within easy rifle range. Every gun was hit, but the enemy's ranks were blown apart. The 29th Lancers swung down into the struggling crowd and took twenty-five machine-guns in a single charge. Eyes of despair turned across the river, here foaming and plunging to where Yarmuk brings a mighty stream racing like a god from ledge to ledge of the dusky mountains. They saw that destruction had gone across before them and that death was as busy on that bank as on this. Three thousand men surrendered, after half as many had died—died not under the shells and spears alone, but in Jordan's exultant waters, that spun and curveted round boulders of glossy shale and shot along through nodding avenues of agnuscastus and oleander. Men reached struggling hands to the flower-fragrant coppices; their breath bubbled up into a swirl of dancing blossoms that the rejoicing river carried downward to his marriage feast with Yarmuk.

Now all the west was clear to the Galilean Lake. The cavalry moved freely up and down the river; the Anzacs from the south met the Anzacs from the north and the Indians and British yeomanry.

Through the night of the 24th the 4th Australian Light Horse Brigade marched for Semakh, the railway junction between Galilee and the line to Damascus. Semakh is on a hot plateau, a little raised above the precipitously flowing Jordan and facing northward across the lake the twin poplars that mark the river coming in from Huleh and Hermon. Hermon's bison-shoulders push into the clouds and loom out above them; to north-westward are Tiberias and Capernaum and the tiny bay of Magdala. Behind a laager of rolling stock in Semakh station the German artisans and engineers awaited death riding stumblingly towards them through the night.

The men who had made that laager made it for defence and not submission, and had counted and in high resolve already paid the price. The battle opened with a burst of fire that struck down Australian leaders whose death now, when victory overwhelming and final was in their hands, came as wrong beyond forgiveness. When all opposition had ceased and every opposing life had been taken, dawn came striding over the hills and glimmering lake, and men felt a revulsion in the sight of that trivial place—a mere line of rails and platform— heaped with so much carnage. It was this revulsion that saved the lives of some score of trembling Turks who were dragged out from the houses where they had cowered throughout the action. This was an abjectness which showed the immensity of conquest fallen to our arms.

A people, being more than the aggregate of so many individuals, is an instinctive inarticulate thing, having desires and fears it does not voice and does not cherish consciously. Since time began, in the Syrian land men have found existence waxing fiercely watchful as autumn draws on. The summer of jaded lilies and faded grass grows wraithlike, a spook whose breath exhales hotly before manifes- tation disappears. Voices inextricably knit with the pulses of the body begin to whisper 'Rain!'

s

This brief interspace between hot and wet, Allenby had known, was the one time when he could 'hop in' and conquer. October would be too late; the brooks would be quags, the roads would be marish.

The tremendous upspringing of the British energy from the hollows where it had lain waiting so long came at the very time when Expectation was working so powerfully (though for what Thought as yet hardly knew) in all the dwellers in the land. It seemed, therefore, as if an intensity not their own, but elemental and borrowed from earth on which they trod, enwrapped the troops moving giantlike and godlike in invincibility. The stars in their courses were again fighting over Kishon and over Jordan. The enemy, outnumbered, outmetalled, outfed, outmanœuvred, outfought, was being driven backward by foes invisible as well as visible. The gods and demons of the land were hunters, roused from their thickets by lust and scent of his blood.

Over Olivet the sunsets of autumn grew ever lovelier. Clouds appeared; the golden light of evening straying widely was impounded and made to mass itself smoulderingly here and to be an amber fountain there. A tender grace of apple-green suffused the upper west.

Earth was gathering herself together in gentleness for her time of flowers.

The War had long ago gone far away. Jerusalem still had wounded, but only from Jordan's further side, and these were mostly Turks. Prisoners came crowding in, wretched and ragged, and with sores and festering places. The Holy City's influx of varied and rigorous life had vanished like a dream.

On the 26th, Valerie coaxed Cynthia into a walk down the Kedron Valley. They would rest by the Virgin's Tomb, where they could see down the deep gorge that is like a waterless stream washing the City's battlements, going on to the Wadi of Fire and the Dead Sea.

They saw filing up from Jericho a host of Turkish prisoners, escorted by a detachment of the 'Jordan Highlanders.' Never on any faces can such expressionless weariness have been seen. The contrast came swiftly to Valerie, of that other march of tired men that she and Martin had watched filing up in moonlight. She realised that there are poles apart of exhaustion. These men's spirits were beaten; it was only husks that were moving there. Their guards were so contemptuous that they had handed over their rifles to prisoners to carry, and were slouching unarmed beside them. Turkish soldiers were carrying rifles for Palestine Jewry.

'That night when we saw the Aussies filing up,' said Cynthia, 'Martin told me what he had been saying to you.'

Valerie started. Martin repeating what he had said to her!

But Cynthia added, 'That those fellows would have to go through it soon. It hasn't been so bad—for them. Val,' she said, rising, 'it all seems like a dream. I shall never believe that I lived through these days in Jerusalem.'

II

British cavalry began to appear north of the Sea of Galilee. There seemed to be no ford, however remote, where the enemy's frightened and footsore infantry or his cavalry and their starved garrons could cross without battle. There was fighting by the Waters of Merom; a flurry of men and a charge, or the whipping of machine-gun bullets over the brook of Jordan, and Damascus would be so much nearer by the number of bodies dead on the stones and sands or prisoners herded together. Probably no other army that ever fought would have bothered to take so many prisoners. It was almost well for the Turks that they were so wretched; even cruelty itself could hardly have steeled itself to slay against such trivial resistance.

Yet continually even these miserable fugitives stood fast and exacted the price of their riding down and slaying. The time when anything could have stopped their triumphant pursuers was long over, yet both in pursuit and flying men still found courage to die. Death brought no service to the cause of the vanquished; theirs was the most foolish mood ever seen in war. Their time went out in useless valour. But valour it was, if ever valour has been.

The Arabs took Deraa, and it was still dawn on the 28th when the desert hosts and Indian cavalry mingled west of the town.

And now the vanquished gained some respite, in the Hauran strewn with basaltic rocks which held up horses from advance except in full daylight. But respite was the merest slackening; the columns drew together converging like a net grasped tight when the quarry is within. The wave of advance presently swept over and beyond; Damascus was visibly lost, and its actual 'taking' a mere formality.

As the lovely city drew into the range of vision its doom thundered heavenward in a race of fiery stars. Ammunition dumps and stores were burning. A horror of illumination overhung it, so that the victors with pity thought that its palaces and temples were flaming out.

On September 30th, it broke into a shower of Arab flags. The Turks and Germans departed, lack-lustre men moving north amid jeers and shouts. Yet even now some sparks flickered; an officer would lift his arm, gravely ironically saluting the Sherifian symbol, in mockery of fate and of the ring of hostile exultant faces.

Over a spur of Hermon Australians led their horses by ways one pile of crag and loose flint. They blocked the city's westward road of escape to the Bikaa and Beirut, where Anti-Lebanon's beginnings tower either side. The road was crammed with troops dragging jadedly along, 'safe' at last; with wheeled transport warlike and unwarlike, with guns, camels, sheep, asses, mules. The autumn splendour was on the foliage of plane and poplar and walnut.

A shot was fired, challengingly; in its throes of flight the column half halted. An Australian stood clear to view, on an outjutting crag that rose free of the fledging forest. There was no mistaking that figure—the drooping emu plumes and slouch hat, the magnificent arrogance of strength and recklessness. Their foes were here too, blocking even this tunnel on the far edges of their flight!

He was demanding that they surrender.

A German tilted a machine-gun swiftly and savagely, and a spurt of bullets, like a covey of birds dipping to shelter, whistled up the hillside. The Australian disappeared.

A flight of answering bullets whipped into the dense crowd. In an open carriage a German lady, wife of an officer, leapt up and back, and her throat was suffused with a gush of blood. Men and women raced madly, screaming for pity in that pass of death. They were clambering and stumbling and being trodden underfoot. You got the impression of a huge creature straining at its centre, and then breaking in two. Most of the mob ran back and back, back to that menacing Damascus which they were striving to leave. The valley was raked with machine-guns. You saw bodies heave convulsively, as the wounded were struck again.

The fliers nevertheless did not dare re-enter the city. Some scattered along hillsides and hid in caverns and groves; some found the one way of escape still open, to the north and Aleppo.

In the city the sick and wounded and dying lay untended and deserted in the wretched, foul hospitals. Every misery that fear and helplessness can lay on the spirit broken by the body's ruin was laid on them. Outside the streets were filled with shouts of festival. Damascus gave itself up to joy and junketing. What did the dead and those who were better dead matter?

At dawn of October 1st, the people of Damascus at last saw the men and horses that had been almost beings of fable. The 10th Australian Light Horse Regiment, riding easily and jauntily, their glorious beasts responding to the mood that called for a victor's carriage in this crowning hour of fulfilment, cantered through the streets and flowed into the big square.

All through this day there were troops enough for battle that seemed ubiquitous (if battle you may call it). Turkish columns wearily moving on to what they thought to be their still uncaptured base at Damascus found dreaded interception across their route. Turkish companies and battalions fleeing widely off the city, through the spaces of the desert that should be hospitable to misery, heard here, too, their foes thundering down on them. If they skirted Damascus, slinking westward, Abana's gorge was choked, and the melée of dead and wreckage told its frightening tale.

Racing in from the south came the Arab Army on their gallant little ponies, firing shots of joy into the air as they galloped. Damascus gave itself up to an 'Armistice Day,' each man and woman a centre of glee to themselves as well as a fountain of delighted adulation to their deliverers. Voices chanted and shrilled, a sea of exultancy swelled and swept majestically and madly, rising in the squares to mighty spouts of acclaim, in the narrow streets falling back like spray. Flowers and scents rained from windows where women sat unveiled. Before and alongside the incoming warriors gambolled and tumbled dervishes, heedless of the excited horses.

is deluged with trash of fiction in which the treacherous Englishman schemes and plots to lead innocent lovers of France astray.

The cat whose paws were burnt might (one thinks) have looked for honourable, if slight, mention from the monkey. But the monkey, though intelligent and nimble and endowed with many ingratiating ways, is not a generous animal.

The Turk, out of pursuit of anything slower than armoured cars, stood at last, and an army began to coalesce. On October 26th, beyond Aleppo was fought the first action deserving the name of a battle since Damascus fell. After charging many times their number the Mysore and Jodhpur Lancers had to fall back and wait for the Australian Mounted Division to arrive from Damascus. But there was no further fighting. On October 31st, the Turk threw in his hand, and was granted an Armistice.

Their warfare accomplished, the Palestine armies, like the Church Triumphant watching the Church still Militant, looked on at the last lurid flames of battle dying down in Europe.

The victors found Syria in the grip of famine so appalling that children were picking over the dung of transport and cavalry animals for stray grains of undigested corn. The amazed Indians saw mobs scrambling for melon rinds they tossed away. The only coin current was food; for a morsel of this women sold their bodies, men their strength.

The American Relief Force immediately transferred three-fourths of their personnel and resources north. With these, early in November, came Cynthia and Valerie, into a grimmer, chillier world. The first snows were settling on Lebanon, fogs and arctic winds drove out not merely the fact but almost the memory of the sun-warmed lands they had left. Every hand was needed to fight such hunger as they had thought was a legend of far-off ages.

In Beirut they found a large community of their own people, whose faces were haunted by many ghosts. The years of war had been a manifold wretchedness, with the fear that their country also might be forced into hostility against Turkey, and they and their families deported to the distant hinterland where their British friends had been sent to die. They had been years of privation, which for some had meant death and for others had left disease which brought death in the next few years. They had not dared to speak frankly of the War and its chances, except in secrecy among themselves; they had had to be silent while Syrians, who had been in their friendship in happier days, were hanged in the public square because their hearts were towards the French Allies of America.

On the evening of Armistice Day the community gathered for thanksgiving. No thanksgiving was ever so quiet and restrained. In the morning the Allied warships in Beirut harbour had announced the news by bursting into a riot of explosion, and the city had answered with crackers and pistol shots. But this reply of exultation had come from Syrians, not from British or Americans.

The room was silent, filled with men and women whose thoughts were straying back over the incredible time that had just passed into history. It was now a tale, that men had borne what had been—a tale that those who come hereafter will not dimly recover from any word that we can say, or even from the authentic words of the long passion itself, its

> ' angry marching rhymes
> Of blind regret and haggard mirth.'

The few British officers present were remembering this man . . . that man . . . who should have been in this completion of strife and endurance, but was dead. You looked round, in this stillness when the guns first closed their mouths, for your friends, and found that they were not there.

One incident sharpened the thoughts of those who waited. A man came late, bursting in melodramatically excited. 'Has the German Emperor escaped?' he cried. 'Is there any news of him?'

No one answered a word.

'What must be that man's thoughts now?' he exclaimed, looking round for encouragement which never came. 'How dreadful beyond our power to imagine his sufferings must be! "My God! my God! why hast Thou forsaken me?" he must be crying out. *What* an event we are witnessing! What horror of loneliness and desolation must be that man's lot! To have been on such a height for so long! And now to have fallen so low! How art thou fallen, Lucifer, Son of the Morning!'

Still no one spoke.

'Can we not *think*—can we not put ourselves in his place, in the awful agony of mind that must now be his! "My God! my God! *why* hast Thou forsaken me?"—that must be his one thought, every minute tormenting him to madness! How *terrible* must be his state of mind! I can think of nothing else!'

Cynthia's heart swelled with almost overpowering anguish of memory and helpless indignation. But in the isolation of that crowded room she caught the illusion of Bunny's voice saying to her quietly, 'Don't—*don't* let yourself be fussed, sweetheart! People either understand or they don't. It's no use talking to those who don't. But you and I understand.'

Captain Wilbur Frobisher's voice broke the stillness. 'Let us pray to Almighty God our Heavenly Father, in the silence of our own spirits—that He would come close this evening to all whose hearts have been left bereaved by the long agony of the War just finished—that He would give them comfort.'

XXIII

MARTIN'S DIVISION MOVED NORTH, SMOOTHING DOWN the land's disordered face as they went, and concentrated at Haifa on October 4th. On the 11th, Austin-Gary, now ranking as Lieutenant-Colonel, pulled aside the fly-flap of his forty-pounder, and announced himself.

'Hullo, Chapman! They told me you were here, when I drew your mess-tent blank. I've run down from Safed for a chat.'

He sat down on Martin's bed, and continued. 'They've appointed me Military Governor of North-East Galilee; and when I was seeing General Money about it he said, "What about that fellow you were telling me about, a man who'd been in the

Londons?" And I put in a strong claim for the body immediately, and said, "It's mine. It belongs to me, sir." But Money said they were wanting to send you over to work with the Hedjaz, since you were such an outstanding Arabic scholar. I said you'd never get on with the Hedgehogs, that you had the devil of a temper and needed to work with some one sympathetic who could soothe you over. So Money, who's the most decent old boy in the world, decided that you should choose. Now, which is it to be, Chapman? If you go to the Hedgehogs they'll probably make you a General of their own, and in any case you start off as a Major. If you come to me you remain an ordinary three-pipped Captain. Money agreed that it was only fair I should warn you.'

Martin, in the exultation of this new door flung wide for escape from regimental drudgery, made a joke.

'What!' he said, fingering the three stars on his shoulder, 'Take away three bits of brass from me and send me to work amid Arabs with only one! No! If I've to work with the Hedgehogs I want all the bits of brass that I can carry; and a whole lot of stripes as well! I'll go only if General Money will reduce me to the rank of sergeant-major, and let me keep my three stars as well!'

'Excellent!' said Austin-Gary. 'But I'll never dare to tell the Chief your reply, or he'll say he accepts your conditions, and that the Hedgehog staff really can't do without such a profound student of Ayrab psychology. Now! Next question! When can you get your kit together and come along with me?'

Martin leapt up. 'Do you really mean it, sir?'

'Of course I mean it! You don't suppose that I've motored down from Safed just for a joke! If you knew the job I have on hand you'd know that I've no time for jaunts and jollities. There's no revenue, to begin with; it's vanished into some bottomless bog, and we have to fish it out. And the whole place is seething with quarrels between groups who each consider that it's *their* turn to do the next massacre. And there's famine. And scrapping about grazing rights in the Huleh marshes. And every kind of devilment and bedevilment that the mind of Oriental man can imagine. Besides, presently, when you and I've got some sort of order going, I look to you to race round North-East Galilee, chucking footballs out wherever you see a quorum of males of suitable age. It's my belief, Chapman,' he said sorrowingly, 'that the people of these regions will never rise to a decent game. But at any rate we can try to teach them soccer. Only—from the one or two half-hearted shots at coaching that I've ventured already—you'll have the deuce of a job to persuade them that the game must be played *without stones*!'

'But what good are stones in soccer?' asked Martin Puzzlewit. His mind was not following closely, it was straying in such delectable byways.

'Why, to register your protest at the other side's success! To chase a naughty referee off the field. But all this' (putting a hand on his shoulder) 'is mere childish prattle. The point is: *Can you come back with me this afternoon?* I've got the whole thing fixed; I've seen your bereaved colonel, and given him halting words of comfort: I've got a car.'

'*Can I come back this afternoon*?' shouted Martin.
'I should say I can!'

During the advance he had had little opportunity
for writing, and less for getting letters to their
address. He had written to both Cynthia and Valerie
from Haifa, but the letters were not delivered until
they had left for Beirut. A letter that he wrote from
Safed took three weeks to reach Jerusalem, and
lay there unforwarded for another ten days. Miserable at what seemed repeated snubbing or, even
worse, to hint at illness, on November 15th he
made a clean breast to Austin-Gary of his reasons—
of three-fourths of his reasons, at any rate—for
his improper request for twenty-four hours' leave.

The intimacy of such jobs as theirs makes men
either loathe each other murderously and con-
temptuously, or like each other beyond the power
of misunderstanding to shake. Austin-Gary respected
a wish of Martin's, even one to escape from chaos
whose control was their every minute's preoccupation. He remembered Martin's agitation when he
had come to beg his help towards transfer back to
the Brentfords when they went to France: he knew
what Bunny's death had meant: Wenyon had told
him something of Warren and Cynthia, and something, too, of Valerie.

So he said sympathetically, 'Twenty-four hours is
no use, with the roads all clogged with rubbish still.
I'll not risk losing a promising young administrator,
wrecked in the mad effort to drive a car at seventy
miles an hour over a mountain of smashed lorries!
I'll manage without you for three days, Chapman,
though I don't know how!'

Martin found merely the skeleton of the Relief
Force still in Jerusalem, and learnt that Val and
Cynthia had left a fortnight earlier, for Beirut. He
was given such address as was known, and advised
that it might be better to write, 'Care of the American
College, Beirut.'

He hurried back by Nablus, through the desolation
strewn yet over Ephraim and Samaria—the shattered
transport, the spaces littered with skulls, the abandoned shell-dumps. It recalled forcibly what at the
time the mind, its gaze caught otherwhere, had let
go by with trivial notice, the agony of an army in
irretrievable ruin.

'Yes,' Austin-Gary agreed, 'it was a pretty
bedraggled Jacko that we saw running for dear life.
I guess that was why we who were in the show felt
so little exultation. Those poor devils that we caught
up with and cursed for giving us the bother of taking
them over looked less like soldiers than any prisoners
since the world began. It was more like the finish of
a highly successful Rat Week than a glorious victory!'

The girls did little more than pass through Beirut.
In the last week of November they were sent further
north yet, to Aleppo, a city of starvation and the
dread shadow of remembered massacre. Here, in
December, Cynthia fell dangerously ill, caught by
the influenza epidemic going round the world.

When she was convalescent, she said, 'Do you know,
Val, I think there can never have been a time when
it was easier to die than now.'

'But why, Cynthia?'

'You feel that all who made the world seem a

T

decent place have gone, and left it full of people whom you either despise and hate or else whom you pity for what they've suffered but can't respect—like our Armenians here. You are most *awfully* sorry for what they've had to endure, and no one will ever believe that it happened. But you can see for yourself that there isn't much hope if the world has to go forward with people whose spirits have been broken. That's one thing certain, Val—that mere suffering by itself does no good.'

Val told her she ought to rest and not worry.

'I *am* resting all I can. You and the doctors, Val, seem to think that I can say, "Now I'm going to rest," and then the resting comes. All the same,' she added to herself, 'it's easier than it was. I think I shall be able to rest more, from now on. Do you remember that time, Val, when you all thought I was delirious? I seemed to myself to see everything more clearly than I'd ever seen it before. And I found Bunny close to me, looking after me so that it seemed too wonderful to be dying like that—just as if he were again looking after me as he did that night by Kantara, when he took me over the Canal that shone so black in the darkness——'

She had never mentioned that night. Val guessed that she was being admitted to deeps of friendship that had been kept from her. She now knew that all through these months when her love and care had been received with what seemed merely kindness and grateful reserve, something had been building up between them, stronger and more intimate than old affection.

'But Bunny said to me, Val, "Go back, go back, Cynthia. The time hasn't come yet." But I know it

will come, Val; and because I know that, I know
that I can go on living.'

'Of course you can go on living!' said Val. She
could not speak for a few moments, then she said,
'Why, Cynthia, of course you must *want* to go on
living! The War's over and we shall never see anything so horrid again. We must think that all those
fine boys who've been killed have done the greatest
job that was ever done. They've ended war for ever.'

'Yes,' said Cynthia dreamily, 'they've done the
greatest job that was ever done or ever will be done.
And there was this wonderful *new* thing about it,
that some of them didn't do it blindly, as men have
done such jobs before. They *saw* they were doing it.
But it wasn't the job that you and I have imagined.
The world will *never* have sense. All we have
gained is that we have seen how, without any of
the things that used to make men madly, furiously
brave—belief in God or in another world or that
their cause was a kind of religion in itself—even
without belief that their country was of course
entirely in the right and the other country entirely
wrong—men could be what we know they have been.
That's what I call the greatest job that ever was done
or ever will be done'.

There was no easy way coming out of the world's
poverty and problems and greeds and passions. In
the years to come mankind were to discover that
after unexampled destruction and waste, burning
up the resources and necessities of fifty years in as
many months, they could not take up what had
promised when War broke out to be an age of easier
comfort. Still less was the ravage of spiritual values
reparable. To-day the world is like a drunkard who

curses for his headaches and depleted powers and possessions everything but his habits.

Cynthia's parents, alarmed, cabled in the last week of January that she must return home. Martin had letters from her and Valerie at last.

'They won't let me write much' (Cynthia said.) 'I've been ill, which is why I never answered your letters. They reached us very late. I guess you didn't know we were in Aleppo. It's a wet, bleak, unhappy place, full of people who've been made almost mad with suffering.

'You don't know what a bad habit I have of letting letters that I simply *must* answer at once wait—until something happens that means I don't answer them at all! But you mustn't think I didn't care about hearing from you. I cared a whole lot, Martin. Val says I must stop writing at once, and that she'll add a note. I'll write again, I surely will. I'm going through England and shall visit at Bunny's home and then go on to the States as soon as I can get a boat. Good-bye, Martin!'

Valerie's note was added to this, and was written later, when she was by herself.

'Cynthia isn't really well enough to travel now, but her father and mother are worrying about her. Mrs. Remfry has written and wants her to stay with them in England until she's better. She feels she couldn't do that, she feels everything that reminds her of Bunny so badly. And of course his home would be hardest of all to bear. But she's promised to visit there for a few days.

'We met Major Wenyon the other day, and he told

us that Colonel Austin-Gary says you are "a born administrator." We are so glad.'

The last four words seemed insufferably patronising, so she scored them out. But he managed to decipher them.

She put the letter by, dissatisfied with its coldness and casual unfriendly tone. Wenyon had said a great deal more than she set down; and said it with an enthusiastic warmth of affection.

In the chilly bleakness of Aleppo's winter, Jerusalem and Olivet belonged to a vanished age of faery. Her work lay among the rags and vestiges of humanity, wretched Armenian women who had endured the Turkish terror and seen their men slaughtered pitilessly and borne every shame and misery that can be put on women. Suffering had crazed their minds to a cowardice more appalling than even their unhappiness.

Her thought strayed far back, to a day of May in Jerusalem, when she had seen Martin and Warren first. The contrast was cruelty almost intolerable, especially now that Cynthia was going and leaving her to this chill after-dusk of war.

'It seems so strange' (she added) 'to be so far from Jerusalem, which used to be such a remote *name* to us, and now means so much. No place will ever mean so much to me as Jerusalem does. And you and Bunny,' she wrote hastily, 'are partly responsible for this. We should never have understood what we were seeing on that walk to Siloam, unless we had had you with us to explain it.

'We shall be coming down from Aleppo to Kantara, leaving here on the 4th of February, and spending two days in Damascus, to rest Cynthia, and a day in Haifa (the 10th).'

The letter was delivered to Martin on the 11th.

There was no mention of walks that he should remember when every other memory had faded out of the dying tissue of his brain. But only of that to Siloam, when Val had been so bored with him, so bored with everything else. When she had wasted the evening with argument that belonged to a world he had left so utterly that he could not even in sympathy or in opposition enter it again!

If only the letter had come in time! He would have raced in to Nazareth and across Esdraelon, to Haifa. The vision of her as she went from him would have stayed his famine while it happened. No doubt it would have been worse afterwards. She was going from him, and for ever; and he had never meant anything to her, except as a fellow to argue with and to ask questions about British ways and customs. But it would have been worth everything to have seen her.

The world was in excitement. In January, men in 'key industries' were hunted out and combed out, and sent to England to restart the engines of national activity. The most important were miners, many of them middle-aged men who in the fervours of the War's beginning had understated their age generously, to enlist. In beanfeast mood they went, and left a trail of shivered glass and ripped-up benches all through Palestine, Italy and France. The stations between Damascus and Kantara looked, even six months later, as if the carpenters and glaziers of the world had fought to the death, and no one had bothered to clear up the splinters. Schoolboys have sometimes similarly misinterpreted the term 'breaking up for the holidays.'

Their less fortunate comrades belatedly followed, and passed through sullen peoples convinced that they were members of a criminal tribe. Italy, especially, insisted that no troop-train should halt in any town, except just once in the north in order that everyone—shepherded strictly to a rest-camp and forbidden to stray beyond it—might have a bath before going on. The city of this rest-camp was selected for its outstanding dullness. On reaching any other town, troop-trains accelerated speed and shot to some miles beyond it before stopping. And they moved not through the veritable 'Italy', not through the names that thrill mankind; but up the dreary desolate sand-duned shore of the Adriatic.

The miners meanwhile, having arrived home, proceeded to start not the key industries but a series of very fine strikes, which continued for some years with brief intermission. They achieved one of the ablest practical jokes on record, and left all philosophers and students of human nature deeply in their debt.

The tide of demobilisation, moving with maddening slowness, began to gather up a few who were not miners. In mid-February, Caleb Wenyon turned up at Safed. He had left the train at Semakh, taken

a boat across the lake to Tiberias, and from there
Austin-Gary had picked him up by car.

'And how's Brother Martin doing as an Empire-
builder?' he asked at lunch.

'Don't mention the word "Empire-building"!'
said Martin. 'All we're doing is sanitary work. You
can't *build* anything, Caleb, on a noisome quag.'

'Chapman shows very great promise as an administrator,' said his Chief. 'The other day I was doing
some ghastly chores on my typewriter while he was
listening to some sort of a row about possession of
land. There was an old woman sitting on the
ground, weeping, and every now and then throwing
up her hands in appeal. And there were two rascals
arguing fiercely with one another and before Martin.
And that distinguished Arabic scholar and states-
man paid no notice, no notice whatever, but just
went on writing.'

'Hard-hearted, unimaginative, British brute!' said
Wenyon.

'Why!' said Martin, laughing, 'you mean those
two pukka rogues who were trying to pinch that
land up behind Capernaum!'

'Don't interrupt my story,' said his Chief. 'Well,
as I say, I watched, and I wondered that any sub-
ordinate of mine could be so uninterested in what
was obviously a tale of terrible oppression, when
suddenly Captain Martin Chapman without any
warning rose and saying with a blood-curdling
scowl, "*Mejnun! mejnun!*"[1] banged the two blokes'
heads together. Whereupon the widow—I'm sure
she must have been a widow woman—abandoned
her sobbing and broke out into wild praises.'

[1] Martin should not have used this word, which is one of abuse.

'A truly shocking story!' commented Wenyon.
'Martin clouts two highly respectable local sheikhs
and gives their land to an old woman who had no
right to it.'

'Will you be going back to Oxford?' asked Austin-
Gary.

'Afraid so. Unless I fall in with a pre-War pal's
proposal to join him in starting a prep. school. He
says there's money in it. Stacks of money! Oceans
of the ready, wealth beyond the dreams of Mond
and Rockefeller! Prep. schools are going to boom
during the next few years! He's been using his eyes,
and he writes that England's stiff with fat children
of fat profiteers. Farmers' sons, munitioneers' sons,
politicians' sons, provision dealers' sons! And their
fathers are determined that these remarkable beings
shall have the education and advantages that they
themselves missed. All you have to do is to buy up
one of the huge derelict country houses that are
going cheap—lay in a stock of chalk and canes—
and then advertise *all* the extras and luxuries, along
with whopping fees! And you can staff with convicts
and lunatics—it simply doesn't matter, so long as
you have the other attractions and necessities! The
parents of the new England to be roll up in their
cars, and lead their ghastly offspring to you.'

'You mustn't do it, Caleb,' said Martin, smiling.
'Oxford needs you too badly.'

'No. I shan't do it. Besides, I don't want to miss
the first post-War generation of undergraduates.
They'll be the most amazing stuff that ever came
into any human academy. Fancy, for once teaching
men—fellows who in age are still boys, but have gone

through experiences that would have taught even an archangel a lot he didn't know before, and have had responsibility which their elders wouldn't begin to understand even if you got H. G. Wells and Kipling both speaking at once to explain it to them. *For four years*, Martin, I'm going to have an epic job! May I perish if I don't put every ounce of brain and will that I have into it! After that, I don't mind singing my *Nunc dimittis*. I'll have had a crowded life, and anything that remains will be merely the lees that are left this vault to brag on.'

Austin-Gary let Martin motor Wenyon to where he could join the train at El-Afuleh, in Esdraelon. When they reached the station, Wenyon said, 'And that's the end of *that*! We've been part of a bigger thing than anyone will guess for years to come; and you and I, Martin, carry to our graves a secret that we can never explain, and shall be fools if we try to explain. Our generation's going to be a pretty lonely one.'

'I know that. The loneliness has begun.'

'We've lost our leaders, though we don't realise it as yet. But we'll find jolly soon that there's only a rabble left to decide what our politics and books are to be like. You're in luck, with a job in Palestine. If you've any sense, you'll do as all the sane fellows in our colonial services do, you'll never open a book from year's end to year's end; and you'll go to your grave happy in not knowing what rot your generation has been acclaiming as wisdom and enlightenment.'

'The job's a pretty risky one. I'd be wiser to go back to my old one,' said Martin doubtfully.

'You would not! The job's not only a heavenly one in itself, but it brings with it the chance of so much else.'

Martin knew what he meant. 'She's gone back to America, Caleb.'

'What! She never even hinted at that, when I saw her! Then get her address—get it somehow—the Relief Force will give it you—and write to her. Write! Act some fashion or other! Or if you don't, *she* won't forgive you. Nor will you forgive yourself. When you finally get to the hell where fools go you'll richly deserve the best brand of brimstone that they can raise. And you'll get it, too!'

'Everything's gone west, Martin,' he continued despondently. 'A whole world, and a whole way of life. We—you, and I, and that good fellow Austin-Gary, and a whole lot of us—saw with our own eyes —I John *saw*, as the Bible has it—a world that was all kinds of unpleasant things, cruel and dirty and insanitary and unimaginative and all that, but still free and fresh and unmechanised and with big chunks of openness and wildness and places for adventure. Now we go forward to the machine, which is the one thing that has really won the War. We've seen every generalisation that mankind looked on as thoroughly sound finished once for all. Even its pathetic dependence on the almighty power of money. Do you remember, when the War started, all our papers were saying like parrots *one* thing, that Germany couldn't stand the financial racket, that she had run amuck like a dog that doesn't know he's tied up and can go only just as far as the end of a very limited string, and not a step further? That she'd have to beg for peace by Christmas, at the latest, simply because she had no cash and could raise no cash? What rot it all was!'

The train came in sight round the curve of Mount Tabor. They continued walking up and down the platform.

'What do you think of the Aussies?' asked Wenyon, his attention caught by a man who leaned out from a window of the approaching train and let off a *feu de joie* with his revolver.

'The finest fighters the world has ever seen,' said Martin. 'Though that's only my private opinion.'

'I don't think it's far wrong. But do you really think this war has knit the Empire as we imagine it has? *I* don't. I feel as if I were going back to the break-up of everything that has held the world together. There isn't one of us, Martin—whether Army or politicians or doctors or schoolmasters or dons like myself—who realises how poisonous we appear in the mass and when together. You know that in America it was our French and Indian wars that started all the trouble, donkeys' years before the actual Revolution? The Colonial spirit found us and our assumptions perfectly maddening then, and they find them maddening still. This puzzled the Regular Army in 1776; it puzzles them now; it'll puzzle them to the hour of the Empire's final break-up.'

'I'm not so pessimistic as you, quite, Caleb.'

'No. Of course you are not. You've got a job in Galilee. Lucky devil!'

'Damn it all, they must have seen what our fellows did. We had the job of smashing up the Turk's defences in Judaea, one hill after another with machine-guns growing on them like grass.'

'Do you think they're fair to us over that? Do you think they'll ever be fair? Have you seen their contempt for our tommies? And you can't blame them, in a way. They've seen our pluck and our patience (though they half despise us for the latter). But they've also seen not only that we carry ourselves like men when it's only death and peril that we have to face, but carry ourselves servilely elsewhere. And they've heard—only too often!—the sharp, shrill, peppery claptrap that makes mess conversation as a rule. It's a damn good thing that in England we order national life in a series of watertight compartments, which those in these compartments have the sense to accept as the only way of saving self-respect and withholding themselves from snubs which they jolly well know are coming if they stir outside their caste! And I'm not sure,' he concluded, 'if *my* particular caste isn't the worst of all, after all my cursing of the Regular Army. Scholars and writers, literary and dramatic circles! My God! what a crowd! Once in a while one of us is saved like Saul before Damascus, by a flash of lightning vision, and he flees just in time, into the deserts of some spiritual Arabia. Oh, well!'

The train's packed freight of men proceeding to the base poured out to stretch their legs.

'Well, this is all rot, Martin,' said Wenyon. 'All I want to say is "Cheerio" and all that! Remember, there's a bed for you at Oxford any time. Wadham will be proud to house Captain Martin Chapman, Orientalist and Empire-builder. Caleb Wenyon, the

poor but proud usher, will be glad to take the great
man round and show him off to his gaping pupils.
By the way, what's this yarn,' he asked, having
supervised the slinging of his kit into a compartment, 'about a skull of Neanderthal Man that you
chaps have been unearthing in Galilee?'

Martin was very pleased. 'Much earlier than
Neanderthal Man! The scientific johnny who found
it explained it all to us. He was frightfully excited as
he pointed out how exactly like an ape's was the
long, pushed-out jaw and the tiny brain-space. He
said it was the lowest form of human—that you could
actually *call* human—that's ever been come across
yet.'

'Sounds to me,' said Wenyon, in the pauses of
packing his pipe for the journey and then lighting
it, 'as if he's hit on the remains of some staff colonel
of ours who died in Allenby's last push. I'd give a
month's pay to hear what old Blundell would have
to say about it. I bet he'd say it wasn't primitive
man at all, but proto-primitive, or some rot like that!'

He looked up; and Martin saw his eyes glaze with
slow horror.

As he turned to trace the source of this emotion,
a well-remembered voice broke in on them.
'You're wrong, Wenyon. And I'll tell you why.
Proto-primitive man—which, by the way, is a foolish
phrase, for reasons which I shall explain to you at
leisure—proto-primitive man is brachycephalic but
not as a rule markedly prognathous. Your theory is
unsound at all possible points of examination.
Furthermore——'

When Martin said good-bye to the train, seven
minutes later, Major Blundell was just warming up

to what promised to be an exceptionally enjoyable
ten hours to Kantara.

XXIV

RELIEF FORCE HEADQUARTERS IN BEIRUT, AFTER SOME
delay, sent Martin Miss Valerie Connett's Virginian
address. It was presumed that the information was
wanted for some branch of the British records.

He had only recently written when Austin-Gary
put him in for two months' leave in England, which
was granted at the end of March. 'Damned little,
after all you've gone through. You've worked like a
Trojan, Chapman. But we'll take a couple of months
each—it'll have to be leave by sections, from *this*
part of the Front—and we'll both get a decent bit
off later on, when things have straightened out more.
Now cut and run, and say "Cheerio!" to your
people.'

The trains across Europe contained four men to a
compartment, in order that no one should have a
good night's sleep. This arrangement displeased
Captain Chapman, to whom it occurred that with
three only, each could use the floor in turn and all
could lie at length. He was lucky enough to find a
pre-War acquaintance in the Railway Transport
Officer at Taranto, and instructed him to chalk up
a fourth fictitious name outside a carriage. He then
thanked his friend and (very unfairly) congratulated
him on being 'the Compleat Wangler.' It made a
difference, for the journey took seven days.

These seven days were unrelievedly dull. But they gave Martin these pictures.

The British Government had many many million pounds' worth of food that it was anxious to throw away—enough for another War, but no war was in sight. So for unending miles, as the train lurched and rattled through northern Italy and France, natives of these regions stood beside the line, begging. They had piles of bread and tins of jam and fruit and bully beef already; but were willing to accept more.

The train waited five hours in the darkness of an alpine tunnel, where a Welsh corporal skilled in farmyard imitations crew hard and to applause— for ten minutes. After that stern voices commanded him to desist.

Paris was in the throes of a railway strike, so an amateur engine-driver took the train on. It stopped frequently and without warning, flinging its human and material contents to great distances. Martin hearing cries of rage and blasphemy looked fearfully into the next carriage, to see the floor deep in golden juice; a case of whisky had been hurled from the rack. After one stop with a bump beyond endurance, the whole train-load of passengers leapt out and yelled at the driver, refusing to go on. He, poor man, uncoupled the engine and fled away. They waited through three hours of delicious dusk, in a forest whose underbrush was innumerable daffodils. Then another engine came, with a driver who ran her smoothly.

As he walked to the quay at Boulogne, a trivial vignette stamped itself on Martin's mind. A private soldier, middle-aged, stolid, complete in himself and in his occupation, sauntered by, a kettle in his right hand, a cup of tea in his intention. He was singing, and all the contentment in the world was in his voice and manner.

> ' Kuk-kuk-kuk-Katie!
> Beautiful Katie!
> You are—the only—gug-gug-gug-girl that I adore!
> When the moon shines
> Over the cowshed,
> I'll be waiting at the kik-kik-kik-kitchen door!'

At last Martin felt that the War was really over.

His mother and young sister were at home; his surviving brother was still in occupied Germany. It was hard to have to explain that he must miss this brother—that he had only three weeks in England.

There was so much that he could not explain, that he was restless. His patience and gentleness were the more disquieting because of his reserves. Never did human relations need more readjustment than in 1919; and it was nobody's fault. But his love and his delight to be home again were deep and apparent. And he was emphatic that he would be returning from Palestine with real leave. After the heart-breaking wretchedness of the partings of the last five years, that life at last was secure sufficed for the present.

All that can be said about his coming has been said once for all. 'Women received their dead raised to life again.' Yet the over-mastering thought in this,

U

as in so many homes, was of the dead who were not
raised to life and were not returning.

Colonel Remfry wrote, in answer to his letter:

'MY DEAR BOY,

'I write for my wife, who is a little under the weather,
but will be all right in a day or two. Come as soon
as you can.'

So Martin spent two nights and the day between
them, at a village nestling under the Bath Cotswolds.
This is a country that holds you for ever if you know
it; you return, however far you wander, as you
return to Florence or Athens or Edinburgh. He saw
what his friend had poured away, dying in Flanders
fields. There were meadows now one cloth of green-
winged orchis and the taller bee orchis. No wonder
Bunny had delighted in the Palestine slopes in
spring! If he had lived to be in the advance into
Galilee, if he and Martin could have walked across
Galilee in April, knee-deep in lilies! When Carmel's
shining front is an excellency of flaming gold! When
Nazareth nestles under hills that are leagues and
leagues of flowers, unendingly!

XXV

WHEN COLONEL REMFRY SUBSIDED INTO HIMSELF AFTER
talking to a guest, you saw the great loosening of
purpose that had come since Bunny's death. There
was nothing now but to grow old.

It was in his wife that Martin thought he could trace the vivid, eager spirit he had known. Six years younger than her husband (who was fifty-one), Mrs. Remfry was still beautiful. 'Mother's no end of a chum,' Bunny had once told him. Even his puckish, gay impudence—it was blasphemy, but you thought that this, too, had lived in the mother before it was vivacious in the son.

It was of her son that she talked; and of Cynthia. 'She was a great comfort to Warren's father. We knew she must be charming, and just as kind as could be; we'd had her letters ever since a perfectly darling one that she wrote when she got engaged to our boy. But I for one wasn't prepared to find her so—so—I can't quite get the word, Captain Chapman.'

'Please!' said Martin. 'Must I be Captain Chapman —to Warren's father and mother?'

'Certainly not, my dear boy,' said Colonel Remfry. 'We've known you for nearly five years, and we've always known you as Martin.'

'As Martin,' said Mrs. Remfry, 'Or sometimes— you'll forgive us, Martin, but you have no idea how intimate an inmate of this household you have been —as Martin Puzzlewit. In fact, it was only about a week ago, just before your letter came, that Colonel Remfry said, "I *wish* we could see Old Puzzlewit soon!"'

'I like it better than *Chapman*,' Martin confessed. 'My own name's such a rotten name.'

'She was a dear sweet girl,' said the Colonel, whose thoughts were back with Cynthia.

'Yes,' said Mrs. Remfry. 'I was saying that we weren't quite prepared to find her so very—*mature* isn't the word, but so very thoughtful for others, so quick to understand, so——'

'*I* was,' said Colonel Remfry. 'I knew Warren would pick a girl out of the very top drawer that there was. He wouldn't have been a Remfry if he didn't.'

There was no hint of a compliment in the handsome testimony; only sincerity and directness of conviction.

Martin hardly dared look at a portrait close to where he sat in the living-room, when they talked. His eyes knew well where it hung, and this awareness was the constant thought behind them. But memory was too poignant to bear revival yet. It was more than the mind would accept, that this presence so vivid even in picture—the very tilt of the chin and sudden challenge, the look that had come when he hit Bunny's first ball for six ('So *that's* what you think you're going to do, Old Puzzlewit! Wait! just *wait*, my boy!')—would not return to them.

For those who lived here the house had passed into history. Nothing existed except in relation to something Warren had said *here*, had done *there*. Despite the generosity with which his father and mother changed conversation to general topics, it came back to the dead boy.

Martin had gone to his room, the first night, when Colonel Remfry knocked and entered.

'I just wanted to make sure, my dear fellow, that you've got everything you want.'

'I've got everything, sir.'

'Quite sure you'll be comfortable?'

'Absolutely sure, sir.'

Then Martin, red in the face, opened his box, and said, 'There's something I brought down, sir, to give Mrs. Remfry and you.' He produced the cricket ball lost and found on Olivet. He told its story briefly.

'I know, I know. Our boy wrote all about it. He said that Old Puzzlewit made a topping catch in the deep field and had the impudence to hit his first ball for six. His mother and I know pretty well what happened to every ball that was bowled in that match.'

This symbol, the tiny sphere of slightly ragged red, made visible the eager brightness they had known and loved. It might have been more merciful if he had left it under its rock on Olivet, to rot with the seasons' passage, into indistinguishable and unspeaking earth.

Next evening, when she was about to retire, Mrs. Remfry drew him aside. 'I have to give you this, Martin. Cynthia left it and asked me not to give it to you until you were about to leave us.'

He took the letter, mystified.

'She wanted us to have you all to ourselves as long as you were here,' Mrs. Remfry explained, 'without anything intruding from outside or taking your thoughts away from us. So she wrote the letter here, and left it to go with you when you went.'

He read it in his room.

'I've been nearly a week with Bunny's people, and I can never say how perfect they've been to me. You would think that it was I who had lost everything and that they had lost nothing. Martin, it makes me realise how very lucky a girl I have been—and how very unlucky too. But I wasn't alive—not really alive—only horrid and selfish and pleased with myself—until I was loved by a *man*. They made me feel that I was their daughter just as much as if Bunny were alive and I were his wife. His mother said to me, "You've made us see that we've lost far more than we knew, Cynthia—not one dear child, but two." And I cried and said, "No, you haven't lost two, you've lost only one. You've got to look on me as your daughter, Mrs. Remfry."

'But it's you I want to talk about now, Martin. You know, Bunny was right when he used to call you Martin Puzzlewit! You are not only the dearest fellow in the world, but you are the dumbest as well! I told Val once that that was perhaps part of your dearness, and she didn't deny it—which is one up for you, if you only had the sense to know it! You are the kind of boy who makes a girl make love to you, you know. You are all chivalry and all decency and thinking about what she wants or *says* she wants—which isn't at all the same thing, Martin dear! Sometimes a girl simply doesn't *know* what she wants; she wants the boy to find out for her and to make *her* know. Now Val isn't a cheap little Yankee girl like me—I guess I'm pretty cheap and mean, I go straight at the boy I want and vamp him without shame or hesitation. She's been brought up till it's in her very *bones* to think that she's someone that the boy who wants her has to force to realise that *she* wants him. Oh, they're not so high and mighty and all-important as they kid themselves, these ladies and gentlemen of Virginia—I guess I wouldn't change my Pennsylvanian blood for theirs, if I had to take on their habits as well—though, mind you, Martin, I'm not saying a word against Val, who's an old sweetheart in every way! But the point is, never mind whether these ladies and gentlemen of Virginny are what they think they are or are not, *you've got to behave as if you accepted it as gospel.*

'(I've nearly finished. I know you're saying, "That's just like Cynthia! rattling on for ever!") I'm going to say something that ought to make you see that we realise what a brick you are. That day you came to us in Jerusalem, the last day you came, the day when we all heard that Bunny was dead, you meant to have come to tell Val that you loved her and were not going to live without her. Now didn't you? Don't deny it, Martin (Bunny used to say, "Old Puzzlewit is the very worst liar that I know.") And you didn't, because my boy was dead. You went away, to the chance of being killed yourself, and you never said a word! It was just like you, Martin. And it was Val who guessed this for herself, though she'd be mad with me if she knew I was letting on to you. You never must let on, Martin. *Never.*

'But my boy's gone and nothing will bring him back. You've been his friend, the best friend any fellow ever had, and when he died he died knowing this. But you have to live your life out. I've told you about Val what should be more than enough, and I know it will be. She wrote to you the same time that I did, when I was leaving Syria. *She wrote to you,* Martin Puzzlewit. Oh, I know, I expect you thought it was a pretty cold and standoffish and snubbing letter. But then, you don't understand women, not the least little bit. And if you choose to fall for a girl who's from Virginny and hasn't been allowed to forget it for one single minute since she was in the cradle, and whose grandfather and granduncles fought under General Stuart, why, you have to take the consequences of your foolishness! The point is, you've made a Daughter of the Confederacy admit to herself—or begin to admit to herself—that there can be something to a Britisher, besides high-

hattedness and solemnity and conceit and dumbness.
She told you, she says, the day we should both be
in Haifa, which isn't so very far from Galilee, where
you were. And you never came! I've told her that
there must have been some good reason why you
never came, and in her heart she knows this too.
But all she'll admit to herself is that she told a
stupid British boy where she was going to be *and he
never came*.

'I can tell you what was behind the letter. There
was a whole lot of wretchedness and loneliness. It's
Val who ought to be going home as ill, and not me
at all. I've just been a burden to her, she's had to
nurse me and to keep up my spirits *and* do her job in
Aleppo, all this winter. It was just one wet misery—
you must have heard how it rained and rained and
rained, all through this winter in Aleppo. And the Armenians gave us a new idea of the Turk whom you
British are so fond of! Val said one day, "Martin
used to say that Jacko was such a gentleman. I wish
I could have him here and show him some of his
gentleman's work! The gentleman's the invention
that the English are proudest of. Well, I *must* say
that what they consider constitutes a gentleman sometimes puzzles those nations who haven't the luck to
possess any of them!"

'And that's what Val had to go back to, after she'd
seen me to Kantara! She went back to it, fretting
because—well, if you are so absolutely dead puzzlewitted that you can't guess that your going clean out
of our lives and *never answering a word*, when you had
not come either—for you *must* have got our letter
afterwards, Martin, and you could have written to Val
and explained! And you didn't, for her last letter
from Aleppo says she never heard from you—if you
can't guess what I'm not going to tell you you are not
the man I take you for. My address is going to be

"Dearhill, Waverley, Penna, U.S.A." Write to me, Martin.

'Good-bye! And *good luck*!

'Affectionately,
'CYNTHIA.'

There was a postscript.

'*Go* to Aleppo, Martin. It's not so far from where you are in Galilee. And if it were a thousand miles you ought to go. And don't give Val time. Make her decide at once.'

He cabled to Aleppo.

XXVI

WHEN HE REACHED ALEPPO, ON MAY 26TH, HE HAD still two days before he was strictly due back at work.

She had met the train, in answer to his wire from Haifa; and she greeted him with the apprehensive look he remembered. A wild thing trapped, except that there was no helplessness—only indecision, uncertainty whether it was fussed with captivity or not. Unless the will were trapped, the net could be broken. His heart had leapt; then he felt wretched to see how worn she looked.

It was late afternoon: a day of deadness, of heat and little swirling puffs of powdery dirt.

'You never came,' she said irrelevantly.

'I didn't get your letter till next day. Then I thought you had gone to America; and I wrote there, Val. It was Cynthia told me, in England, that you were here. You look dead tired,' he said anxiously. 'You've proved that you're not fit to be left to look after yourself. Val darling, you've got to let me take care of you! I love you, Val; you know that I've had only one thought since I first saw you.'

She laughed, nervously and happily. 'But, Martin! in this dreadful place—all dust and starvation and sickness and horrors!'

'Anywhere that I can find you! What's wrong with you'—he was going to sin boldly, borrowing his lines from Cynthia—'is that you always think of yourself in a setting of moonlight and mountains. You don't need them, you bring them with you. But I'm going to take my chance here, with no Olivet to help me. I know I look nothing without it, but I've come to risk it.'

'You look a *man*, Martin!' she said gratefully, 'as you would anywhere! And I've almost forgotten what a man looks like, in this place where everyone's been beaten down and made miserable!'

'I am a man,' he said humbly. 'And it's you who've made me one. Will you marry me, Valerie? I've got only these few hours before I must start back to my job.'

"You've given me a strict time-limit!'

'Cynthia said I had to. You escape if you are given longer.'

She met his eyes full, which always had a disconcerting effect. If she was to continue to tease him, she wanted to have the right to see that no damage was done.

'So you and Cynthia are in league against me! And I am helpless in this horrid, foreign city, not even British! Oh, Martin!' she pleaded, 'don't make me answer here, but give me a chance somewhere else! It's Aleppo in May, dusty and hot and dirty and just *horrid*!' She shuddered. 'You don't *know* what this city has seen! But it's got other places besides this station. Lines of cypresses and tall white asphodels that go on for miles and miles! I'll be good, Martin, I will really! Only not here!' She looked away from him. 'Will it do if I swear by moonlight on Olivet?'

'I should say it would.'

'The Frobishers are here,' she told him as they found a taxi. 'And Wilbur insisted on fixing up a room for you. You can keep Galilee waiting for just one day longer.'

At the post office she stopped the taxi. 'You've got to send a cable for me. It gets through quicker if an officer sends it.'

'There!' she said presently. 'I've announced our engagement before it happened, a thing no decent Virginian girl would do. But after all, Cynthia was an accessory before the fact. I don't think you *ought* to read it, Martin! But you can send it for me.'

'Never guessed Martin could be so bullying— Valerie,' he read; and wrote in the space for information 'not to be cabled unless required'— 'Captain Chapman, British O.E.T.A., Safed, Palestine.' He thought a minute, then added to the cable message: 'You have been a dear—Martin.'

THE END

Printed in Great Britain by PURNELL AND SONS, *Somerset*